BY NINA SADOWSKY

Just Fall

The Burial Society

THE BURIAL SOCIETY

THE BURIAL SOCIETY

A Novel

Nina Sadowsky

BALLANTINE BOOKS

NEW YORK

Published in the United States by Ballantine Books, an imprint of Random House, a division of Penguin Random House LLC, New York.

BALLANTINE and the HOUSE colophon are registered trademarks of Penguin Random House LLC.

LIBRARY OF CONGRESS CATALOGING-IN-PUBLICATION DATA
Names: Sadowsky, Nina, author.
Title: The burial society : a novel / Nina Sadowsky.
Description: New York : Ballantine Books, [2018]
Identifiers: LCCN 2017053842 | ISBN 9780425284377 (hardback) |
ISBN 9780425284384 (ebook)
Subjects: LCSH: Secrets--Fiction. | Psychological fiction. | BISAC: FICTION /
Psychological. | FICTION / Romance / Suspense. | FICTION / Suspense. |
GSAFD: Romantic suspense fiction. | Mystery fiction.
Classification: LCC PS3619.A353 B87 2018 | DDC 813/.6—dc23
LC record available at https://lccn.loc.gov/2017053842

Printed in the United States of America on acid-free paper

randomhousebooks.com

2 4 6 8 9 7 5 3 1

FIRST EDITION

Title-page image: © iStockphoto.com

Book design by Dana Leigh Blanchette

This book is dedicated to my most excellent children,
Raphaela and Xander (neither of whom is anything
like any of the characters contained herein).
You inspire me always and in all ways.

Burial societies exist across cultures.

Their members are committed to ensuring that death and burial rites within a community are conducted with dignity and compassion.

The society's duties are considered the ultimate acts of benevolence, and may include being present at a death, watching over the corpse, cleansing and shrouding it, accompanying it during the funeral procession, conducting the burial service without charge and with appropriate religious ceremonies, and providing support to the deceased's family.

Part One

CONVERGENCE

If I could tell the story differently . . .

It would be a tale of courage. Honor and loyalty.
Sacrifice and righteous vengeance.

And love. Of course love.

But what really went down is this.

Catherine

FOCUS

I can do this. I will do this.

I've done this many times before. And under trickier circumstances, I reassure myself. I've calculated timing and approach, extraction and escape. It will be hazardous, perhaps fatal—if not for the benevolent graces of luck and perfect timing.

But it's what the client ordered, and the customer is always right. Plus, the payoff? Huge. I don't care about the money, but there will be other rewards for me in this.

Why am I so nervous?

I hate the waiting. Gives me too much time to think. My heart thuds in my chest.

Focus.

I scan the street.

Two skinny Americans, weighted with backpacks, fingers entwined, eyes soaking in every last precious crumb of Parisian detail. A little boy, maybe three, still unsteady on his chubby legs, wobbling behind his sleekly dressed and fiercely bickering parents. A fine-boned shopgirl, just relieved of her shift, her face hardened by the disdain she holds for the countless Chinese tourists she has serviced today. Indeed, a crowd of them is now jostling back on board their gaudy tour bus, juggling their haul from Ralph Lauren, Hugo Boss, Façonnable, Gerard Darel. An expensively punked-out rocker dude with a fluffy Pomeranian on an embellished leash side-steps the throng, cursing at his dog (or maybe the Chinese) in angry bursts.

There's a hunger about this part of Paris, despite the broad Haussmann-designed boulevards, the elegant shops, the leafy trees. The money, the designer labels, the thirst for status, they all feed a rapacious maw that is persistently desperate for "more," that will never know satiation. And then there are those who scavenge off the leavings of that hunger, the salespeople and doormen, chauffeurs and personal assistants, beggars and thieves. Boulevard Saint-Germain may look like the epitome of discreet wealth and understated luxury, but I know better. I know the darkness obscured by the glitz.

It is only because my client is well-heeled that I find myself here. Paris has been my home for a little over three years, but this arrondissement is not my usual stomping ground. Still, today I look the part—Givenchy black leather skinny jeans, a perfectly distressed four-hundred-euro T-shirt, Robert Clergerie platforms, my light brown hair swept back in a sleek ponytail, diamond studs in my exposed ears, eyes shadowed by oversized Chanel sunglasses. I am ostentatious, but I am also invisible. Wherever I am, whoever the target, I must blend in like a chameleon.

I've been doing it for so long I don't quite remember who I am anymore, not the real me, the *me* I left behind. But more on that later. I must concentrate on my current objective.

Focus.

I've done my homework. I always do. The facts check out. The first installment, a direct deposit to a Swiss bank account, is confirmed. I've followed my target for two weeks now without being detected. I've assessed her patterns and habits and, perhaps more important, those of the bodyguard who is never far from her side.

I've enlisted Delphine as my driver for the day, always grateful for her steady, silent acquiescence to plans and payment.

I move into position. The Sonia Rykiel storefront is attractive. Behind the pristine plate glass, wooden shelves laden with hardcover books rise from floor to ceiling. The rich colors of the books' spines are mirrored in the ornate ensembles draped onto bald alabaster mannequins. Layers of complex embroidery on the most luxurious silks, fringes and furs, palettes that glimmer under the artfully directed lights. It's dusk, and as the day darkens, the shop windows glow.

I buy myself time to linger by extracting a pack of Gitanes from my Louis Vuitton handbag.

The chubby toddler and his squabbling parents cross in front of me. The little boy totters. Lands on his plump butt as his parents continue on, absorbed in their heated fight. His small mouth curves into an indignant O as his face goes pale.

"Nice fall!" I compliment the toddler cheerfully in French. *"Next time, be sure your parents see, you'll get more attention."*

The kid's watery eyes take me in. Should he cry? Be afraid? He's undecided. Then he gives me a sly, delighted smile. He scrambles to his feet and rushes in front of his parents, only to plop down dramatically before them and wail, mouth open, eyes screwed shut. I choke back a laugh.

And suddenly, there she is. Exiting the boutique. My target. High Slavic cheekbones. Thick, shiny blond hair. A full mouth and a strong jaw that gives her face a tinge of hauteur. Elegantly dressed, Alexander McQueen. Sky-high stiletto heels. A stunning pair of cabochon emerald earrings. Skittish despite all her sophistication and grooming. Like a high-strung Thoroughbred awaiting the starting gun.

She's empty-handed. To give truth to the lie, the day's purchases will be delivered to her apartment on avenue Montaigne. As if she always expected to go home. As if he expected the same.

My target's bodyguard follows her out, thick-necked and dead-eyed.

My nerves fade. I'm stone cold, as I knew I would be when the time came. That's better. This is how I like me. Moving into action and reaction, calculated and sure. Ruthless.

I pretend to dig in my purse for an errant lighter or matches. Approach her. I ask in French if she has a light. I extend my pack of cigarettes, an offering.

Her eyes meet mine from under a heavy fringe of black lashes. I know she sneaks smokes when she thinks no one who matters is looking. I've watched her do it thirty-seven times in the last fourteen days. Now thirty-eight.

Behind her, the bodyguard steps protectively forward, but she waves him off. I am nothing to fear, just another rich, spoiled coquette in need of a nicotine fix.

She reaches into her purse and extracts a Cartier lighter, accepts a cigarette from my pack. When she snaps the lighter, our heads bend toward each other, near the flame, and my hand closes around hers. The door to the van parked behind us slides open.

"Don't resist," I whisper in English. Her eyes dart to mine, instantly wary.

My hand tightens around my target's wrist. With one cruel jerk, I bundle her into the van, flicking my lit cigarette into the bodyguard's face. He bellows and bats away the burning ember, too distracted to anticipate the thrusting thud of my platform shoe into his gut. He stumbles backward, reeling, cursing, as I scramble into the van.

I plunge a hypodermic needle loaded with fentanyl into my target's neck just as she opens her luscious mouth to cry out. She wilts in my arms. I slam the door shut.

We peel away, Delphine expertly navigating the boulevard. I imagine the bodyguard, frantic, furious, recovering his balance, running after us, pulling out his cellphone, but we are prepared.

Three swift turns and we stop in a narrow alley. Load our unconscious target into a waiting taxi. Delphine takes the wheel of the cab and we pull out, blending anonymously into traffic. Tucked in the back with my target, I settle her limp form comfortably against the velour seat. Strap on her seatbelt. I brush a wisp of blond hair away from the sharp angle of her cheekbone. Her life has been hell. But now that hell is over.

BRUISE

Natalie Burrows pivots, scanning the horizon. She glances at her phone to check the time. He's late.

Parc Monceau is magical. The heavy gates are gold-tipped wrought iron; the swaths of manicured grass a stunning green. Wildflowers bloom exuberantly. Nestled in the 8th arrondissement, the exquisite little park features such delights as a miniature pyramid, a Dutch windmill, a grand rotunda, and a classical colonnade facing a man-made lake, at the center of which squats an island sprouting a majestic weeping willow. The park had been conceived as a "folly" in the late 1700s, its design intended to delight and amaze. Its wandering paths, luscious blooms, and sudden architectural surprises do just that.

It feels good to be back in Paris. Natalie loves this gem of a park, and she loves the richly appointed apartment just off it that Brian's rented for the summer. (She's just started calling her father "Brian." Even inside her own head it feels weird and unfamiliar. But at eighteen she is an adult now; she's trying it on for size.)

Natalie catches sight of the miniature windmill, its blades spinning lazily, then more urgently as the wind kicks up. A smile tugs at the corner of her lips as she remembers Derek, the Brit backpacker with whom she'd spent the last few days (and nights) in Amsterdam. And they say that Brits are passionless and pasty! Derek had been full of energy, able to tour all day, hit the clubs till the early hours of the morning, then make vigorous love as the sun rose. Natalie thinks Derek might have fallen a little bit in love with her.

Not that he knew her as Natalie.

Her smile broadens as she bids adieu to "Carolyn Somers," rising sophomore at the University of Chicago. Natalie had toyed with Carolyn's major, first trying out international relations with a minor in economics. But then she saw the panicked look on Derek's face and gently punched his arm, saying, "Just kidding. Art history." At least she knows something about art history.

Natalie doesn't quite know why she felt compelled to lie to Derek. They both knew the parameters of their hookup from their first meeting in a beer hall. Four days. Tulips and windmills and herring served from street carts. Canals and the Anne Frank house, bicycle rides and cannabis coffee shops. Nightclubs and a giddy tour through the red-light district. A lingering kiss, an exchange of contact information (all of Natalie's false), and goodbye. It had felt wonderful to be somebody else. Freeing. Even if just for a few days.

But now she is back. She is Natalie Burrows, raised in Westport, Connecticut; recently of New York City; based in Paris, France, for the summer; and heading to RISD, in Providence, Rhode Island, in the fall. Daughter of Brian. Sister of Jacob. Youngest child of Mallory Armstrong Burrows (missing and presumed dead). A dark cloud scuds across the sun and Natalie shivers.

Where is Jake? When they had split up in Amsterdam they promised to meet in the park and return to the apartment together. Brian doesn't need to know his little girl has been having passionate sex with a stranger. And Natalie doesn't need to know what her brother has gotten up to. Still. They need a little rehearsal to get their stories straight for Dad. *Brian.*

Natalie checks her phone again. Now Jake's *really* late. She frowns. This isn't like him. She's about to text him when the dark cloud overhead splits. Plump raindrops splatter. Natalie tucks her phone in her pocket and runs, her backpack thumping against her shoulders. The day is still strangely sunny, even as the rain pelts down harder. Natalie laughs out loud, exhilarated by the sudden storm, the bright sky. She dashes through the exquisite park and out its wrought-iron gate toward their apartment on rue Murillo, sneakered feet slapping against the wet pavement. Raindrops drip from her nose; she tilts her head up to catch them on her tongue.

As she nears her building, a woman emerges. Light brown hair in a high ponytail, a tightly belted khaki trench coat, a black bag under one arm. She radiates that effortless chic French women achieve so easily. The woman pulls her coat collar up and dashes through the downpour, away from Natalie. The woman's not someone Natalie's seen before, but Natalie is oddly drawn to her. She makes a mental note. *Find out if that woman lives in our building. Befriend her. Learn her stylish secrets.*

Natalie pauses in the meager shelter the doorway provides, sliding her backpack from her shoulders. Black umbrellas pop open on the sidewalk. Pedestrians caught in the sudden shower squeal and curse. One fuchsia umbrella unfurls across the street and as it does, a rainbow streaks the sky.

Remember to be grateful, Natalie thinks. *For every single day.*

Well. She can't stand out here in the rain like an asshat. She'll text Jake, tell him to say he stopped to do an errand on the way back to the apartment. Then they can plead exhaustion and have a chance to compare notes before they debrief Brian in the morning. Natalie fires off the text before she inserts her key into the front door.

She bounds up the stairs, backpack be damned. Unlocks their front door and opens it.

History resounds in their summer apartment. In its gracious rooms, high ceilings, and crisp white walls iced with crown moldings, its chevron-patterned wood floors and leaded French doors, its paintings (mostly dour portraits clasped by ornate and heavy frames), its built-in bookcases, graceful antiques, and thick cream-colored curtains. Countless lives breathed in these very spaces. Natalie loves conjuring stories about the apartment's past residents; her sketchbook is full of imagined scenes set within the apartment's gracious walls.

"Brian," she calls. "I'm home!"

No answer. Hmm. Dad had said he would be sure to be here when they got back. Maybe he got delayed at work. That at least solves the problem of Jake being late.

Natalie kicks off her wet sneakers. She dumps her backpack and dripping windbreaker. She pads toward her bedroom in her damp socks, stripping off her T-shirt as she goes. She catches sight of her half-naked body in the gilt-framed mirror on the wall. *I am super hot,* she decides, the mirror reflecting back the same desirous gaze she had directed toward Derek the Brit.

She studies her tapering waist, delicate shoulders, and perky breasts. B cup. Not too small and not too large. Her ribs are faintly visible under the caress of her soft skin, as are the bones of her spine when she twists to examine the rear view. Turning back toward the mirror, she studies her face. It's a good face overall. She got the best of her mother—full mouth, widely set gray eyes, sharply arched eyebrows—and the best of Brian too—defined aquiline nose and a squarish chin that gives her a look of happy determination.

It's a pity that look is frequently deceptive.

Is that a lump of fat over her left hip? Natalie pinches at the skin, weighing, testing. Her eyes drop from the girl in the mirror. She kneads at her flesh until it darkens with a bruise.

Sickened, Natalie examines the damage she's inflicted. She gives the mottled skin over her hip one last sharp pinch. Certainly not the worst she's done to herself. She raises her eyes defiantly back to her reflection. *I can stop this. I can.*

Remember to be grateful. For every single day.

Catherine

MARSEILLE

We've driven for seven hours. Delphine pilots us smoothly in the direction of the Old Port. I peer out the windows only to see indistinct shapes muffled by the soot-black night; still, I can imagine what we're passing. Tenements housing the city's countless immigrants. Synagogues and mosques and Greek Orthodox churches. Expansive "urban renewal" projects, grim even before completion. And then, more optimistically, the opera house, public gardens, and burgeoning industrial parks.

I close my eyes briefly, fighting the exhaustion that threatens to overwhelm. As soon as I hand off my target, I will check in to a hotel and sleep the sleep of the just. Or at least the sleep of the justified.

A low moan pulls me back from the brink of slumber. I open my eyes. My target is stirring. An elegant hand flutters up to touch her forehead. She moans again.

I study the planes of her face. She'd been a model before her marriage, having traveled from her hometown of Vologda, Russia, to an open casting call in Moscow at only fourteen. Even then, she was a willowy blond beauty, with a gravity in her cobalt blue eyes that reflected an old soul. I know from my research that both the flight to Moscow and her somber smile were caused by her stepfather, a government official who strenuously denied her assertion that he'd begun molesting her at age eleven.

Signed by an international modeling agency, she spent the next seven years crossing the globe for fashion shows and photo shoots. She walked the runways in Paris, Milan, New York, São Paulo, and Tokyo. She appeared in the *Sports Illustrated* swimsuit issue and on the cover of *Vogue* twice. She took a stab at acting, playing a version of herself in a Hollywood action film. She made money and she spent it lavishly. She was hounded by the paparazzi, her romances (some of them disastrous) dissected for the prurient delight of tabloid readers around the world. She never lost the wariness in her eyes.

She met her husband while vacationing in Ibiza. He was a fellow Russian, older, extremely rich, charming, intelligent. He told her he manufactured engines. It was the first of many lies.

After a whirlwind courtship, they married in a lavish celebration in London. Tabloids reported the reception cost more than a million pounds. Exclusive photographs were sold to *OK!* magazine for hundreds of thousands. The three dresses she wore over the course of the evening were favorably scrutinized by fashion bloggers who admired her politic choice to honor three of her favorite designers: Monique Lhuillier for the ceremony, Stella McCartney for the cocktail hour, and Reem Acra for the dinner and dancing.

The couple honeymooned on the groom's yacht, a leisurely six-week tour of the Greek islands, mostly notable for the photograph that later emerged of the bride sunbathing completely naked (in what she had presumed was total privacy).

Do you see now why I worry about making this woman disappear? She possesses one of the best-known faces and bodies on the planet.

HOWL

The shower is glorious, hot and steamy. Natalie emerges, fragrant with jasmine-scented body wash and shampoo, and bundles up in her plush rose-pink bathrobe. She wipes the steam from the bathroom mirror and brushes her teeth. It's lovely to feel so clean. Muffled in the huge robe, she looks all she wants to be: petite, almost elfin. She cinches the belt of her robe tighter.

Where is Jake? And where is her dad? Natalie starts to feel a little anxious. She exits the bathroom calling for them. Maybe they came in while she was in the shower?

Passing the door to her father's bedroom, Natalie catches a glimpse of her dad's briefcase. "Brian?" she inquires as she pushes open the door.

Rain-filtered light passes through the skylight, washing the room in shades of gray. Brian is splayed across the bed. His face is strange, empty, ashen. His eyes stare blankly. His head hangs at an odd tilt.

Blood, dried to a dull rust color, is caked onto the cream-colored coverlet.

Natalie sinks to the floor as an agonized howl escapes her mouth.

Catherine

SALVATION

My target's eyes flutter. She licks her dry lips.

I reach into the case tucked by my feet and extract a mask that I pull over my head. It's a glow-in-the-dark alien head, slanted almond-shaped eyes, a slit of a mouth, mere suggestions of nostrils. It's silly, I know, and uncomfortably warm, but has the benefit of obscuring my voice as well as my features. This close to the target I can't be invisible, so I must be obscured.

"*Elena,*" I growl low in my throat. "*Are you awake?*" My Russian is serviceable.

Elena's eyes peel open. She's dazed and blinks to focus. When she catches sight of me, she recoils.

"*Have some water,*" I order in Russian, as I hand her a bottle. She chugs it obediently.

"*Don't be scared,*" I continue. "*Everything should work out just fine as long as the ransom is paid.*"

I see the panic flare in her eyes. She glances toward the door of the taxi; I know she's gauging the speed of the car, the possibility of escape. I grip her wrist tightly.

"Don't even think about it," I mutter as I plunge another syringe into her neck. She doesn't know it yet, but I am her salvation.

This is what I do. I am the Burial Society.

Jake

ORPHANS

Natalie's frail body curls into a corner of her bed, her breathing finally rhythmic but shallow. The doctor had given her a sedative.

Jake watches her sleep, knowing her drug-induced peace is only temporary.

Brian's corpse has been removed, his bedroom examined and sealed. Two gendarmes wait for Jake in the salon. He's not even really sure why they are still here; he's told them all he knows. He came home, found his sister hysterical and his father dead.

He can't stay in here much longer. The young flic, the one with the acne-pitted face, had even wanted to come into Natalie's bedroom with him. But Jake assured him he would be only a minute, he just wanted to be sure Natalie was finally sleeping. Now Jake wonders if the cop had been less concerned with his welfare and in fact suspicious of his actions. As if he could ever hurt Natalie! His sister is the only person on earth he loves without reservation. Natalie is the only person he has left.

We're orphans now, he realizes. It seems an old-fashioned word, conjuring up images of workhouses and Oliver Twist, ragged clothes and sad-eyed faces hollowed by hunger.

Is Natalie too thin again? Where her spine emerges above the butter-yellow blanket, he can see the sharp knobs of her vertebrae. He never should have let her go off with that boy in Amsterdam. Even as he chides himself, he knows it is irrelevant. The young Brit didn't hurt Natalie; it's this new devastation that might break her.

Jake's mind races. There are the practical questions: Can he and Nat stay on in the apartment? Should they? For how long? At least tonight, since Natalie is finally sleeping, but surely not beyond that. Where will they go? How much money do they have? Can they access their dad's accounts? Oh god, will they be hounded by the press again? Shit. Should he call Uncle Frank? Do they need a lawyer? A translator? Should he contact the embassy? How will they get Brian's body home? Did he leave a will? A burial plan? How can Jake *not know* these things?

Then there are even more troubling thoughts. What will people think about him and his sister now, with *both* of their parents murdered? Will they pity them even more? Jake hates pity. Will people believe they are tainted? Cursed? Are they cursed? Is his whole family linked in a daisy chain of tragedy? *How could this have happened?* The memory of Brian's savagely torn neck makes Jake shudder.

He holds his hands up in front of his face. They look foreign to him, the hands of a stranger. Hands can do so many things. Build a fire, make a sandwich, paint a landscape, toss a football, fly across a keyboard. Caress a lover, soap a back, rub out a solitary orgasm. Wield a razor, swing a baseball bat, punch a heavy bag. Pull a trigger. Choke a neck until all breath is stilled.

Slit a throat.

Jake snorts back a rush of tears. He has wished his father dead many times. Even before Mallory disappeared, they had butted heads. Mallory was the parent who *stayed,* while Brian roamed the world for the sake of one commission or another. Jake became the "man of the house" while Brian was away. And his resentment only grew when Brian came home because of the angry voices that emanated from his parents' bedroom at night, the harsh creases carved into his mother's face in the aftermath.

But wishing someone dead and actual death are two entirely separate things.

Aren't they?

Catherine

HANDOFF

Bruised pink sky heralds the arrival of morning. The Old Port is stirring, fishermen and pleasure-boat crews readying for the day ahead. Delphine stops the taxi at the designated spot. Zahida, a moonfaced Bosnian girl, darts from the shadows.

Z works the cleaning crew on a small cruise ship (capacity 300), and she will see that my still-unconscious target is safely deposited into an unused first-class stateroom (where she will likely sleep until the ship docks in the Ligurian port of Genoa). Z will also deliver my target to the next handler when she arrives. Z doesn't know whom it is she's hiding and she doesn't care. I helped free Z from a desperate situation once upon a time (perhaps a tale for another telling). I won her gratitude and loyalty then, and now I pay her well.

Z and I lift my target from the taxi. Delphine shoots me a smart salute and is on her way. We load the target's limp form into a waiting dinghy. Once she is settled, Z casts off. I pause on the dock and watch them head out to open water.

I pop on my sunglasses. Tug a slouchy hat low on my forehead. I walk away with purpose and determination, a woman with somewhere to go.

Frank

ANOTHER MAN'S CHILDREN

Frank Burrows is sick to death of arguing with his ex-wife. The script of each skirmish is punishingly familiar. Bottom line: She hates his fucking guts and wishes he would die.

Frank sighs, trying to hang on to his composure as Della goes on the attack, her voice shrill through the telephone. Then he erupts. His brother has *died*, for god's sake. In Paris. Jake and Natalie, his nephew and niece, are there alone. Frank is still trying to wrap his head around it all, he tells her, but any reasonable woman would understand that he has to go, that it isn't, as Della claims, "yet another excuse" to avoid seeing his own children. She's being outrageous! He has been looking forward to the two weeks with the girls, the reservations are made, the plane tickets booked. And, he adds (his tone growing louder and harsher, knowing that there will be no logic or compassion to be found in *any* conversation with Della, so really, what is the point of even trying to modulate), *his brother is dead*. Brian has been *murdered*.

"It's just like you to abandon your own girls to take care of another man's children," Della snipes.

"How can you be so callous?" he finally shouts as he slams the phone off.

How had he ever married that woman? That's what comes from

acting on the rebound. He had realized she was batshit crazy, but only after she was pregnant with their twin girls. Now he is shackled to the bitch for life.

The twins, Analise and Adelaide, are eleven now, still little girls, on the brink of the roller coaster of adolescence. He loves his daughters wholly. He caught Addy wearing lip-gloss a couple of months ago. She'll be the one to watch. Ana still loves her dolls.

He'll make it up to them, Frank promises himself. When this is all over, they will do something spectacular. But for now, his focus must be on Jake and Natalie.

As he begins to plan getting to Paris, comparing flights and train schedules, notifying his office, he is conscious that he is avoiding the very thing he should have done first.

Call his mother.

Or at least let the nursing home know. Susan Burrows suffers from dementia. There are still some good days, but after she set a fire in the galley kitchen of her garden apartment two years ago, Brian and Frank moved her to Meadowfield, "the finest in adult care facilities." Frank had always thought the name of the place was wack—aren't a meadow and a field basically the same thing? It was like an ironic etymologic joke carried on the backs of those who could no longer remember their words.

And who would pay for Meadowfield now? Brian had borne the expense without a thought, knowing that not only did he make far more than Frank, but that child support and alimony payments slivered Frank's income.

Frank piles clothing on the hotel room bed, carefully refolding his belongings. What a stroke of luck he was in London for the trade show. He can be with Natalie and Jake in a matter of hours.

Maybe he won't call the home just yet. Or his mother. Maybe a little ignorance truly is bliss, at least for the time being. Still, the American news is bound to pick up the story soon enough. And once the journalists realize that Brian is *the* Brian Burrows, husband of Mallory Burrows, whose disappearance three years ago sparked its own salacious headlines, they are bound to have a field day. Unable to decide what to do, Frank pushes away the question.

He pauses, hands filled with balled socks. Brian. Truly gone. Their relationship hadn't always been easy. What brothers' is? But the finality hits him hard. There will be so many things left unsaid.

Catherine

LET'S GO

I welcome the sight of the unpretentious little hotel that is my destination. My back is sore. My legs ache. The day will be scorching. Already the cobblestones are radiating an obnoxious combination of reflected heat and pungent stink.

The hotel is decrepit, crumbling stone, broken steps, its weather-beaten door a faded turquoise. I step inside into the cool, dim lobby, blinking to adjust my eyes.

"Ah, mademoiselle. Welcome." The greeting comes from Gabriel, the ancient and cantankerous proprietor. Gabriel and I have an understanding. I pay cash and he asks no questions.

Gabriel's hands, knotty from arthritis, move quickly enough when pocketing the wad of euros I give him. In return he hands me a key. Room 3. My favorite.

I mount the warped and creaky stairs to the second floor and fit the key into the door of my room. An iron bedstead is made up with threadbare sheets and a faded paisley coverlet. There is one chair, with a busted rush seat. One rickety table. The robin's-egg blue paint on the walls is cracked and peeling, the floor and base-boards scuffed, the one floor lamp, with its curling wrought-iron tendrils and fringed cobalt-colored shade, dusty.

So why is this room my favorite?

I stride to the window and peer out. From here I can see up and down the narrow street. The walls are thin enough that I can hear anyone coming, but the shutters are thick enough that I can block out all light. These are the reasons this room is my favorite.

I close the door and turn the lock. Pull the shutters, plunging the room into darkness. I kick off my heavy platform shoes and sink gratefully onto the bed. My eyes close.

"*Cathy.*" The feminine whisper tickles my ear. "*Let's go, Cathy. Let's go.*"

I bolt upright, eyes raking the shadows. My heart feels like it will explode right out of my chest.

Where is she? Can we get out in time?

I am alone.

ON A DIME

Frank settles into his seat on the Eurostar. Checks the time. They are scheduled to depart in seven minutes. He has spoken only to Jake; Natalie had been sedated. Frank is worried about her, anxious to see her in person. Jake sounded deeply dazed. Shock, no doubt.

Frank once again counts the blessings that landed him in London on business. Lucky timing in the midst of a grotesque horror.

A sturdy, Nordic-looking woman tucks into the seat next to him, and Frank gives her a cursory nod. He hopes she's not a talker. He wants to be left alone to pick through his memories of his brother.

Frank had been eight, so that would have made Brian fifteen. Frank walked all by himself from the school bus stop to their house. The walk meant crossing only one street, but this was the first year Frank had been allowed to do it solo. He was proud and careful as he checked for traffic and crossed the road.

He let himself into the house, dropping his backpack and his keys on the bench in the front hall, calling for his mother. No answer.

He found her slumped on the tiled floor of the kitchen, her face slick with tears, a half-empty bottle of frozen vodka spilling its icy contents onto her blouse. She became enraged when she saw him, and although Frank now understands that she had been deeply ashamed, at the time all he'd felt was fear and panic. She'd scrambled unsteadily to her feet, brandishing the bottle, slopping vodka as she shrieked at him to go to his room.

Frank was stunned; *he'd* done nothing wrong! He refused. His mother grabbed him by his arm and dragged him to the front door, throwing him out into the street.

"You can just stay there, then!" she'd snarled, slamming the door shut and turning the lock.

Locked out of his house and terrified by this monster that had taken control of his mother, but still pricked by the righteous belief in his own innocence, Frank had pounded on the door yelling to be let in. His mother didn't come. She wouldn't come.

Brian found him huddled there four hours later when he came back from baseball practice. Frank's tears had long since dried. The hem of his T-shirt was striated with snot. Brian brought Frank inside and told him to take a shower. When Frank emerged from the bathroom, their mother was tucked into bed, asleep, a bottle of aspirin and a glass of water on her bedside table. Brian was in the kitchen making sandwiches.

"Let's not tell Dad," Brian offered. "He doesn't need to know." Their father was at a convention in Hilton Head, due back in two days.

Frank was silent. He had yelled and cried for hours, he had no words left.

"You know about Laurie?" Brian asked. Frank managed a shake of the head.

Brian sighed. "There was another baby between you and me. A girl. Laurie. Today's her birthday. She would have been twelve. Usually Dad is here, you know, but . . ."

Frank had a thick, gummy bite of PB&J in his mouth; he couldn't swallow so instead spit it into his hand. "What happened to her? Laurie?"

"That thing where babies just don't wake up. SIDS? I was too young to remember, but, you gotta understand, Frank, some days are just harder than others for Mom."

Frank couldn't sleep that night.

But inevitably, the rhythm of their family life normalized. Frank went to school and Little League, out on the family sailboat, away to summer camp.

And even though his mother went back to being the mother he always knew, this incident marked the first time he understood that things, and people, could change on a dime.

And so they have again.

Catherine

RANSOM

The sweet little outdoor café in the 1st arrondissement is three-quarters full. Marble and brass tables. Cocky green umbrellas provide shade while promoting *pastis*. A balmy breeze, the warming sun. A spectacular Parisian day.

I fall in love with this city all over again; it's impossible not to. I wear old boyfriend jeans, a man's button-down knotted at the waist, sneakers. Perfect clothes to move fast.

Tucked in a corner, my back to the wall, I scribble in a notebook, broad-brimmed hat tugged low over my forehead. Pick at a slice of chocolate cake.

The image of Brian Burrows's bloodied body ricochets through my mind, unbidden, unwanted.

The coagulated blood. His splayed palms, open, beseeching.

I have a job to do. When it's finished I can think about discovering Brian Burrows's corpse. Not until then. I let a creamy morsel of decadent chocolate icing melt against my tongue. Sip my bitterly rich espresso.

The object of my interest sits with two pals. He chain-smokes and coughs, gulps red wine. When he throws back his head and laughs, I suppress a frown. That's not the behavior of a man whose beloved wife's been kidnapped. This whole scheme is predicated on a series of assumptions, one leading to the next with researched certainty. There is no room for me to have made a mistake.

There she is, right on schedule. Delphine.

She looks magnificent. I knew she would; she's come quite a long way since we first met, and even then she had mad raw skills.

I chance a quick glance at him. His thick lips and nose would be ugly on another man, but the broad planes of his cheekbones and jaw anchor these features with an unexpected grace. He has a thick mane of hair about which he is vain; I can tell from the way he strokes it. Dark circles under bloodshot eyes reassure me that maybe the laugh was just a stress release.

It's go time.

Delphine sashays by him. Her navy sheath dress at first appears chaste, but skims close enough to reveal every sinuous undulation of her exquisite body. High heels pitch her ass up, her tits forward. Prada sunglasses shield her face. The wig she wears bounces a mane of shiny blond curls down her back. We know he likes blondes.

It unfolds just like I planned. His eyes follow her. He grunts something in Russian. His buddies laugh, then turn to stare at her. A dusky-skinned teen in waiter's garb (Jumah, a friend of mine, you'll meet him later) glides past their table, drops the thick ivory-colored envelope onto my Russian's lap, and exits the café without anyone taking notice.

Casually, I tuck my notebook into my purse. Lay down twenty euros for my cake and coffee. I saunter out of the café. Join the ebb and flow of the pedestrians savoring this glorious summer afternoon.

I hear it: the shout of excited rage. I smile. The note has been read. The note itself is old school, formed of letters cut from Russian newspapers bought in Finland, glued to a piece of stiff vellum purchased at an art supply shop in Madrid, all touched only while wearing gloves.

The payment methodology is new school: bitcoin.

Nothing like mixing it up when making a ransom demand.

Natalie

REUNION

Jake had insisted she get some fresh air; when she'd resisted he'd explained that when Uncle Frank got there it would be necessary to go over some "details" that it might be best for Natalie to miss. She would have fought harder but she was lethargic, a combination of shock and the sedatives the doctor had prescribed, so she slouched out here into Parc Monceau. It's now a hateful place. The last space in the world that held Natalie's *before*.

The problem is, her brain shrieks with gruesome imaginings about the "details" she's supposedly been spared. What could be worse than seeing her father's slit throat?

She takes some comfort from the bloody shred of cuticle worried between her teeth, from the hidden burn of the tiny cuts she's incised along her inner thigh.

A young cop with a weight-lifter's build is positioned where he can observe her. She glares back at him with laser eyes, imagining his eruption into flame, cinder, and powdery ash.

Be grateful for every day? Fuck that shit. Natalie shivers despite the humid warmth of the afternoon. Then she sees them: Jake and Uncle Frank.

Thank god. Uncle Frank will know what to do.

She is over to greet him in a flash. The three of them form a spontaneous circle. Arms around shoulders, foreheads meeting; an insular curtain of shared love and grief.

Natalie is startled to learn they have to move to a hotel. But of course they do. The apartment's a crime scene. It's a relief, in a way.

They have a police escort to a functional, modern, all-suite hotel. Through the window of the sedan, Natalie watches as the streets of Paris drift by. Cafés and shops and bicyclists. Restaurants and monuments and tourist traps. Paris is a city that has reclaimed and reinvented itself from war, occupation, terrorism. She envies that resilience, although she doesn't share it. She would like to die, she thinks. Just curl up and die.

Natalie feels poisoned. Or maybe like she *is* poison. She's not sure which.

They check in and are asked by the officer in charge to stay put for a while. The weight-lifter gendarme is stationed in the hallway outside their suite, just to be sure.

Finally, they are alone in their suite with its functional, modern furniture and orange and brown décor. There's a dining table that seats four and Uncle Frank gestures that they should all take a seat.

No one says anything. Natalie thinks ruefully that they are beyond the platitudes of grief. It's unbearable, this weight of loss and sorrow. *Unbearable.*

She's relieved when Uncle Frank begins with logistics. Obviously they will cooperate with the police. He has also made an appointment for them at the American embassy first thing in the morning. From those two statements he goes on to order a meal for them from room service. Natalie is struck by a sickening sense of déjà vu. She had thought Uncle Frank taking charge would bring the same reassurance it had when Mom disappeared. Instead its familiarity is making her ill.

Silent tears spill down Natalie's cheeks. She drops her face onto her crossed arms. Uncle Frank rubs her back. Murmurs those very platitudes about everything being all right that Natalie hates, having heard them too many times before when nothing was *all right* at all.

A crash makes her jump. She lifts her head to see Jake hoisting a chair over his head. He smashes it again into the already shattered full-length mirror. Shards of mirror shower soundlessly to the carpeted floor.

Uncle Frank is on his feet, his face white. "Jake. Stop that. It's not going to help a thing."

"Fuck him!" Jake screams hoarsely. "Fuck that asshole!" His face is mottled with rage; his body bristles with aggression.

Natalie huddles into herself, making her body as small as possible. She doesn't know whom Jake is cursing: Their father? His killer? God?

She doesn't know. She doesn't care. She just wants the violence to stop.

Catherine

GHOSTS

It was fifteen days before I extracted Elena from Paris that I first saw the Burrows family in the Marais. I saw the girl first. She looked familiar, not in a vague, where-have-I-seen-her-before kind of way, but in a punch-to-the-gut kind of way. My eye was caught by that particular shade of auburn hair, by a glimpse of those wide gray eyes.

She looked older now, of course, more womanly under her oversized shirt and loosely slung jeans, still almost painfully thin. But it was Natalie Burrows. My eyes scanned the two men with her. Yes, that was her brother, Jake. And her father. Brian.

What the hell were they doing in Paris?

I shuddered and forced myself to breathe slowly. I'd thought I would never see any of them again. They are why I fled to Paris in the first place. My failure to save Mallory Burrows after she reached out to the Burial Society is a splinter in my heart. My greatest failure. I've always felt I owe Mallory, owe her family.

But I couldn't afford this distraction, not with Elena's abduction looming. I had just met with Delphine and given instructions for a nondescript van and an equally anonymous taxi. My other plans for the day included a rendezvous with Gerard, my lover, before he headed home to his understanding wife, and then confirmation of the shipping route out of the port of Marseille.

I had an hour before I was to meet Gerard. It was against my better judgment, but also a scratch I had to itch. I followed the three Burrowses through the cobblestone streets.

They were shopping for their supper. A stop at the *fromagerie,* the *patisserie,* the *boucherie.* Watching, I examined them for the telltale, ashy residue of tragedy.

Brian pointed out selections to his children. Natalie was the one who responded to him, asking questions, acquiescing, or making alternate suggestions. Jake stayed sullen and slouched, his hands buried in his pockets, his neck and shoulders a vulture's hunch.

It would be easy enough for me to find out where they were staying and for how long. I offered up a little prayer that they were in Paris only briefly. Seeing them had sent my stomach roiling, set my brain spinning.

I was due to see Gerard in eighteen minutes. He can be so pouty when I'm late.

I hurried into my apartment on rue des Archives. Dropped my keys into the china dish on the console table near the door.

An image floated before my eyes. Radiant gray eyes under sharply curved eyebrows. Natalie's eyes. So like her mother's. I pushed the image away.

"Baby," I purred as I pulled off my shirt and slipped out of my shoes.

Gerard sat majestically in the middle of my bed, naked. Unhooking my bra and sliding off my skirt and panties, I climbed onto the bed, just grazing his body with mine, teasing him with brushes of my flesh.

Gerard kissed me. Then flipped me over and smacked my bottom with his open palm. *"You are late,"* he scolded in French as he struck. The pain was pleasure and just what I needed right now.

"Again," I begged in French. *"Hit me again."*

When I was satiated, I sent Gerard home. Went back to work on the plans to kidnap my Russian supermodel. Pushed the Burrows family out of my brain.

I never dreamed that Brian Burrows would be dead by the time I got back to Paris. Or that I would be the one to discover his body.

Part Two

ORIGINS

How do we ever really know what's true?
Memory is a kaleidoscope.
History transforms with each telling.
So believe what you will. Don't we all?
Let's go back in time, just a little bit.

Natalie

MISSING

There was something in the air. Even before she opened her eyes, Natalie felt it, even though she couldn't put a label to what "it" was exactly. She snuggled deeper into her down pillows and silky comforter. Late March and there was still a chill in the mornings.

It was the quiet. The house shouldn't be so quiet. Deep unease settled over Natalie as she slipped away from her cloudy dreams and into the reality of this particular morning.

Jake was just home for spring break, so no surprise he was sleeping in. But Mom should be up, making coffee, sorting the mountain of laundry Jake had brought back from school, buzzing with anticipation for the moment her older child woke so she could ply him with food and grill him about his classes, the city, his friends (and, with only slightly more veiled probing, his love life).

Natalie's eyes flew open.

She glanced at the digital clock on her night table. Over half an hour until her alarm was set to go off.

But the quiet.

Going back to sleep seemed impossible.

Natalie threw back her covers and sat on the edge of the bed. She looked around her bedroom, really taking it in as if it wasn't the same room she had woken in for all of her fifteen years. She loved her bed, with its ruched and beribboned canopy that she knew she should have outgrown but hadn't. She loved the deep lemon paint on the walls, her giant corkboard pinned with concert tickets and dried roses, stickers and inspirational quotes, photographs and poems. She loved her window seat with its thick yellow-and-white striped cushions, how it looked out over their backyard, which was just now budding with early spring. She loved her bookcases overflowing with novels, travel books, memoirs, and biographies, and her old-fashioned desk with its neat little cubbyholes for pens and rulers, pencils and paper clips.

But the quiet.

Mom never stayed away overnight. Mom would *never* not be here to make pancakes and bacon for Jake on his first morning home.

Natalie padded out of her bedroom. The cool wood of the wide plank floors felt reassuring underneath her feet, as did the rough texture of the woven rag rug. But even as she comforted herself with their familiarity, she knew something was *wrong*.

Natalie found her father downstairs, pacing in the living room, wearing the same clothes he had worn the day before. His face was ashen. Morning light glinted silver off his stubbled jaw. When had Dad's beard gone gray? Overnight? Or had Natalie just not noticed before?

"Daddy?"

Brian gave her a weak smile. "Morning, pumpkin."

"Where's Mom?"

Brian just looked at her.

"Dad. Where is she?"

"I don't know, honey. We had a bit of a fight last night and she took off." Brian rubbed at the corner of his eye with a knuckle. "I'm sure she'll be back soon."

Natalie knew he was mistaken.

Something terrible had happened and it was all Natalie's fault.

Jake

24 HOURS

Deep navy shadows crawled away from the house and into the gathering night, even as golden light flowed from every window, unanswered beacons.

Jake perched on the porch railing, hands shoved into the pockets of his hoodie, shoulders hunched, staring at the suddenly unfamiliar street in front of the house he had lived in all his life. Nothing felt the same, looked the same, was the same. He checked his watch.

It was twenty-four hours since Mom had gone missing.

He longed to reverse time itself, dial it back a week to when the stress of midterms and whether he would get to bone David, the hot sophomore from North Dakota, were his most pressing problems.

Jake unfurled his body. As he entered the house, he called, "It's just me."

After all, why let the creak of a door hinge lure Natalie to false hope?

His father, on the other hand, could go fuck himself.

The fucker was just where Jake had left him. On the sofa, head in hands, cellphone by his side. Natalie was curled into a corner of the loveseat, wrapped in an afghan, chewing raw the skin bordering her left thumbnail.

"Call." Jake was surprised venom didn't spill from his mouth as he spoke. "It's twenty-four hours. Call the cops."

Brian raised his head. His eyes were glassy.

"Do it," Jake spat.

Brian's eyes locked on Jake's stony face. Drifted to Natalie's wide-eyed stare. Finally, Brian grabbed for his cellphone and nodded. Stood. Hesitated. Then he picked up the blown glass hummingbird from the coffee table. It was Mom's favorite, a birthday present from Jake and Natalie. "I'll call from the kitchen," Brian said, pocketing the glass figurine.

"It's his fault, you know," Jake muttered as much to Brian's retreating back as to Natalie.

"Don't," his sister shot back. "Just *don't*."

Brother and sister. Closer than many. In fact, closer than most. Three years and two months younger, little Natalie had worshipped her big brother from babyhood. Toddled after him. Played with trucks because he played with trucks. Cheered herself hoarse at his Little League games. Tailored her Halloween costumes to his whim. And of course, in return, he abused her. Teased and tickled her mercilessly. Shut her out of his games. Played pranks and pulled her hair. She had adored him throughout it all.

As they got older, though, Jake became protective. Dad was away all the time. Mom was unhappy and distracted. Jake had felt *too* responsible for Natalie these last few years. She was fragile and Jake felt both responsible and burdened.

It had been a relief to start college, to move to New York City, to get out of this house. He came home often enough. And Natalie had spent a weekend with him in the fall term. It was all right. She was all right. She was. Until last night. Until today.

He'd been about to go out last night when he heard his parents fighting. It would have been impossible not to, what with the volume at which they were going at it. They fought a lot, they always had, so Jake had learned to tune out much of it. But last night, his mother had sounded different. Jake had hovered by the garage door, arrested by her tone and words. She wasn't angry. She was *afraid*. She had said as much, out loud. She had actually uttered the words, "I'm afraid for my life!" as she slammed out the front door.

Afraid of his father? Jake could believe it. Everyone thought Brian was such a paragon of virtue. A pillar of society. The respected architect with the international career, the gorgeous wife, and the two picture-perfect children. A staunch supporter of the fashionable charities (and even of one or two more personal projects, just to prove how individual and forward thinking he was). A handsome, affable guy, a rock star in his field, blessed with the ideal family, the ideal life.

He was also the guy who had backhanded Jake across the mouth so hard he had sent him flying to the floor and knocked out a tooth.

True, it had only been the one time, and Brian had sprung tears of apology even before Jake was back on his feet. But Jake couldn't forget it. The incident festered and smoldered. From that day forward Jake knew his father was capable of sudden, terrifying violence.

Mr. Brian Fucking Perfect Burrows wasn't perfect after all.

Frank

3 DAYS MISSING

Frank Burrows's life was literally one of buttons and bows. With a wife and twin daughters of the girliest sort, as well as a job selling beauty supplies, Frank was surrounded by the accoutrements of female adornment. He sold hairbrushes and ponytail holders, barrettes and bobby pins, combs and clips for a company called Good Hair!! (two exclamation points included on every package). He had risen through the ranks and was the manager of a tristate sales staff, so all good there, but the unvarnished truth was that Frank hated his job. How could he get excited about moving flimsy pieces of plastic and rubber encrusted with cheap rhinestones and plastic beading? He couldn't.

But Frank had a way with people; he could bullshit with the best of them, always found a conversational way in. And his staff loved his "low-key yet supportive brand of motivation." If only they knew it was simply the path of least resistance. Remembering a wife's name or that a kid just got an orange belt in tae kwon do went a long way in the world of sales. This, Frank was willing to do.

As he piloted his Volvo closer to his brother's place, Frank tamped down the rage that had simmered during his entire drive to Westport. Frank knew he had to let go of the argument that had erupted when he told Della he was using his vacation days to be with Brian and his kids. Had to forget her flashing eyes, the smack of her hand on the kitchen counter, the way she came at him with the poultry shears she plucked from the center of the butcher's block. Even more frightening, how her mask of adoring mother, *normal person,* dropped into place when the babysitter came into the room with the girls. Della would never hurt the girls. Never. He believed that much at least, but her lightning-fast ability to swerve from harpy to happy was unnerving to say the least.

He tried to remember a time when he'd loved Della, or even lusted for her, and failed. Instead he conjured the swelling bubble of pride, love, and anticipation that had consumed him when his newborn daughters were placed in his arms. Frank sighed.

That delicious bubble had popped pretty quickly under the relentless pressure of his wife. More, more, more, she demanded. The best doctors, the certified nanny, the luxury double pram she'd seen in a celebrity magazine. Then on to the best toddler programs, private music lessons, Japanese classes. His girls would want for nothing even if it killed him. Some days he thought it might. Frank had to admit he never would have risen so high at his company without the cattle prod, but he also had to admit he wouldn't have cared.

Mallory had been missing for three days. Frank needed to get his head on straight. He was needed here.

Turning the corner to Brian's street, Frank was struck by the real/unreal quality of the vibrating pack of reporters and cameramen lurking across from the Burrows house. Of course there would be reporters. Why did he feel so shocked?

Frank sucked in a nervous gulp of air as he pulled his car over to park.

Reporters surged toward him. Frank slung his duffel bag over one shoulder. Patted his pockets. Keys? Yes. Wallet? Yes. Good to go.

Frank opened the Volvo door. Lights flashed in his face. The air thrummed.

As Frank slid from the car and slammed his door shut, he was swallowed by a surging mass of bodies. Cameras whirred to life. He raised one hand, shielding his face against the thrusting microphones, and muscled his way through the crowd. Questions were shouted. "Who are you?" "Are you Brian Burrows's attorney?" "Did Brian kill his wife?"

What? Brian kill Mallory? Completely absurd. Frank's shoulders rose indignantly. Brian would never. Not Mallory. And he wouldn't be capable anyway. It just wasn't the way Brian was made.

Frank wheeled around sharply. "Have some respect! Their children are in this house!"

The flash of a camera caught Frank mid-yell, one eyebrow raised, so vitriolic he looked like a comic book supervillain in the resulting snap.

Jake

---

19 DAYS MISSING

Jake was spying.

His perch on the second-floor landing was the same one he had picked since he was a little boy. To the left of the sightline of anyone seated in the deep burgundy leather sofa that anchored the living room. Behind the backs of those occupying the facing pair of cushy upholstered armchairs.

His father and his uncle were on the couch. A pair of detectives occupied the chairs, their cheap, somber garb forbidding against the cheerful geometric design of ochre, orange, and egg-yolk yellow.

Jake had trolled the Westport Police website. Seen the statistics. Traffic accidents, vandalism, burglaries, bar fights, and noise complaints. Kids smoking pot. The occasional domestic disturbance. Not a hotbed of criminal conspiracy, his hometown.

This domestic disturbance, this missing woman, his mother, the whole of it, seemed beyond them.

They had no leads they said, no new information. They'd conducted local door-to-door inquiries, checked area CCTV footage, spoken to the employees at the women's shelter where Mallory volunteered, interviewed all her friends. They'd deployed the department's two K-9 officers with their dogs. But it was as if Mallory Burrows had simply vanished off the face of the earth.

"We want to go over the night your wife disappeared one more time."

The speaker had coarse black hair. He raked his fingers through it. Detective Benson.

Uncle Frank spoke first. "Again? For god's sake, what else could he possibly tell you? It's been almost three weeks and you just keep asking the same damn *questions*. How about some *answers*?"

Jake pressed his hot forehead against the cool wood of the banister. Everybody knew the statistics. After forty-eight hours the likelihood of Jake's mother being alive was slim, so by now . . .

There was always the possibility that Mallory had just taken a breather, the lady cop, "Call me Karen," had assured Jake and Natalie. "It happens, sometimes even the best moms need a break," but Jake knew that couldn't be true. He had just come home for spring break. Mom wouldn't have. Not now.

"Just take us through it one more time," Cop Karen wheedled.

The detectives' high beams were trained on Brian. This both sickened and thrilled Jake. If his father had done it—and he was only thinking *if*, mind you, he wasn't sure—but if he *had* done it, Jake wanted him to fry.

"No, it's all right," his father said. "Anything, if it will help."

Brian's story had a weary cadence to it now, freighted by multiple tellings. He had gotten home the night before Mallory disappeared. The business trip to Barcelona had gone well, he'd been awarded the commission. He was jet-lagged, slept in late. It was a Saturday. He had lunch at home with his wife and daughter. Their son came back from the city for spring break later that afternoon. They all had dinner together. Jake and Natalie went out afterward to see friends. Brian was tired and admittedly short-tempered. He and Mallory had words. She slammed the door as she left.

"And said nothing about where she was going?"

"No."

"She didn't mention going over to the yacht club where we found her car?"

"No."

"Do you know why she would have gone to the club that night?"

"We've been over this a thousand times. We keep our family's sailboat there, but as to why that night I have no idea."

"What were her last words to you?"

"As I've already told you," Brian spat through a tight jaw, "she told me to go fuck myself. I'm being completely transparent with you. We had a bad argument, yes! But that's all I know. . . ."

Brian's face clouded over, his voice choked with tears.

Either his father hadn't done it or he was a damn good actor. But why didn't Dad tell the cops that Mom said she was afraid? *Afraid for her life.*

"What was the fight about?" Benson pressed.

"I've told you. The amount of traveling I was doing for work."

"In the course of your argument did your wife tell you she was afraid of someone or something?" Benson's tone was mild.

Jake tilted forward in anticipation. *Let's see what Dad has to say about this.*

"What?" Brian's face mottled red.

"Did she?"

"Where did you hear that?"

"Answer the question."

"Yes, but I didn't take her seriously," Brian choked out.

Frank put a consoling hand on his brother's shoulder.

"Is there a reason you kept this information from us, Mr. Burrows?" Cop Karen's voice was as creamy as butter.

"I was ashamed." The words caught in Brain's throat. "Ashamed that I belittled her fears. And then, the longer I went without saying anything . . ." He trailed off. Shrugged.

"Do you know who or what she was afraid of?"

"No. I . . . I wouldn't listen to her. I told her she was being ridiculous. Overly dramatic. That's why she told me to fuck myself." Shame and pain strangled Brian's words.

The two detectives exchanged a sidelong glance.

"And then what happened?"

"Like I said. Mallory left. The kids came home, Natalie close to midnight, Jake a little after."

"Kinda late for a fifteen-year-old, isn't it?" Benson made the question an accusation.

"What are you implying?" Dad's face contorted.

Cop Karen leaned toward him. "We're just trying to understand the rules of your household. Does Natalie have a curfew?"

"Of course she does." It was Uncle Frank who answered. "It was the first weekend of spring break. Home by midnight as requested."

His father shot Uncle Frank a look, startled, grateful. It occurred to Jake that Brian didn't actually know whether Natalie had a curfew or not. Why would he? He was never here to enforce it. And Uncle Frank was so quick to cover for him.

"Please continue, Mr. Burrows."

"I told both kids their mom had gone to bed early. That was unlike her, Mallory was a night owl, but I didn't want them to worry."

"But you were worried, right?"

"Yes."

"Yet when you spoke to us you didn't think to mention that your wife expressly told you she was afraid for her life?" Benson pressed again, this time with a sharper edge.

"I know I should have said. But I don't know anything, so it can't really matter, right? She never told me anything specific." The naked desperation on his father's face turned Jake's stomach. "Where did you hear that? Please. What else do you know?"

"We'd like to ask you the same, Mr. Burrows."

The air vibrated with an ominous silence.

Jake was disgusted by his father's needy weakness. It was almost as bad as believing him capable of murder.

Uncle Frank rose, decisive. "You need to go now. We need to get the kids their dinner. We've given you all the information we can." The finality in his voice was not to be denied.

The detectives stood. Made a show of shaking hands. Said good night in tones that rang with warning as Frank eased them toward the door.

Uncle Frank had earned Jake's respect these last couple of weeks. He'd handled everything. Taken complete charge. Even helped Jake and Natalie post "missing" flyers emblazoned with Mallory's photograph all over town while Dad stayed at home hunched by the phone. And Jake knew Uncle Frank was as worried about Nat as he was. Natalie just wasn't *right*. She wasn't eating much, sure, but Jake suspected that was the least of it. It was like there was something rotten festering inside her. It was the only way he could think to describe it.

You heard about these stories, these horrors, all the time. Women abducted. Imprisoned. Killed and discarded. But it wasn't supposed to happen to you. Not to your family. Never to *your* mother.

Jake retched, coughing up a string of yellow bile that he caught in his cupped palms. He made it into the bathroom just as he heard the sound of the front door closing behind the cops.

22 DAYS MISSING

The longer it went, the more isolated Natalie felt.

Jake thundered and glowered when he was around the house, but came and went as he pleased, often without even a word. Dad was slow to respond, a half-step *off* all the time, just missing the point.

Uncle Frank took care of everything: the shopping, the cooking, the laundry, the press, the cops, the neighbors and friends, both nosy and concerned. He arranged a leave of absence from NYU for Jake. Called Natalie's high school and arranged to have her work sent home.

How could she care about biology and English lit? Advanced algebra or U.S. history? It all was a crock of shit. Her mother was *missing*.

She couldn't face it, the sea of curious, salacious, pitying faces. The gossip and whispers. The crude remarks and sly, ugly jokes. Even her close friends didn't seem to know what to say and that pissed Natalie off. Their hesitancy and recoil. Their skittish eyes. Even her best friend, Melissa.

Natalie gnawed down the bloody, ragged side of her left thumb. She welcomed the metallic tang of the blood, felt a stinging relief with each shred of skin worried away by her nimble teeth. A stab of hunger hit and she tried to remember the last time she ate. This morning. Half an apple, sliced into delicate, paper-thin wafers.

Her stomach clawed at itself, but she didn't dare eat more, deeply convinced of the urgent necessity of self-denial.

She curled into her window seat and watched as her cousins, Addy and Ana, set up a tea party in the backyard. Normally Natalie would have indulged them and played along, but.

She hadn't left the house in thirteen days. She hadn't left her room in four.

Aunt Della's whiny screech disrupted the gentle murmurs of Addy and Ana pouring "tea" and sharing cookies. Della had brought the twins for a visit. Natalie got that Uncle Frank wanted to see his girls, but bringing anyone into the toxic cloud that had descended on their home felt like a bad idea, much less someone as already poisonous as Della.

Uncle Frank's voice rose in response. Natalie couldn't make out what he was saying, but he was angry. Aunt Della's strident reply was clear as a bell, though. "You just try it. You'll never see the twins again!"

How could she? How could Della even think about leveling that kind of threat, now of all times? There she went, expertly demonstrating her tone-deaf response to the emotional delicacy of any situation. Natalie despised her.

Anger fueled Natalie downstairs and into the kitchen. Uncle Frank stood at the sink, hands gripping the stainless steel rim. Dad perched on one of the four stools lined up at the kitchen counter.

"What's going on?"

Uncle Frank turned, unable to hide his relieved surprise at seeing Natalie out of her room.

"Aunt Della and the girls are going home."

"You're staying, though, Uncle Frank?" Natalie heard the rising lilt of panic in her own voice.

"Of course, honey. As long as you guys need. It's just hard on Della and especially on the girls. They're really too young to understand what's happening."

What did "young" have to do with it? How could *anyone* understand?

Natalie burned to know why her father hadn't stopped it. How could he have left the family flanks vulnerable to a predator? Wasn't Daddy supposed to protect them? Wasn't he supposed to *fix* everything?

Uncle Frank laid a hand on her shoulder. "Hard for any of us to make sense of this, Nat. I know."

Natalie jerked away. Could Uncle Frank read her mind now?

"But the police are doing everything they can," Uncle Frank assured. "And we have each other."

Natalie managed a quick nod.

Brian's eyes rose to meet Natalie's, as if Frank's words somehow blazed a light through a dense fog, allowing the father to fully see the daughter in front of him for the first time in days.

Natalie stared back at him, but found no comfort in his gaze.

Still, she understood. She and her father sipped from a shared elixir of fear, guilt, rage, misery, love, and loss. She'd heard him prowl the house during the thickest hours of night, when she too was restless and haunted.

She couldn't blame him for how he had disappeared into himself—hadn't she done the same?

Part Three

CONVERGENCE

If I could tell the story differently . . .

It would be a tale of bravery. Noble motives and nobler deeds.

A story in which regrets were redeemed and the past forgiven.

But one can only twist the truth so much.

Catherine

SPICE

I haven't slept. With the ransom note delivered, my only task now is to wait. Patience is not one of my virtues. I've been prowling around my apartment for hours. I feel jittery and unfocused.

I draw the curtains open and peer down at the street below. Akili, my earth-brown neighbor, lifts the roll-up gate guarding his Moroccan spice shop. His son is Jumah, whom I enlisted for yesterday's ransom drop.

So many lives. So many stories. Perhaps tales for another time.

With no definitive action to take, my thoughts are too free to roam.

Mallory Burrows. Despite my many successes, it's that failure that haunts. And now her husband, Brian, is dead? Murdered. Improbable. But true.

Two nights ago I'd brushed past Natalie Burrows on my way out of their family's apartment near Parc Monceau. I did nothing to stop her, even though I knew that girl was walking in to discover her father's bloody corpse. My breath quickens remembering it. But I needed to get out of there. Brian's laptop was tucked under my arm. I couldn't afford kindness.

I'd manufactured a persona, an expat running an organization for Americans living in Paris, arranged a meeting. I wanted to see how Brian Burrows was faring three years after Mallory's disappearance. To look into his eyes and take his measure. There was no answer when I arrived at the appointed time. I picked the lock to allow myself a discreet look around.

And found Brian with his throat slashed.

I grabbed his laptop and bolted. Force of habit, I guess. I wanted, no, *needed* to trace his digital fingerprints.

Brian's computer awaits me, tucked into one of the two desks in my command center, my apartment's second bedroom.

I run the Burial Society from this sun-flooded room with its banks of monitors and multiple keyboards, numerous hard drives and neat stacks of supplies (medical, tactical, office), the two desks (both for me), and the austere hard-backed desk chair on wheels which I use to zip between them. I am known by face and (various) names to some of the people in my network; to many more I exist only in the cyber realm. I prefer it that way.

I traffic in others' secrets, but don't want anyone knowing mine.

I unlock the door to the command center by pressing my thumb against the fingerprint-activated biometric door lock. Pop open Brian's computer. Crack his password, trying "Mallory," her birthday, their anniversary, and a dozen other logical possibilities before hitting bingo: "jake&nat."

I'm into his email easily enough. Lots of work-related correspondence. Promotions from Barneys New York, Amazon, Maxim, Uber, American Express, *Architectural Digest*. Missives from friends back in the States. An invoice from a place called Meadowfield, an elder care facility. An email from Brian's brother, Frank, about his unexpected trip to London, suggesting they spend a couple of days together when Frank's trade show was over. Brian's enthusiastic reply.

They would have a very different sort of reunion now.

I snap Brian's computer closed and fire up one of my own.

Going through encrypted and secure Tor channels, I am assured that Elena is safely deposited in Genoa. The tomato-red warehouse where she is now housed nestles anonymously among many others of similarly brilliant hues that clutter the rocky beach. Four floors of the warehouse are devoted to the storage of olive oil before it is loaded onto ships for distribution. The top floor has been fitted out as a luxurious apartment. Elena will be comfortable. I've stayed there myself.

The enormity of what I'm trying to accomplish abruptly overwhelms me. I'm putting others in danger as well as myself. The whole plan is risky, possibly insane. I can't afford a single mistake.

The last thing I need is the complication of the Burrows family.

_____

COPS AND ROBBERS

Frank has insisted on the meeting at the prefecture. He wants to rouse those two dazed kids from the hotel room, get them some fresh air. Remind them that *they* are still alive.

For his own sake, Frank craved action, *information*. He needed a sense of what the police know, what they are doing. But now that he, Jake, and Natalie are cooling their heels in the waiting room, Frank feels less sure.

The room reeks of desperation and institutional indifference. Threadbare gray carpet, dun-colored walls. Posters announcing police initiatives against such things as graffiti and subway groping, which Frank can only decode based on the brightly jarring artwork. He speaks no French. He's been assured of an English-speaking translator. This is all hard enough without the language barrier.

They arrived on time for their appointment, but have been kept waiting almost forty-five minutes. Natalie sits on the bench next to him, knees pulled up to her chest. Jake slouches against the wall, tapping at his phone.

Frank reflects that these kids are well trained in the art of patience in the face of a dreaded unknown. That's a sorry fact.

The inner door swings open. A woman greets them in a soft,

lightly accented tone. "Monsieur Burrows? My name is Aimee Martinet. I am your liaison."

Aimee Martinet's in her forties, striking, gray-streaked dark hair pulled back into a chignon, frank brown eyes, a permanent furrow between her brows that makes her look as if every single word has been carefully deliberated before utterance. Her skirted uniform fits her superbly. Her navy leather heels are surprisingly high.

Aimee clicks, clicks, clicks down the hallway and ushers them into a room. A blond wood table surrounded by molded plastic chairs. Three stark white walls, a fourth painted red, a mirror in its center. Frank wonders if it's the kind that allows someone unseen to observe them. He wonders if someone unseen *is* observing them.

A pile of yellow legal pads and a ceramic mug full of pencils grace the center of the table. Frank takes a legal pad and then opens his own pen, a **fancy Cross** number that had been a Christmas gift from his brother. Frank glances first at his nephew and then his niece, flanking him at the table. Jake pretends indifference. Natalie gnaws a cuticle.

Aimee sits opposite them. When she speaks, her voice is intended to soothe. "Are you sure you want the children here?"

Frank nods. He promised them this. He understands. The desire to make sense of a senseless universe is one of humanity's most urgent needs, and it's been developed to an especially fine edge in these two young people whose mother disappeared off the face of the earth three years ago, whose father has just been murdered in cold blood.

Aimee opens a file. The police have interviewed the other residents of the building as well as neighbors along the street. Run fingerprints found at the scene. Talked to Brian's co-workers. They're checking CCTV footage. However, as of now she's sorry to say they have no specific leads. They suspect it was a robbery gone terribly wrong, as Brian's laptop is missing. Surmise that perhaps someone saw him with his computer bag, followed him home.

Either tricked or forced his way into the apartment. Her voice drops (reverence for the dead? compassion for his loved ones?) as she announces they believe the robber killed Brian, then panicked, grabbed the computer, and ran. Aimee is terribly sorry. They will continue to do all they can.

Natalie shifts in her chair. Expels a gusty breath of dissatisfaction. Frank places a hand on hers. Is surprised to realize her fingers are trembling.

Is more surprised to realize that so are his own.

Catherine

MUSCLE

Lights pulse in the near darkness. Red, violet, and golden-amber flicker and glow, revealing tantalizing glimpses of breast, hip, ass. On the stage, platinum blond Louise Brooks wigs and provocative strips of barely-there black patent leather are the order of the day. Electronica throbs through the sound system; the girls arch and stretch, spin and twerk, open their thighs, lick their lips.

Other beauties thread through the crowd flirting and sipping, encouraging private dances, rounds of drinks. The club is upscale. The patrons are as well dressed as the performers are undressed.

The crowd is white, brown, black, yellow. Straight, gay, trans, fluid. Lots of couples. Several polyamorous clusters. A man who looks like he could be with his granddaughter. A regal African woman in traditional garb leads two naked Chinese men in collars and leashes. There are no rules here if the price is right.

Gerard's delighted eyes and slack jaw show I have done well on my offer of a surprise. I run one hand up along his inner thigh and gesture to a passing girl with the other. A sheer black negligee flung over hot pink panties, tits bare. In her six-inch heels, she's taller than both of us. She crooks a finger and shoots me a smile.

"*Let's go, Cathy. Let's go.*" A slivered whisper of memory twines through the pulse of the music, brings me to my feet.

Gerard's eyes lift to mine, as if to ask, *Really?* My lover looks so happily shocked when I give him an impish nod that I can't help but laugh.

We follow Pink Panties back into the recesses of the club. To the private rooms.

I don't know that you need all the details of what transpires next; let it suffice to say that lips, tongues, cocks, ears, pussies, necks, toes, assholes, mouths, breasts, and thighs are thoroughly explored. Backs are turned, asses slapped, tummies licked, calves stroked, wrists tied, orgasms had.

Gerard and I stumble out into shocking pink dawn. We've been here all night. The street's shops and cafés, the movie theater, the travel bookstore, the *tabac,* they are all still closed. I kiss Gerard goodbye. He has to go. Face work. Face his wife. He breathes a satiated *merci* into my ear and hurries away.

I'm not ready yet to face what's in front of me. I squint my eyes against the sunshine.

Then head back into the club.

DOUBT

Aimee Martinet, the police liaison, told one story, but Natalie can't help but wonder: How many other versions could also be told? Robbery just *feels* wrong. Yes, Dad's laptop's missing, but his watch and his wallet weren't taken. Nothing else from the apartment was stolen.

So what are the other ways to look at it? What other scenarios could have led to Dad's vicious murder?

Natalie burns with the need for more information. She must find out what was happening right before Dad was killed, while she and Jake were out of Paris.

Who was Brian spending his time with? Did anything unusual happen at work? In the apartment building? How can she find out?

She's determined to investigate. But how? Where to begin? She can't ask Jake for help. He's too volatile. Natalie finds it difficult to admit, even to herself, but she's afraid of her brother when he's angry. And he's been angry a lot. Not that she blames him.

Natalie contemplates her reflection in a mirror identical to the one Jake smashed their first day in this hotel. That very night, a pair of maintenance men clad in navy coveralls had come in, swept up the debris, hung a duplicate mirror, and departed, all without saying a word. It was like Jake had never broken the mirror, like the whole incident had never happened. Natalie finds it simultaneously reassuring and disturbing, this evidence that damage done can be so easily erased.

Uncle Frank will know what to do; he always does. Wasn't he the one who took care of everything when Mom disappeared?

Natalie knocks on her uncle's bedroom door. Frank calls to her to come in. He's propped up on the bed, a *New York Times* international edition open on his lap, a soccer match playing on the TV, the sound turned off.

She starts by posing questions, getting a feel for Uncle Frank's impression of the robbery theory before she advances her own qualms about its validity. She listens intently to his answers. Nods as if his words about faith in the system and the determination of the police actually reassure her.

With a sick twist of loss she remembers that it was her dad who taught her this technique. Listen first, in order to disarm your opponent with his or her own words. Different context, of course. Model United Nations negotiations in eleventh grade.

But Uncle Frank is on to her.

"I can tell you're up to something, Natalie. And all I can say is let the police do their jobs. You're not some kind of secret agent."

"I'm not saying I am! It's just his watch and his wallet weren't taken and—"

"You don't have superpowers."

"Am I saying I do? I'm just asking questions. Why was nothing else taken from the apartment? How did the killer get in? Why was the door locked when I got home?"

"That's enough, Nat! Stay away from this investigation! It's not safe for you."

Natalie pales. "Why do you say that? Do you know something you're not telling me?"

Uncle Frank swings his legs over the side of the mattress. Gently grasps Natalie's wrist and pushes up her sleeve. Natalie averts her eyes.

"Look at your arm, Nat. Don't pretend they're not there." He touches her chin with his index finger to turn her face. She refuses to look. She knows what she'll see. She carved them there: tiny incisions sliced by the precise blade of a razor into the thin, bluish skin of her inner arm.

"It makes me feel better," she manages to whisper.

"Not really," Uncle Frank whispers back before he releases her arm. He reclines against the headboard.

"Look, Nat," he continues in a level tone, "I know this is awful for you. It's awful for all of us. But it's not your job to fix it or solve it. Your only job right now is to take care of *you*."

Natalie capitulates. She lets Uncle Frank suggest a nearby rustic bistro for dinner. She goes through all the motions. Dices her food into bits and pushes it around on her plate so it looks like she's eaten just enough. Makes desultory conversation with Jake and Uncle Frank. Tries her French on the waiter. She hears herself laugh at a corny joke Frank floats out, registers his pleased flush at her response.

All the while, she is dreaming of her escape. Of diving into the streets of Paris, seeking out her father's murderer, and bringing him to justice, her journey protected by the shining beacon of truth.

Catherine

SNAP

Bone weary, I stumble into my apartment. Avert my eyes from the image greeting me in the mirror over the hall table as I drop my keys in their accustomed place. Pale skin, raccoon circles around my eyes. Strands of fine, light brown hair escaping from underneath my honey blond wig. My torn Versace dress reveals a purplish bruise rising on the soft flesh of my upper arm. I don't even remember it happening. I step out of my strappy Jimmy Choo snakeskin stilettos, my feet aching and raw. Pad into my bedroom.

I throw myself on top of my bed. Pull my favorite heavyweight chenille throw on top of my throbbing body. Burrow my head deep into a down pillow. All I want to do is sleep.

A phone vibrates. Shit. No.

Sleep. Please, just let me sleep.

The phone buzzes again, deep from the recesses of the black leather Céline handbag I used tonight.

Shit. The phone in the Céline is the emergency number for all things Elena.

I claw into my bag and extract the cell. Stare at the new text message without comprehension, at first too shocked and exhausted to make sense of it.

I'm on my feet and running a computer search the moment it sinks in.

There she is, Elena, radiant, laughing, pulling a scarf over her exquisite blond head, out and about on the Italian coast in an Instagram posted by a teenage fangirl from New Jersey on vacation with her parents.

Shit.

BARGAIN

The music is deafening, propulsive. Euro-disco at its finest. Laser lights split the darkness, streaking the mirrored surfaces, bouncing off shiny bodies. The dance floor throbs; it looks like a single gigantic organism composed of writhing torsos and twirling limbs.

Jake's bare-chested, slick with sweat, his T-shirt lost god-knows-where. He throws back another shot. He has never seen so many nearly naked men.

He's lost himself in this club, in the pure sensual pleasure of dancing, in the moody, theatrical lighting, among the hundreds of moving bodies.

He pushes damp hair away from his forehead.

A sleekly muscled guy in a pair of royal blue satin shorts and not much else grinds up against him. Whispers something Jake can't understand in his ear, though the message is clear enough in the man's smile.

The guy seizes his hand and leads him to a dark corner.

Later, when he stumbles out of the chaos of the nightclub, Jake hurries through the cobblestone streets, dipping in and out of the sulfurous pools of light cast by the iron streetlamps.

God, he needed that. Needed to feel anonymous and free and wild, even if just for one night. The pressure has been incredible.

Natalie fading and wilting before his eyes, Uncle Frank short-tempered, yelling into the phone at colleagues, embassy workers, Aunt Della. The three of them cooped up in that hotel suite, driving each other mad.

Jake enters the plaza in front of the Pompidou Centre. The building is always jarring to look at, its modern architecture with loops of exterior tubing anachronistic against the formal elegance that defines most of Paris. The plaza in front of the museum seethes with darkened forms: homeless settling in for the night, huddled couples moaning in release.

A mural covers the side of a building on one end of the plaza: a huge face, eyes widened in surprise, one finger placed against lips in a gesture that means "shhh," in any language. Jake quickens his steps as he passes.

He's been sleeping on the foldout sofa in their suite, freeing one bedroom for Natalie, the other for Uncle Frank. He knows Frank gets up early, around dawn. He'd better hurry if he wants to slip back in without anyone being the wiser.

The night clerk at the hotel doesn't bat an eye when Jake rushes in half-naked, just offers up a polite *"Bonsoir."* Jake greets him in return and heads to the elevator.

His key card slips in easily, the release light turns green. Jake pushes open the door to their rooms, intending to slip into bed as quietly and quickly as possible.

Wide awake and wide-eyed, Natalie perches in the center of his rumpled sofa bed. Knees drawn up to her chest, long-sleeved oversized nightshirt tucked around her legs.

"So, where've you been?"

"Out."

"I can see that, asshole."

"Give me a break, will you, Nat? I went dancing, all right? I wanted to, you know, just stop thinking about everything for five fucking minutes."

"I get it, all right? I'm not mad. I was *worried*."

Jake sits down next to her. "You don't have to worry about me, okay?"

"Sure I do." Natalie's tone aims for light, but there's a hardness in her words.

Jake gestures at Frank's closed bedroom door. "Are you going to tell him I went out?"

Natalie shakes her head. "Not if you don't want me to."

"I don't."

"Okay, then. I won't. I want something in return, though."

Jake raises an eyebrow.

"I want to get out of here on my own for a few hours too. Uncle Frank means well, but he's hovering all the time. I just need . . . I need . . . a little time to myself."

Jake nods, understanding. "Where do you want to go?"

"Just out. For a walk. You'll cover for me, right? Later today? Tell Uncle Frank I'm taking a nap or something?"

Jake hesitates. Should he worry about Natalie walking around alone in Paris? He hasn't much wanted to put his suspicions and fears into words; they've teased the corners of his brain, tickled at the back of his throat, without being allowed to fully flower. But now they rear up fully fledged.

What if death had followed them here? What if that motherfucker who killed their mother murdered Brian too?

Or are the police right? Was Brian's murder a random robbery gone south? Isn't that the more likely scenario? And if it is, would the greater danger to Natalie come from her continued confinement? He studies his sister's face searching for signs she is telling the truth, that this isn't some ploy that will allow her to hurt herself again. Finally he nods.

"Okay."

Catherine

RUIN

I book the first flight I can to Budapest. Out comes the Canadian passport in the name of Rhonda Daly. I send a Tor email to Gillian with our intended rendezvous point and head to Charles de Gaulle Airport. I stride through the broad, gleaming corridors lined with shops selling everything from luxury handbags to pastel-hued macarons and make my way to my gate.

Waiting to board, impatient, scrolling through one of my phones, I realize it's worse than I thought. The Instagram of Elena has gone viral. Countless websites spew innuendo about Elena's smiling appearance in an Italian resort city without her powerful husband, fueled in part by prior observation by the same gossip-mongers that since her marriage she has rarely been seen without him or a bodyguard. Her image is everywhere, smiling, thick blond tresses blowing in the wind.

Elena had been discreetly escorted off the cruise ship in Genoa and transported by car along the coast to Santa Margherita Ligure by a confederate of mine in Italy, Gillian Spencer. Gillian's a former client of mine, the first I had when I left the States and came to Europe. (Of course Gillian Spencer is not her real name. Perhaps a tale for another time.)

That all went according to plan.

Gillian's husband, Giuseppe Tonorelli, generates the most pristine false documents I've ever seen. Passports, driver's licenses, birth certificates, diplomas—he can do it all, at a level that passes even the most sophisticated scrutiny. The passport I carry today is Giuseppe's exquisite work. He comes from a long line of papermakers, famed for their beautiful marbled prints. Still operates a storefront on a narrow side street near the harbor selling paper and leather-bound journals to tourists.

The plan was for Elena to stay in Santa Margherita long enough to have new papers generated in the name of a dead double (the identity of a deceased woman of similar background and age— good old Rhonda Daly from Manitoba is one of mine). When the papers were ready and the ransom paid, Elena was heading to Australia, where she would no longer be my problem.

Stupidity got us where we are now. Elena was smitten by the beauty of the port city of Santa Margherita, the curved marina with its bobbing boats, the red-roofed stucco buildings, the rock beach cluttered with candy-striped umbrellas. She begged Gillian for a chance to walk outside, "to taste her freedom." I can just see poor Gillian, a solidly built British woman of red nose and comfortable shoes, dazzled by the beautiful, imperious Elena, helpless in her sway.

One American teenager with an iPhone later and we're screwed. I study the pictures of Elena again. Behind her, there are glimpses of cobalt water, a yellow building with forest green shutters. It's Giuseppe's shop.

Shit.

When I arrive at Ferenc Liszt International Airport, I brush through the terminal and hail a taxi. Recite the address of my destination in passable Hungarian.

Despite the circumstances, I'm pleased to be back in Budapest. Not all of the memories are good, and the city itself has a haunted quality for all its old-world glamour, but I've always felt at home here. Something about the way the elegance of the old city knocks up against the rigid blandness of the Cold War–era architecture, the subversive atmosphere that permeates the nightlife here, the fierce traditions of public art and protest.

The Danube River crests into view. A shiver crosses over me as I remember the sixty pairs of iron 1940s-style shoes constructed on its bank to commemorate those murdered by the fascist Arrow Cross Party. Shoes were scarce during the war, so the victims were ordered to step out of theirs before being shot in the back, their bodies dumped in the river.

I killed someone at that site two years ago. Threw that body into that same stretch of river. Definitely a story for another time.

I check my messages. Through the encrypted email address I provided in the ransom note, the Russian (let's call him "Boris," just for fun) has requested proof that I have his wife before he makes the transfer. Nothing unusual there, but I don't understand what he's asking for. It's not a photo of his wife with a current newspaper, or even the chance to talk to her on the telephone. Boris wants to see a picture of "his monogram." His email says Elena alone will know what that means.

I've come to Budapest in person to impress upon Elena that from here on in, she must do exactly as I say. I still haven't let her see my face, and I won't now, but she needs to hear the steel in my voice. Truth is, I don't care if Elena lives to see another day as much as I care about taking down her husband, but above all I need to be in control.

After Elena reached out to me through the darknet channels that lead to the Burial Society, requesting a disappearance from her "abusive husband" and a relocation to a new, anonymous life, I researched, as I always do. She was telling the truth. He is abusive to her. But I also found that Boris traveled in the same cyber world I did, the shadowy recesses of illegality and encryption, where life is bought and sold cheap along with drugs and guns. Boris, I discovered, is an arms dealer.

I hate guns. It's personal. I don't use them in my work. I have distaste for those who do.

I decided I'd give Elena her new life while dismantling Boris's business as a bonus.

Just because you have your own agenda, it doesn't mean you're not servicing someone else's.

The taxi pulls up to the gaping metal roll-up door of the given address. My driver looks doubtful. Asks if I'm sure. I am.

It's daylight so there are no burly bouncers manning the front entrance. I pass through the rusty gate and into the ruin pub, struck again by how the vast, empty place transforms from day to night.

At night, the pub seethes under the darkness, sparkling with the energy of countless people desperate to reinvent themselves by morning.

The light of day reveals why this is called a ruin pub. Chicken wire seems to be the only thing holding up large sections of the ceiling. Exposed silver ductwork crawls along graffiti-sprayed walls. Scaffolding rims the perimeter. Broken bicycles and mutilated store mannequins hang from the three-story-high ceiling. Fairy lights wrap around a bank of televisions displaying only static. A foosball table dominates one corner of the enormous room; a tireless and topless Trabant sedan has been converted into a kind of booth.

I nod to Balint. The bartender nods in return. We go back, Balint and I.

I pass through one dim room into the next, each one decorated differently, the walls covered in yellowed newspapers and sepia photographs or dominated by abstract canvases, a collection of huge stuffed giraffes or mirror balls and battered chandeliers. The place is an enormous, crumbling rabbit warren that can hold up to a thousand revelers on a good night.

A courtyard emerges at the far end of this tangle of rooms. I cross through it, blinking at the sudden sunshine, and ascend the creaky metal staircase. At the top, a battered door, rusty and weathered. I rap softly: two knocks, a pause, then three in rapid succession.

The door opens.

Natalie

HAPPY FOOLS

Thrilled to be out and *free,* anonymous, *integrated* into the world, Natalie speaks to no one. She observes.

She watches mothers with their children, shopgirls with linked arms. Street artists and beggars. Tourists with sensible, ugly walking sandals and bulging tummy packs. Tough guys on motorcycles. Women wrapped in hijabs, men with yarmulkes and sidelocks.

She drops down on a sunny patch of grass. Her body aches. She realizes she had forgotten how *physical* grief can be.

An elfin-looking girl of the Audrey Hepburn/Audrey Tautou variety poses for photographs. Dark hair parted in the middle, two braids hanging down the back of her simple white shift, the girl seems the quintessential Parisienne. The young man with her, scruffy beard and lanky limbs, Converse sneakers and a worn T-shirt, croons and clicks away as she skips and pouts.

Natalie feels bitterly sorry for the two of them, so nakedly, blindly happy. Disaster can strike at any moment. It *will.* That's life. It's just what happens. No one should be as happy as those two fools.

The young man sweeps the elfin creature up in his arms and kisses her in the hollow of her throat. The girl wraps her legs around his waist. *Get a room,* Natalie thinks, turning away.

She's irritated now. The dazed fog that shrouds her lifts. She's out alone and unsupervised. Why is she wasting her time drifting around Paris like a wraith?

Natalie springs to her feet and heads toward Brian's job site with a new kick in her step. She checks the time. Just past four P.M. Her dad's co-workers should still be around.

Lilja Koskinen is just leaving for the day. The Finnish project manager pulls the silk scarf from her head when she sees Natalie. Unexpectedly, she enfolds Natalie in a hug before murmuring in her ear, "I'm so, so sorry about your papa."

Natalie had liked Lilja right away when they met at the Burrows family's "welcome to Paris" dinner. She's married to a Frenchman, a painter, and has lived in Paris for five years.

Lilja links her arm through Natalie's and steers her into a café. She orders thick, warm sipping chocolate for both of them as well as an array of cream pastries, their crusts flaky with butter. Lilja chides Natalie for looking thin, but in a way that doesn't make Natalie feel defensive. Natalie bolts down one pastry and a half of a second. Lilja looks pleased.

When Natalie sips the very last drops of her chocolate, Lilja leans back in her seat and crosses her arms.

"Much better. You know, I am convinced that chocolate and pastry can fix just about anything."

How Natalie wishes that were true. The sweets in her stomach turn suddenly sour. Natalie is horrified to feel tears brimming. Crap. She swipes them away.

Lilja leans forward. "Not the death of your father, I didn't mean that."

Natalie gives a nod. She knows Lilja doesn't mean to be unkind.

"What do the police say?" Lilja wants to know.

It's the wrong question or the right one, depending on your point of view. The words gush from Natalie's mouth, all her frustrations about the robbery theory, her own helplessness. Lilja nods and listens. Pats Natalie's hand.

"I can tell you this," Lilja says when Natalie finally pauses for breath. "Your papa was scared of something."

Natalie's pulse quickens. "What do you mean? How do you know?"

"The last day, you know, that he was at work . . ."

Natalie nods. The last day he was alive.

"He stopped by in the morning to check on progress. I realized he had forgotten a bid he was to analyze that night so I ran after him." Lilja pauses, as if debating exactly how to describe what happened next.

"He had just turned the corner when I caught up to him. I was out of breath, so I tapped him on the arm. He jumped nearly clear out of his skin! He turned on me with a look like he was going to . . . I don't know. Take my head off."

Lilja rushes to continue as she sees the confusion on Natalie's face. "It was nothing like your papa. Nothing at all! And he apologized right away. Said he was jumpy, distracted, that he had things on his mind. We laughed it off. But of course later . . ." Lilja trails off. They both know what happened later.

"Did he say what was on his mind?"

"No. He made a joke about being paranoid."

"Did you tell the police?" Natalie is disgusted with the squeak that emerges as her voice.

"Of course. But I will tell you this, I don't think they made much of it." A frown creases Lilja's angular face. "What was he afraid of, do you think? Or who?"

Natalie doesn't know. Not yet. But she will find out if it kills her.

MONOGRAM

Elena is blindfolded, ramrod straight on the purple velvet sofa, her right hand splayed on the tufted armrest. While her bearing is regal, I can see the tension in her long, thin fingers, the color draining from her cheeks.

"Tell me about the monogram, Elena," I repeat. Gillian shoots me a glance.

We're in my Budapest safe house, at the back of the ruin pub. Thousands of locals and transients pass through here every week; it's a perfect place to hide short term. The rooms themselves mirror the eclecticism of the pub: a mix of shabby antiques, art nouveau mirrors, Turkish lamps, and 1960s kitsch. One of those cat clocks with bulging eyes and a swinging tail hangs on the wall, next to a series of heavily framed bold prints: communist-era propaganda posters.

"We had been married four months," Elena begins, her voice soft and heavy with Russian inflections. "We had argument. I was tired and didn't want to go with him to party. He gave in. Brought me drink, to help me sleep, he said."

The cat clock's eyes swing back and forth, sightlessly scanning the room.

"When I woke up, I was tied with ropes." Elena pushes off the armrest to stand, unsteady and uncertain with her eyes covered by the blindfold. I grip the Taser I hold more tightly.

She unbuttons her pants. Slides them down so her taut lower belly is exposed. "He did this to me. With branding iron. While I was tied like pig."

Burned into the very spot even the tiniest of bikinis would cover are the Russian's initials.

"You know how many times he hurt me? Where no one can see?" Elena buttons her pants back up and sinks down onto the sofa. "Next he say if I cross him again, he throw acid in my face. You see now why I want him blame for my kidnap? He should burn in hell."

When Elena had hired me, she'd communicated the broad outlines: Shortly after her marriage she'd learned that Boris wasn't exactly a clean-living modern captain of industry, but a ruthless and sadistic gangster. Their relationship soured; he became controlling and abusive, she felt like a prisoner. She summoned her courage and asked for a divorce. Then she found out Boris planned to have her forcibly taken back to his home in Moscow. Terrified, she contacted the Burial Society to arrange a "kidnapping" in advance of Boris's "arrangements." The plan was to extract a sizable ransom, pay me, and use the rest to make Elena disappear. Then I was to release the evidence Elena had collected of Boris's plans to abduct her, placing him under suspicion for her disappearance and presumed death.

It was a good plan, and my private intention to dismantle Boris's gun-smuggling operation along the way made it even better. Until Elena proved unpredictable. And Boris even more sadistic than I anticipated.

"He want monogram? Give me knife! I slice off for him!" Tears dampen the maroon silk wrapped over Elena's eyes.

Gillian's face goes slack with alarm. I think her reserved British sensibilities may actually be more unsettled by Elena's histrionics than the horrific story of the branding. But then again, Gillian's survived her fair share of horror.

A photograph is taken of the monogram. I send it off to the Russian via my usual onion routing. Elena's signature blond tresses are cut and dyed a mousy brown, her blue eyes concealed by brown contacts, her new passport photos taken.

Gillian heads back to Giuseppe with Elena's new photos. My old friend Balint will take over from here, babysitting the model until her traveling papers are ready.

Frank

DENIAL

Frank feels a heavy pressure on his chest. A tight, grasping pain, like steel claws. Maybe he's having a heart attack. *That would top things off perfectly,* he thinks acidly.

He needs to get out of here.

He cautions Natalie and Jake to stay in the hotel suite. Tells them he is going out to get some snacks. Asks if there's anything in particular they want. Natalie requests English-language magazines or newspapers. Jake, Doritos and Coke.

Natalie starts to give Frank a little grief: If he can go out, why can't she? She's been locked in this stupid hotel for four days. Frank shuts her down sharply. Things are spiraling out of control. He has to pull it together. He doesn't have the time or the energy for her crap right now.

He slams out of the room, all jittery anger, and clatters down the stairs, too impatient to wait for the elevator.

Frank thunders down the avenue, rage about the conversation he's just had with his ex-wife blinding him to the bustle and shine of Paris on a beautiful summer evening.

Della is suing for full custody. She's claiming abandonment because of Frank's cancellation of his promised trip to Disney World with the twins. She's arranged for an accelerated court date. Della's found a new sugar daddy who's agreed to bankroll an expensive attorney with a reputation as a shark, she informed him gleefully. That fucker has moved them all into his house. His girls? In another man's house!

She thinks she's going to deny him his children? And the bitch is making these obscene plays while he's here in Paris, dealing with his brother's murder? If Della suddenly appeared in front of him, Brian wouldn't be the only one dead.

Frank stops and blinks against the waning sunlight, registers his surroundings. The streets are thronged. The cafés hum with diners and drinkers. A fresh wash of people emerge from a nearby metro stop, laughing and chattering. A man walking a pair of flat-faced pugs smokes a cigarette and yells into his cellphone in angry French.

Frank ducks into the nearest café and orders a beer. The enormity of what he's facing overwhelms. The upcoming battle with Della. The potential loss of the twins. Responsibility for his niece and nephew.

He has to get them back stateside as soon as possible. He will go to the embassy first thing tomorrow, explain the circumstances. Of course they all want to find Brian's murderer, but what can he and the kids really do? And surely they have rights as American citizens. It's not like any of them are suspects here. They are *victims*!

As he rehearses his speech in his head, he imagines cooperation and alacrity in arranging their return to the U.S. He will make the court date. He will annihilate Della on the stand as he exposes her callousness.

He slugs down the remainder of his beer, orders another. He fills with steely resolve. He is not losing his children. He's worked too hard and too long to keep everything together. He's damned if he's going to allow it all to fall apart now.

Catherine

NEEDS MUST

I hail a taxi at CDG. As we near the city, I direct my driver to pass the hotel to which the Burrows family has moved. I realize I'm hoping for glimpses of Natalie and Jake, even as I'm unsure why I feel so compelled.

Pulling up, I see news vans and reporters. Gendarmes keep them in line. I ask my driver to stop. Pay him. Exit the taxi. Circulate through the crowd listening for valuable nuggets among the babble.

The link has been made between the murdered Brian Burrows and Mallory Burrows's disappearance back in the States, unleashing the mob of press I am now navigating.

But it gets worse. The lives of the Burrowses have been threatened, first by Internet trolls and then an ugly crowd at the hotel accusing them of bringing a serial killer to Paris. One religious group has offered them exorcisms. Others offered prayer vigils on their behalf. Publishers and news outlets are throwing money at the family for interviews; the kids and their uncle have remained barricaded in their hotel.

I need to help them.

I make my way around to the service entrance of the hotel. I'm in luck. The shift is just changing. A bevy of maids exits the building.

I focus on one woman in particular, bony, fair skin, mousy brown hair. She of all the exiting workers is not chatting with a friend or calling out cheerful farewells. She has the hangdog look of someone who has known real hunger and is desperately afraid deprivation is around every curve. Eastern European would be my guess.

It takes me only sixty euros to get the scoop about the Burrows family and the drama they have brought to the hotel. The management wants them out, but the police insist they stay. Other guests are fleeing, of course, who would stay in a hotel that has turned into such a circus? And, she confides in me, they can hear the Burrows family arguing all the way out in the halls. Yelling, yelling, yelling all the time. And the teenage girl? Weeping. What a mess.

I ask more questions. Shift changes? Hotel layout? Staff lockers? Room numbers? For another twenty euros she tells me everything. I elicit her name: Nyura. She's Ukrainian. I scribble the number of one of my burner cells on a piece of paper and press it into her hand.

"My name is Hannah Potter," I tell her, using a dead-double alias I've not had occasion to employ for a while. "I think we will be of value to each other."

PARIAH

At least now the outside world views Natalie the way she views herself: as a pariah.

It's a relief in a way. She doesn't have to pretend to be brave or stoic or *normal*. The shattered remains of her family have been shut away in this hotel suite to wallow in solitude. A family touched twice by pure evil. At least they all know what they are. Tainted.

There are two cops stationed outside their door and more on the street outside the hotel to deal with the hungry press and the (enraged or solicitous) loons. Natalie knows she should be scared of all the frenzy, but she seethes with impatience and regret.

Right after she spoke with Lilja she should have gone directly to Dad's job site and quizzed the other people there. Instead, nervous about how long she had been gone, she came back to the hotel to find Uncle Frank frantic, furious at Jake for letting her slip out, equally angry and relieved to see Natalie return safely.

She'd apologized. Tried to explain how stifled she felt in the hotel. Swore she would never sneak out again. Tried to shift the blame away from Jake.

Natalie kept secret the information she'd gleaned from Lilja. She wanted to puzzle it through on her own first. *Who could Daddy have been afraid of?*

Gradually Uncle Frank cooled. But Natalie didn't dare sneak out again too soon and then the press descended. It's been a freak show ever since.

Despite the watchful eyes of her brother and her uncle, Natalie spends a little time each day locked in the bathroom, slicing minute incisions into her skin with a razor blade she's secreted by taping it under the lid of the toilet tank. The ritual provides a much-needed release, first the feel of tantalizing pressure, blade to skin, then the glorious cut, the welling blood, the sweet relief the pain provides.

Char. Scar. Trich. Bit. Charring, scarring, pulling, biting. The rotation serves Natalie well. Some of the other girls in treatment were purists, proud in a perverse way that trichotillomania, say, was their sole methodology, derisive of Natalie for her range. Natalie is less judgmental.

If only her tension didn't build up again so quickly. The three of them are fighting all the time now. About the stupidest stuff.

Natalie grabs the ice bucket and heads out to the hallway. She's worked hard to earn the sympathy of the uniformed cops guarding them. They let her disappear down past the ice machine and into the stairwell for a few minutes of peace. How could they refuse her, this skinny young girl with the big eyes and tragic life? The cops can hear the fighting booming from inside the suite; they know how hard she has it right now.

Natalie slips into the stairwell and sits on the landing, tucking the empty ice bucket next to her. She winds a strand of hair around her index finger. Tugs. Is filled with a pleasing pop of painful euphoria as the hair comes away.

The woman's voice is soft, American. "Natalie? Natalie Burrows?"

Natalie starts, instantly guarded. "I can't talk to the press," she says automatically.

"No, no, I'm not press. I'm a friend of, well, I was a friend of your father's."

Natalie examines the woman. In her early thirties, maybe? Light brown hair falling in soft waves to her shoulders. Comfortable in her own skin is the powerful first impression. Fashionable, understated clothing is the second. Vaguely familiar is the third, although Natalie can't place her.

"Really? From where?" Natalie can hear the snide suspicion in her question.

The woman introduces herself as Hannah Potter, an American living in Paris working for an interior design firm. She goes on to explain that she and Brian met at a violent-crime survivor's counseling group.

If Dad was going to a support group in Paris, it's news to me. How did this woman get into the hotel? What the hell does she want? Natalie's eyes narrow.

With a smile Hannah continues. "I know you must think I'm nuts; I actually bribed a maid to get in here! It's just that you and your brother were all your dad talked about at our meetings. He was missing you something fierce while you were away. Where was it? Amsterdam?"

Hearing Hannah speak of her father with this unexpected intimacy brings a rush of tears to Natalie's eyes. She's flooded with the urge to cut or pull or pinch or burn. She clasps her knees together tightly. Wraps her arms around them.

Hannah sits next to her. "My husband and my son, Ben. That's who I lost. They were shot and killed in a gas station robbery last year. Back home in San Diego. That's why I took this job in Paris. Supposed to be a fresh start." Hannah pauses. "My boy was only six."

Someone else who knows what it's like to have everything suck. Natalie murmurs a genuine "I'm sorry." She knows from experience there's little use in saying anything more.

"Thank you, Natalie. I'm sorry for your loss as well. *Losses.* Your dad talked about your mom a lot too."

Natalie shoots her a quick, appraising glance.

Hannah shrugs eloquent shoulders. "It's just different, isn't it, when it's violent crime? When the natural order of things is disturbed by a gun or knife?"

Or by a body that seemingly evaporated. Natalie still thinks about it all the time: where the remains of her mother could be.

"Anyway," Hannah continues, "I just wanted to reach out. Let you know that when I last saw your dad, all he could talk about was how much he loved you. How proud he was. I thought it might be helpful for you to hear that."

Hannah wipes her palms on her thighs and stands. "I won't take any more of your time."

"Wait!"

Hannah looks down at her with surprise. Natalie hesitates. This woman is a complete stranger; Natalie has no reason to trust her. She should have run the minute she saw her.

But Natalie has been cooped up with Uncle Frank and Jake for days. Neither of them will talk about Dad's murder. Natalie is sick as fuck of being told to sit down and shut up. She wants to *fix* this.

"Do you know if my dad . . . Was he afraid of someone?"

Hannah looks quizzical. "Why do you ask that?"

"I saw the project manager over at his building site. She told me that he was scared of something."

"Did he tell her who or what?"

"No. But I've been dying to talk to the other people he worked with. Someone else might know more. Lilja, that's the project manager, she said the cops blew her off when she told them, so maybe there's more they dismissed. They're convinced it was a robbery for his stupid laptop! Won't look at anything else. And my uncle! He was furious when I just left the hotel for a walk. He doesn't want me to investigate and he won't either. Particularly because of what's happening out there . . ." Natalie indicates the pious, the angry, and the rapacious with a gesture to the outside world.

Hannah sinks back down next to her on the stairs. "What would you do if you *could* get out?"

"I'd go to Dad's job site. Talk to everyone. Find out what was going on with him. He must have said *something* to *someone* if Lilja's right."

"I could go around . . . ask some questions for you."

"Why would you do that?" Natalie's tone is sharper than she intended.

"It's up to you," Hannah offers, hands raised. "I won't do anything at all unless you want me to."

Again, Natalie hesitates. Uncle Frank and Jake will go ballistic if they find out. She doesn't know this woman from Adam. On the other hand, maybe this Hannah Potter can find out something useful.

"Do it," Natalie decides. "Please. And then come back here and tell me everything you find out."

Catherine

TRUST

I wasn't surprised by the ease with which I'd bribed my way into the hotel. Nor about how simple it was to learn of Natalie's "secret" forays to the stairwell. Nyura was eagerly pliant for the money.

I feel for Natalie, this frail woman-child at the center of a tragedy. God only knows what she's been seeing online about herself and her family, how she's withstanding the enormity of her loss. But while I had calculated my angle of approach with the girl, I still question how easily I gained her trust.

Perhaps Natalie leapt to trust me because of her frustration about being on the hunt and then suddenly finding herself locked up in the hotel by her uncle?

Or could it be that she is attempting to manipulate me in some way? Does Natalie believe she's using the poor, grieving widow "Hannah" for her own ends? I need to be careful with this girl. I have the sense there is something I'm not yet seeing. I fear for my objectivity, given my guilt.

My antennae are up. What does her willingness to trust a stranger tell me about her psychological and emotional state? What can I use to my advantage in our next encounter?

If my manipulations make you squeamish, remember my goals are worthy.

I shake off my misgivings. Natalie had shared useful information, which was also unexpected. Brian Burrows was afraid before he died. This presents me with a trail of sorts, a start. I need to talk to Brian's co-workers right away.

Part Four

ORIGINS

There are so many stories.

This is only one.

Tales transform in the telling, are both shined and scuffed with time.

But still. Let's go back in time just a little bit.

23 DAYS MISSING

Frank folded the last of the laundry and tucked the neat piles into a basket to be carried upstairs. He missed his girls, but he was also glad they'd gone home. This house was no place for them.

Brian barely slept and slipped out of the house for a long walk at sunrise each morning. He said he needed to be alone, to work the tension from his body, to think.

As the outside world came awake, Brian returned, made coffee, settled at the kitchen counter, and then drank cup after black cup, meticulously consuming a hard copy of *The New York Times*, which was delivered daily.

He checked in with the detectives in charge of the case every morning at nine. Spent the rest of the day scouring the Internet. He looked for stories of missing women, turning over the shards of the cases as if they might shine a light on his wife's disappearance. He dove headlong into reports of sick obsession. For a brief while, he became fixated on the news about a place called "the Farm," some kind of a cult for renegade fathers and their abducted children that the FBI shot up.

Brian did not call his office. The Barcelona commission had been postponed in light of the circumstances.

Jake came and went. The boy still had a couple of close friends in the neighborhood, or so he said. Whether Jake was seeing them or not Frank had no real way of knowing. Jake was eighteen, he had his driver's license, they couldn't keep him locked in the house. And with the tension between Jake and Brian so very palpable, Frank figured it was probably a good idea for the boy to get out, work the tension from *his* body, have *his* time alone, *his* time to think.

Natalie told Frank she was sleeping a lot, and that might have been true. Or she might have been just hiding. An upper-middle-class suburban teenager, she had a bedroom equipped with satellite TV and an Internet-based sound system. She had an iPhone and a laptop and a bathroom en suite.

Now she was asking to have her meals in her bedroom too and Frank was on the fence. Should he refuse to let her? Insist she join them downstairs?

Brian had stared at him blankly when he'd asked his opinion; Frank was on his own.

Frank had taken compassionate leave and was prepared to stay as long as necessary, adding to Della's list of complaints. But *here* he had a purpose. It was beyond the drudgery of maintaining the household; he was *needed,* depended upon in a way that Della, who seemed to view him purely as a cash machine, never allowed.

He'd kept them *functioning,* Brian, Jake, and Natalie. Kept them upright.

Frank had even successfully suggested that Natalie use her art to process her feelings. Yesterday after Della and the twins had left, he'd lured Natalie out of the house with the promise of a new sketchbook. He'd bought her several, plus charcoals, pastels, pencils, and watercolors, overspending in a compulsive, compensatory rush and considering the excursion a great success.

He hoisted the basket of laundry and headed upstairs. Jake was out, he'd left without a word right after dinner. Brian was hunched over the kitchen countertop, the blue light of his laptop illuminating his haggard face.

As Frank climbed the stairs leading to the bedrooms, he heard an indistinct mewling. He followed the kitten-like sound to Natalie's closed bedroom door.

Frank set down the basket and knocked softly.

"Nat, you okay?"

To his surprise the door swung open immediately, almost as if she was waiting for him. Her eyes were red, her cheeks blotchy. She retreated to her canopied bed and curled under a blanket, leaving the door open for him to follow.

Frank swiped away the flower-bedecked silk ribbons that descended from the bed's canopy and perched next to her.

"Talk to me, honey."

"I know something about Mom. . . ." Natalie whispered.

Frank's blood ran cold.

Twenty-three days in and now *she announces this?* He kept his voice even. "What do you know, Nat?"

"I'm afraid to tell you."

"Natalie, if you know something related to your mom's disappearance, you have to share it with me."

"I don't know what to do," Natalie whispered.

"Tell me. I'll help you figure it out."

She wiped the tears from her eyes with fists. Grabbed a tissue from the box on the bed and blew her nose.

"There was a man. He was her, I don't know, boyfriend? Dad doesn't know."

Frank felt the flush color his cheeks. "Why do you think that?"

"I saw texts! On her phone. Between her and some asshole called Will C."

"Are you sure he wasn't just a friend?"

"I'm not an idiot!"

"I know you're not."

"There's more. I have Mom's phone."

"What?" Surely he had heard wrong.

"I'd seen some texts. I wanted to know. I swiped Mom's cell, that day, you know on the day she . . ."

Natalie lunged under a corner of her mattress and extracted the cell.

"I turned it off so it couldn't be, you know, traced, after. I felt so guilty about taking it. And so worried about Dad finding out about Mom and that guy, and then the longer it went on the more I didn't know what to do."

Natalie scooted back into a corner of the bed. Hugged her knees to her chest. Chewed on the side of her thumb.

"We have to tell your father," Frank said gravely.

"It's going to kill him!"

"And we have to tell the police."

"Am I in trouble?" The girl's anxious eyes locked on his own.

"It would have been better if you had come forward about this earlier, Nat—"

"But we can fix it, right?" Natalie interrupted. "I mean, Mom didn't have her phone on her, so it's not like they could have used it to find her."

Frank's heart ached with sympathy. The poor kid had been sitting with this painful secret all this time. Trying to protect her father, her mother, the fiction and fabric of her family. "I'll say I just found the phone. In the laundry room."

"You'd do that for me?"

"Of course."

What difference did it make at this point? What was done was done.

Frank carried the phone back down into the laundry room. "Found" it. Charged it. "Realized it was Mallory's." Marched up the stairs and told Brian of his discovery.

Frank handed the cell over to Brian and watched as he thumbed through her texts. Frank knew what he would see; he'd read through them first himself. Will C.'s exchanges with Mallory spoke of an intimacy built over time. Pet names. Private jokes.

Brian set the phone down. "You know the worst part?" Memory clouded his eyes. "I'm not even really surprised. Maybe I fucked it up. Maybe I never really had her. I don't know anymore."

"I'm so sorry." The heft of Brian's pain left Frank feeling hollow. Useless.

"I should call Detective Benson."

Brian and Frank both knew what this phone call would bring.

The press had finally abated, there was fresher meat for hungry jackals. But now there would be more scandal. Newly inflamed accusations and suspicions. Further invasion of privacy.

Slicing of new wounds, infection in old ones.

In other words, another round of hell.

Natalie

---

35 DAYS MISSING

Natalie had seen him on the news, hands raised to shield his face from the pack of reporters shouting questions as he emerged from his neat brick colonial.

Will Crane. Forty-one years old. Separated from his wife of six years. No kids. Owner of a local nursery. Natalie remembered the first time she'd seen him, buying a Christmas tree there last December. Crane had helped them tie the tree to the top of Mom's SUV.

Natalie needed to see him in person. She needed a *real* look at him, to see his face, to read his eyes. To reconcile the man from the nursery with the benign smiles and canned holiday cheer, with *this* monster, destroyer of her world.

As dawn broke, Natalie pressed herself into the shrubbery dividing Will Crane's yard from his next-door neighbor's.

The toe of her sneaker dug into the freshly turned earth at the base of the bush.

Letting the soil breathe for spring. The phrase floated through her mind; it was something her mother used to say, crouched by a flower bed, invigorated and glowing after a morning of spading the earth.

The neighborhood was quiet. A solitary light glowed over Crane's door, the house otherwise dark and shuttered tight. Two local news vans were parked across the street, satellites atilt like the half-cocked ears of a dozing dog.

Fuck Mom. Maybe her glow was from trysts with her plant-nursery-owning lover, not from the pleasure of turned earth and vibrant buds.

Mallory had always been on Natalie, accusing *her* of being secretive: *Who are you texting; put your phone away; not at dinner; be here with me now, please; what are you hiding?*

Maybe a plan to sneak vodka into junior prom. That was the worst of Natalie's sins. She felt virtuous in comparison to her mother.

The Adulteress. The Harlot. Strumpet. Floozy. Hussy. *Whore.*

Maybe I'll fuck him. I'll fuck Will C., she thought viciously. *That'll show her!*

As if she ever could. As if he would even want her.

A Lincoln Town Car pulled up in front of Crane's house and disgorged a florid man in a navy suit and a striped silk tie. He rang the doorbell and was admitted. Other cars and news vans arrived, as if summoned. Reporters staked out positions on the sidewalk, conducted sound and battery checks. Natalie realized they *had* been summoned.

The guy in the navy suit opened the door. Flashes popped, cameras whirred. He spoke formally, his voice thin and unexpectedly shrill. "My client William Crane will now make a short statement. There will be no further questions or comments beyond that statement at this time."

The air buzzed with curiosity, apprehension, titillation, a tinge of sickening dread.

The lawyer nodded back toward the shadowy recesses of the house and then there he was, Natalie's quarry, Will Crane, tall, gray-flecked dark hair, strong hands that twisted at one another. His voice, though, rang true and steady. "I would like to set the record straight with respect to Mallory Burrows."

Her mother's name tumbled, familial, out of Crane's unfamiliar lips. Natalie hadn't known what she expected, but it wasn't this.

"Mallory and I met a little over a year ago. We became friends. I will not comment any further on the extent of our relationship."

What a white knight, sneered Natalie, *how charming and discreet—to fuck Mallory but refuse to talk about it.*

"I am completely innocent of any involvement in her disappearance. I am cooperating fully with the investigation. The police will confirm that."

Believe me, his eyes implored, dancing from one listener to the next, *believe me.*

For a razor-thin second Natalie thought he looked right at her. She shrank deeper into her hiding place.

"I pray for Mallory's safe return. And I ask that anyone, anywhere, who knows anything about her . . . where she is . . . how she is . . ." Crane's voice cracked. "I love Mallory, her children love her. We need her to come home. Please help us if you can."

Natalie reeled. It was his casual assertion of love, the presumption he knew *anything* about her or Jake, speaking as if *he* were Mallory's family, she and Jake drafted along, lucky them, from a prior chapter, but her father disappeared into nothingness like a cheap magician's trick.

Jake

---

91 DAYS MISSING

How could a woman just disappear?

Jake wandered their house, eyes urgently searching for glimpses and hints of his mother. Not that it even looked like their house anymore, filled as it was with cardboard boxes, piles for Goodwill donation, oversized black plastic garbage bags headed for the dump.

Dad had this plan, he hadn't even discussed it with them, had merely announced it. They were putting their house on the market, moving to Manhattan. That was it. And so it was. Today was moving day.

Jake stared down the squares and rectangles of a brighter citron marking the sun-faded hallway wall, the last of the framed family pictures recently removed and carefully swaddled in bubble wrap. He tried to remember where particular favorites had hung. Already he was forgetting.

The shifting and moving and packing of things that had long held permanent locations revealed scuff marks, loose change, old receipts and ticket stubs, the faint residue of that time Natalie colored on the wall with Sharpies. A lost sapphire earring of Mallory's, fiery and brilliant, that Jake had slipped into his pocket. And memories. A billion memories.

Jake brushed a finger over the empty mantelpiece in the dining room, coming away with a film of gray dust that he wiped hastily on his jeans.

Jake had expected to feel sad, but what he mostly felt was guilt. He knew the likelihood of Mom ever coming back was slim to none. But still, leaving the house felt like they were all abandoning her. As if she did come back from wherever the hell she was to find her house empty, her family gone, she would think they hadn't loved her.

"Bye, Mom," Jake whispered.

Their new home consisted of two Upper West Side pre-war apartments knocked together. Palatial by Manhattan standards, tiny by Westport's. Jake had his bedroom on one end, with his own separate entrance, thank god for small favors. It was only until school started again, then he was moving back downtown into the dorms.

The movers loaded in furniture and mountains of boxes. Brian ordered pizza for everyone. The cable guy miraculously showed up in the promised window. All the necessary steps to erase Jake's old life and paint-by-numbers a new one took place with orderly progression.

That night, over too salty take-out Chinese, Brian pretended that this move was exciting, that things were *returning to normal.*

But while Natalie praised the moo shu and Brian shoveled in chicken with broccoli, Jake picked at his pork fried rice. The specter of the missing Mallory still hung over them. How could it ever be different?

Jake retreated to his room, pushed aside the stacks of unpacked boxes, settled on his bare mattress with his laptop. How was he going to survive until school started? He hated being around his father. He hated thinking about that prick Will Crane; the very idea that his mom had had an affair made Jake's skin crawl. He hated worrying about Natalie. He hated *this,* all of it.

Jake scrolled through photos on his computer: family birthdays and vacations: Kauai, Vermont, St. Croix, Greece. Natalie mugging for the camera. Mom smiling despite the shadow in her eyes, cocky, confident Brian draping a possessive arm around her shoulders.

Jake enlarged a photo of his father and peered into the depths of his captured gaze. Brian's temper was infrequent but powerful. Oh yes, Jake had seen that firsthand. He would never forget the night his father knocked him down for taking his mother's side. The *family's* side, really. Jake could see Brian erupting in jealousy, taking it out on Mallory before she had a chance to defend herself.

If Brian did it, Jake swore he would kill him.

Frank

96 DAYS MISSING

Frank had been living on the Burrows family boat in its dock at the Saugatuck Harbor Yacht Club for three weeks.

When he returned home from Brian's, Della had served him with divorce papers. She'd also changed the locks on the doors to their house and drained their joint checking account. He had been allowed to see the twins exactly once since he'd been back, Della wielding access to the girls like a bludgeon in order to get swift acquiescence to her outrageous demands.

He didn't care about divorcing Della; that relationship was long over. But the girls. Girls needed their fathers. And he needed them.

A rush of memories came along with being on the boat, feeling its sway in the water, listening to the creak of rope, wood, and metal.

He remembered the first time Brian brought Mallory home to meet the family. It had been a long weekend, the Fourth of July. Mystic, Connecticut, was exploding with its usual patriotic fervor, bunting and flags and the parade down Main Street. Mallory had been charmed by the way the town embraced the holiday: lawn bowling and mock Civil War military exhibitions, boat races down the Mystic River, old-fashioned spelling bees for the kids.

They had taken the boat out too, of course. Had a picnic supper that Mom prepared. Watched the fireworks from the deck. Cracked open more than a few beers. Dad and Mom wholly approved of Mallory, that much was easy to see; besides, when didn't they approve of golden boy Brian's choices?

But Frank had to admit he'd been equally charmed. She was so beautiful. And she stood her ground with Brian, didn't worship him the way so many of his prior girlfriends had. She seemed genuinely interested in Frank. She had asked questions, but more important, had listened to his answers.

Frank plucked a bottle of bourbon from a cabinet. A long pull of the burning liquid coursed down his throat.

He mourned Mallory. He rued the pain that held his brother, niece, and nephew in its cold, tight grip. He longed for his daughters. He grieved for lost chances, doors closed, decisions made.

He wondered if any of them would ever be happy again.

Natalie

___

101 DAYS MISSING

None of the various and sundry objects in the battered wooden box would appear as treasure to another's eyes, but to Natalie each and every one of them was sacred.

She unearthed the box from its hiding place deep in her closet. Once burnished wood, now scuffed and scratched, bound with brass fittings and a neat little lock. She inserted the key and felt a rush of anticipatory pleasure as the mechanism caught and turned. The lock sprung open.

She lifted the lid of her treasure box and contemplated the wealth inside.

There was a tube of Mallory's favorite lipstick, a deep rosy pink. A heart carved from a spectacular chunk of deep blue lapis lazuli. Filled sketchbooks, each dated and carefully labeled. A certificate proclaiming Natalie's first-place finish in the middle school spelling bee. A colorful Menehune doll, a souvenir from a family winter holiday in Kauai. A half-smoked joint, carefully inserted into the fold of the program for her high school's Cabaret Night (a memento from that magical evening, during which Adam Nash pulled her behind the gym in between acts, got her high, and then kissed her).

Cabaret Night. The last great memory she would ever have, she thought bitterly. The last night of promise *before* . . .

Adam Nash had averted his eyes and shuffled away when he saw her *after*. And who could blame him? It wasn't like they were *a thing*. It had just been a kiss.

Natalie toyed with her Menehune. Long brown hair, a neon green "grass" skirt, caution-yellow bandeau, and a crowning halo of flowers. The Menehune were the leprechauns of Hawaii, they had been told on that magical vacation. On that trip, there had been laughter and affection; her family had been *whole*.

They'd stayed at a sweet cottage on the north end of the island with a spectacular view of the ocean and an open-air lanai where they ate their meals. They'd played games, watched DVDs, laughed *a lot*. They'd hiked and kayaked. Grilled fresh local ahi, chopped pineapple salsa, and made tropical fruit slushies in the blender.

And then there had been the jellyfish.

Dad had arranged for a day of sailing and snorkeling along the magnificent Napali Coast. Their catamaran had pulled into a little cove and dropped anchor. Outfitted with a mask, flippers, and a snorkel, Natalie had been among the first to dive into the turquoise water.

In the ocean all was silence, except for the sound of Natalie's own breath through the tube, rasping in her ears. She saw tiny bright yellow fish darting quickly, and larger, flat, iridescent blue fish that swam with lazy purpose. Long, thin fish with orange and white stripes. A sea turtle as big as her torso.

Excited to share her find with her family, Natalie raised her head above water. Voices thundered in. Kids squealing, the ripple of her mother's laugh. Mallory was on the boat, head thrown back as one of the crew, the one with the tattoo sleeves and shaggy blond hair, held her leg in his calloused hand. He helped her strap on the unwieldy flippers, his hand too high on her thigh. Natalie had yelled, "Mom, a sea turtle!" But Mallory hadn't heard. Disappointed, Natalie had slipped back under the water.

The sting, when it came, was alarmingly painful, utterly unexpected. A piercing in her right shoulder. She swiped at it with her left hand and pulled away what looked like sticky blue threads. Lifted her head to cry out in confusion and hurt.

"It's a jellyfish bloom," the tattooed guy had yelled, pointing. "Swim away."

Disoriented, Natalie swam right *into* the bloom. She was stung everywhere: her right cheek, her nose, the side of her neck, her shoulder blades, her left armpit. The pain was excruciating, but also somehow exciting. Natalie had never felt more alive.

They'd pulled her onto the boat, hosed off her body, and applied medication to ease the sting. Joked about peeing on her as Natalie recoiled. Mom had wrapped a towel around her, hugged her tight, stroked her hair, murmured reassurances.

Now, in her new bedroom, in an apartment she was certain would never feel like home, Natalie swiped her palm across her skin, unconsciously tracing the path the stinging beasts had inflicted upon her that day in paradise.

Would she ever stop missing her mother?

She heard the sound of a phone ringing. Her dad's greeting.

It was Detective Benson.

Natalie closed her box of treasures and shoved it back into its hiding place. She edged into the hallway. Peered into the kitchen. Her father grunted a few replies and questions into the phone before clicking it off. His face was stricken.

"What is it, Daddy?"

A letter had been received at the station, he informed her flatly. Addressed to the officer in charge of the Burrows case. The writer claimed responsibility for the death of Mallory Burrows. He taunted the cops, informing them he'd moved on and would never be caught. The letter was typed, but claimed to be from Will Crane. In it, he said he'd killed Mallory because she was going to leave him, had chosen her family over her lover. Her father's voice broke with emotion. Mallory had chosen them. And it had cost her her life.

And now Crane was "in the wind." That was the phrase Detective Benson had used, Daddy said. "In the wind."

Natalie wanted to scream. But if she started, she might never stop.

Part Five

CONVERGENCE

If I could tell the story differently . . .

It would be a tale of hope and faith and happy endings.

Where love conquered all and good won out.

After all, we can tell ourselves all the lies we want.

Even if they always catch us up in the end.

Catherine

MUD

I come around the corner just as a sludge-caked prosthetic leg is thrown up on the bank of the canal. I jump back to avoid its spatter.

In the partially drained waterway, workmen in rubber waders and fluorescent safety jackets dredge up filthy bicycles and rusty motorbikes, wine bottles and plastic containers, traffic cones and sodden clothes. It's disgusting, but I can't look away. The bottles and general garbage I get, but how and why did all those bicycles and motorbikes end up submerged? The fake limb?

I pause to watch as the workmen joke and holler. One pulls a soggy inflatable sex doll from the muck. It brings about a fresh round of hilarity.

Canal Saint-Martin was once a neighborhood occupied by working-class laborers. Now it's on a trendy upswing. New apartment buildings, restaurants, and bars sprout like mushrooms in the rainy season. The restaurant renovation Brian Burrows was overseeing is one such growth.

Construction is under way at full force; Brian's death seems not to have stopped the march of progress. Located in a long-abandoned and antiquated power plant, the building is stripped down to its bones. Welders' flames burn blue; concrete mixes and pours.

I seek out the project manager, Lilja Koskinen. I introduce my-self as Hannah Potter, a friend of the Burrows family. It's almost sort of true.

Lilja's kind face crumples in distress and she asks me into the construction trailer for a coffee.

Once we're inside, she gestures to the two folding chairs arranged by the single metal desk. I sit in one as she removes her hard hat and fluorescent jacket. She goes about the ritual of coffee. A French press. Finely ground beans. A hotplate. Boiling water.

She expresses concern for Natalie and Jake, those *"pauvre enfants."* I use this opening to explain that I've come at Natalie's request.

"Could you repeat to me what you told Natalie? Something about her father being scared? I'm sure the poor girl misunderstood, so I'd like to put her mind at rest."

Lilja hands me a mug of coffee. She pours one for herself before taking a seat. I sip. Bitter. Strong. Delicious.

Her story is consistent, but not so much that it arouses any suspicion. In fact I determine Lilja Koskinen is probably truthful about most things. It's the way she's made.

"It was such a brief exchange, and then Mr. Burrows was on his way. Maybe I should have—"

"Don't beat up on yourself," I interrupt as her bright eyes dim with memory and regret. "We make choices every day, turn right, turn left, miss the bus, take the call. . . . If we second-guessed all of them we'd go mad. There's nothing you should have done differently."

Lilja rewards me with a relieved smile, but then stands abruptly. "I need to go back to work. . . ."

I ask her if there is anyone else on the job who might have some insight into what Brian was experiencing the last few days of his life, who might know just what had frightened Brian so much. Lilja demurs. She's happy to do whatever *she* personally can do to help, but since the murder, and all the press about Burrows . . . well, some of the men have gotten superstitious, and the project can't afford any more delays.

"Superstitious?" I can't hide my surprise.

Lilja swings open the door to the trailer and gestures outside. I turn in time to see a shower of sparks rain down in a glittering, sweeping arc from a welder's torch.

"It's the history of the building," Lilja explains. "Tunnels under the plant were used as a hiding place for Parisian Jews during World War II. This was especially daring because while the plant was operated by locals, it was under Nazi supervision." Lilja puffs out a breath. "But shortly before the city was liberated, the hidden families were betrayed. Men, women, and children—marched into the street and shot dead, the bodies left there to rot as warning."

My breath catches in my throat. Even after all I've seen and done, man's capacity for barbarity still shocks me.

Lilja continues, "Members of the French resistance retaliated, planting a bomb on the site. The explosion rendered the power plant inoperable but also killed seventeen people."

I am silent, muted by sorrow for the innocent dead.

"After the war, the building fell into ruin. It was a squatters' paradise for decades."

But reconception and renovation were inevitable now that the area was growing so hot, Lilja explains. Brian's design of the club/restaurant had paid respectful but daring homage to the building's history. A fierce press and political battle debating the design's merits had delayed construction, and they are in even deeper trouble now after the delays caused by his death.

"Some of the men on our crew feel the building's ugly past is somehow tied to Brian Burrows's ugly *now*. I'm having a hell of a time keeping things on track. I don't know if I can afford to have you talk to anyone else." Lilja ushers me from the trailer.

I raise my voice to be heard over the noise. "I can see you care

about those two kids as much as I do. So sad. Natalie, especially."
I catch Lilja's eye. "I'd do *anything* to help her."

Lilja chews her lip. Then asks me to wait.

"Just don't meet around the site," she instructs a few moments
later, thrusting a square of paper into my hand. After all, *pauvre
enfants*.

Jake

CRANE

Locked in the suite's bathroom, perched on the edge of the bathtub, Jake lays out his theories for his friend Rami over Skype. Jake misses Rami. It feels great to look into his expressive eyes, see his brow narrow in concentration as he listens to Jake's deductions.

Rami's face fractures into digitized squares; his voice scrambles into static. Jake thumps his fists on his thighs in frustration. He was only midway through his theory!

There's a knock on the bathroom door.

"Give me a minute," he calls. With Jake sleeping in the living area of the suite, the bathroom is the only place he has any privacy.

"I have to pee." It's Natalie.

From the laptop screen, a pixilated Rami tries to reassure Jake. "Listen to the cops. If they say it was a robbery, it probably was. All this speculation . . . You're just making yourself crazy."

Jake knows he's making himself crazy. But he can't help it. He can't stop.

"Jake!" Natalie is pissed. She pounds on the closed door.

Jake flushes the toilet he didn't use and says goodbye to Rami. Exits the bathroom, snapping his laptop shut.

"It's about time," Natalie huffs as she darts past him and slams the door behind her. Jake wonders if she's going to hurt herself in there. More making himself crazy.

Natalie emerges just a few moments later, zipping up her jeans.

"Why were you hiding in the bathroom? Who were you talking to?"

"Rami."

"He your boyfriend now?"

Jake feels the scarlet stain his face. Turns away and grabs the remote, snapping off the babbling TV.

"Hey! I was watching that."

"And now you're not."

"You're in a mood."

"Can I ask you something, Nat?"

"If I answer, will you give me back the remote?"

"Do you think that what happened to Dad was . . . related to Mom?"

"How do you mean?" His sister pales. "Like what the nut jobs are saying? That we're cursed?"

"Of course not. But what if Crane was back somehow—"

"No!" A cry of pure terror bursts out of Natalie, loud enough to draw Frank from his bedroom.

"What's going on in here?" he demands.

Jake puts an arm around Natalie's narrow shoulders. Realizes she's shaking. "Sorry, Nat," he says to her. "I didn't mean to upset you."

He draws Natalie over to the sofa and eases her onto its cushions.

"What on earth did you say to her?" Frank hisses at Jake.

"I raised the possibility of whether that prick Crane could have had something to do with Dad's murder."

"Why on earth would you say *that*?"

His voice urgent, Jake lays it out for them just as he had for Rami. "Crane disappeared three years ago; he could be anywhere now. Why not here in Paris? Maybe he came after Dad? Or maybe Dad was on Crane's trail? Trying to lure him out . . ."

Frank takes an involuntary step away from him, his lip curling with—anger? Disgust? Jake can't tell.

"Shut up!" His uncle's voice has an edge as sharp as a blade. "Don't you see what you're doing to your sister?"

Her knees are drawn up to her chest, her arms wrapped around her shins, her spine curled tight, as if she wants to fold into herself and disappear through the other side.

Jake sees the edges of a bruise (or is it a burn?) on the tender inner flesh of Natalie's right wrist. Her left thumb snakes under her cuff in order to press deeply, rhythmically, at the wound over and over again. Her eyes are unfocused. Her jaw slack.

Jake shuts up.

Catherine

CURRY

Lilja had given me two names: Ursine Fournier, the secretary/assistant who was Brian's local hire, and Hank Scovell, a junior on Brian's team from New York, who is now the acting head of the renovation.

Scovell is in the States for a few days, scheduled to return by the end of the week.

Ursine Fournier is just where Lilja said she would be, at an Indian restaurant on nearby rue de Lancry, eating green curry and flirting with the sexy waiter who's serving it. Ursine is a pretty girl in her early twenties with glossy dark hair and almond-shaped eyes.

I again introduce myself as Hannah Potter, friend of the Burrows family, and tell Ursine that Lilja told me where to find her. I ask if I might join her for a few moments, ask a few questions about her former boss. The girl puffs up in importance for the sake of the hot waiter. *"It's a murder investigation,"* she boasts to him, as she gestures for me to take a seat.

Ursine answers my questions readily. She'd been working for Brian since the project started; she was his "woman on the ground here in Paris," even when he was still traveling back and forth to New York in the preliminary stages.

And yes, she liked him *very* much. Her eyes mist. He was very good to work for, Monsieur Burrows. Fair, communicative. But he'd seemed different this summer. Worried. It made him irritable and distracted.

She lowers her voice and confesses that Hank Scovell is not nearly the man Brian was. He's got a temper, that one. Her eyes darken as she pushes a pile of curry-soaked rice around on her plate with a fork. I make a mental note to learn more about Hank Scovell.

I steer her back to the subject of Brian. What did he tell her? What was he worried about?

"I don't know. When I asked what was wrong, he said it was personal. But he used the word *afraid*. And that struck me. Because, you know, he was such a *vital* man. It was hard for me to imagine he was afraid of something. Or someone."

Ursine nods sagely as if she has uttered some great and fundamental truth.

Mallory Burrows had been afraid. Had reached out to me. And I had failed her. And now her husband? Also afraid. Also dead. Were these two tragedies connected? If I had prevented the first, would I have also prevented the second?

The curry spices rise through my nostrils, making me suddenly feel stifled and queasy. *"L'eau, s'il vous plait,"* I command the sexy waiter.

I gulp the cool liquid down as soon as he sets it on the table. "Do you have any idea who Brian might have confided in, if not you?"

Ursine's eyes narrow. "He didn't confide in you? I thought you were his friend."

Sharper than she appears, Ursine.

"He shut me down too," I lie solemnly. "I wish he hadn't been so closemouthed. Maybe one of us could have saved his life."

Ursine nods at me in mournful agreement.

"Here's my number." I slide over a sheet of notepaper with a burner cell number on it. "If you think of anything else, please call me."

I thank her for her time. Add a whispered, "He likes you," about the waiter. Ursine blushes deeply as I leave.

Natalie

TREATMENT

It's after three A.M. and she hasn't slept. Natalie's heart thuds against her rib cage. Trapped. Just like her. Caged within a cage within a cage. Ad infinitum.

She longs to char her flesh or slice into her skin, anything to relieve her urgent fears and electrifying anxiety, but Uncle Frank searched the entire suite and confiscated her carefully hoarded tools. After he yanked up her sleeves and splayed her scarred and scabbing arms in front of Jake.

She thought she'd been clever. She ate enough to keep her weight from alarming anyone and restricted her injuries to areas covered by pants and sleeves. The thing on the wrist, well, it was an aberration. She couldn't help herself.

And the simplicity with which she had convinced one of the gendarmes to smuggle the lighter to her! Sneaking cigarettes, she told him. He didn't care if she smoked. He was French.

Jake was horrified when he saw the burn and the other injuries. Worried, of course, and contrite about upsetting her. But Natalie could tell he'd also been repulsed. She doesn't judge Jake (or anyone else for that matter) for finding her repulsive. She finds herself repulsive.

Will Crane. *No.* She can't even think about him. Natalie shudders. Presses her thumb deeply into the open burn on her wrist. A satisfyingly painful curve of nausea arcs through her, and then, oh rapture, that past-pain thrill of pure ecstasy.

Treatment.

Uncle Frank threatened to ship her right back when they got home to New York.

No wonder she can't sleep.

The memories surge over her. The late-night intervention.

Daddy. Uncle Frank. Jake. Her best friend, Melissa Masterson, along with Melissa's mother, Sunny. All of them so pious. So riddled with guilt. But also lit up with the drama of it all.

The orderlies, the doctor, the syringe.

Jake fighting tears as they carried her out. The salty stream leaking from her own half-mast eyelids.

A long ride in a featureless van.

Drifting off. Bouncing back. Into a reality that was completely unreal.

A forbidding brick building in the middle of fucking nowhere.

Feeding tubes. Restraints.

Sleeping.

Weeping.

It got better. It did.

The place wasn't so scary in the light of day. The grounds were actually quite beautiful and shifted with the seasons, crayon-colored summer flowers giving way to the cinnamon-hued leaves of fall.

Natalie mourned her missing mother. Raged at her too. She forgave her wounded father and perhaps even more essential, forgave herself the irrational fury she harbored toward him.

Uncle Frank brought her cousins to visit and they played doubles Ping-Pong in the break room. She cried in Jake's arms when he came alone.

She shared in Group and went to art therapy. Endured the lectures on nutrition. Explored the grounds. Made a friend or two.

She experienced a different way of feeling in control of her own body, more nurturing, less harmful. She shut the doors to the past. Locked them. Tossed the keys.

She learned to be in the present. Began to plan a future. Was grateful for every day. She learned to love herself.

Mostly. Until she just couldn't stand it anymore.

Char. Scar. Trich. Bit. Old habits die hard.

She glances at the time. 3:27 A.M.

Let's try a patented Dr. Bloom challenge: *Make a list and do ten other things before you let yourself self-harm. If after all ten, you still want to, go ahead.*

At first, that had shocked Natalie. Thrilled her too. Dr. Bloom was giving her *permission* to hurt herself.

Natalie learned fast it was a mind fuck—more often than not the compulsion, that indescribable achy *need* to Char, Scar, Trich, Bit, was stilled by number 8.

Okay. One. *Ask for help.* She twiddles her phone between her fingers. Makes a decision. Taps a text.

To Natalie's surprise, the dots indicating a reply in progress flicker on her screen. She waits for what seems like an impossibly long time.

The text finally comes up: *Spoke to Lilja and Ursine. Waiting to talk to Hank Scovell. More soon. Hang in there.*

Natalie fires back: *What did they tell you?*

She waits, staring anxiously at the phone screen, but there is no further reply.

Catherine

MALWARE

I toss my "Hannah Potter" burner cell into the deep recesses of a drawer, deeply conflicted about having responded to Natalie.

I should shut that whole thing right down. Let my hastily resurrected alter ego disappear into the ether and not contact any of the Burrowses again. At least until after the Elena exchange. Despite my guilt, despite my profound sadness about the way I failed the Burrows family, I have bigger fish to fry right now.

The photo of Boris's loathsome brand, his "monogram," that I dutifully emailed him from Budapest was infected with a particularly vicious malware of my own creation.

Boris got his proof that I had Elena but also unwittingly allowed my spyware to transmit huge data dumps from his computers to mine. For hours I have been tracing correspondence and transactions, recording passwords, logging lists of associates, and following the complex money transfers designed to wash Boris's blood money clean.

He's been careful and clever, but I'm determined to take him down.

My computer pings, a signal that I've received a message on the Tor account I set up just to communicate with Boris. My heart quickens. Here we go.

I open the message. It's blunt and to the point. Boris requests a telephone call with me. He's received the picture of the monogram. He's willing to deal.

Now it's my turn to let him wait. I want him anxious, off balance. Besides, I'm still data mining.

Hours later, I emerge from the Conciergerie, site of Marie Antoinette's Parisian prison cell. It was a brief visit, but the queen's chamber is a touchstone for me, a reminder that all history is in the telling.

The sky is just blushing into sunset. If I hurry I can make the last group allowed for the day at Sainte-Chapelle.

The cathedral is magnificent as always, soaring arches of intricate stained glass, a dazzling crystalline array of artistry in the name of faith.

I step outside to the small balcony just off the chapel, holding the door open for the young Chinese couple heading back inside. Rest my elbows on the balustrade and eye the sleeping-till-morning cranes and earthmovers at the construction site one lot over. Casually, I affix a voice changer to the cellphone I've reserved for Elena business. It's a cheap commercial model, ordered online for a trifling four hundred euros, but quite effective nonetheless.

I will sound like a man to the Russian, which will play into his assumptions.

I make the call. Boris and I come to terms quickly. He will transfer bitcoin. I will deliver Elena. We will go our separate ways.

Or so I let him think.

Frank

THE GIRLS

Despite Frank's well-intentioned resolve to enlist the U.S. embassy's assistance in going back to the States, they are still stuck in this damn hotel in Paris. Mumbo jumbo about the ongoing police investigation, mutter, mutter, blah, blah, but bottom line, they won't release Brian's body yet and don't want the rest of the family to leave until that formality is resolved. It's been eleven days since Della told him she was suing for full custody. Frank's stress level is skyrocketing as their court date ticks ever closer.

On the phone with his daughters, Frank hears his voice as the twins must hear it: whiny, weak.

How could he have allowed Della to make him feel so impotent? They are angry, his girls, and Frank was taken off guard by the level of their rage. Della is doing a fine job of tainting their perception of him.

He settles his body on the edge of the bed. Taps two fingers of his left hand nervously against the meat of his thigh. "I promise I'll be home as soon as possible. By the end of the week probably."

Sweet Analise whines a petulant and elongated "Daaadddy," while feisty Adelaide delivers a tart "Fuck you."

"Watch your language," he snaps at Addy. "That's not acceptable. Your cousins need me. And you should show a little more compassion, given what we're all going through here."

Addy unleashes a few more choice phrases at Frank before he hears a click.

"Ana?" he inquires cautiously.

"I'm still here." Her voice is small and subdued. "Daddy, I miss you."

Frank's heart swells. "I love you, baby. And I miss you too. I promise everything is going to be all right. Tell your sister that too. I'll be home to take care of you just as soon as I can."

Catherine

THE DAMAGE DONE

There's a divine pleasure in watching something one has planned unfurl elegantly, properly, just the way one envisioned.

With my spyware granting me access to all of Boris's accounts, passwords, and associates, I have spent the day wreaking havoc on his carefully clandestine operations. I'm going to turn him over to Europol, but first I'm fucking with him a little, I just can't help myself.

He's a vain man, weekly pedicures, fingernails shined and buffed twice a week. That mane of hair he is so proud of is meticulously styled on a bi-monthly basis to conceal an incipient bald patch. His wardrobe is tailored by one of Paris's finest artisans to disguise the swell of his belly. He likes to live large: expensive meals and pricey hookers.

I mentally filed away these tantalizing details before I got to the real business of the day: the diversion of a bitcoin payment for a shipment of automatic weapons. The intended recipient of the money is enraged, but Boris doesn't know that, as I have intercepted and deleted the recipient's furious tirades. The guns won't be delivered to Boris as scheduled and with a tickle of pleasure I anticipate the oppressive heat that will rain down on him when he can't fulfill his buyer's order.

I know I shouldn't be playing like this. My concentration should be on getting Elena safely away. After that, I can do anything I want with Boris. But if I stop thinking about entertaining ways to upset the Russian (I've also screwed with his account records at all of Paris's finest shops), then I will be thinking about the Burrows family.

Just wrap this up.

Jake

SEARCH

The day is hot. Jake's damp T-shirt clings to his skin; sweat trickles down into his jeans from the small of his back. A baseball cap is pulled low over his forehead; oversized sunglasses shadow his eyes.

With the help of a flirty room service waiter, he'd escaped through the hotel kitchen and into the throbbing, thrumming streets of Paris, avoiding the lingering members of the press camped out in front. There's a good half a dozen still there, smoking and spitting, perched atop motorbikes and car hoods, senses attuned for the shot or the quote.

The police, on the other hand, as of this morning, are no longer a constant presence outside their suite door. This happened with no prior notice. Just a brief phone call from Aimee Martinet to Uncle Frank, after the fact, when the gendarmes were already gone.

The cops had felt like jailers. But now that they're gone, Jake realizes the cops also made him feel safe.

People surge and eddy around him, but he has never felt so lonely.

He's afraid to talk to Natalie, who's an alarming mess. Or to Uncle Frank, who shuts him down every time. And Jake's French sucks. Even if it was better, who could he talk to here anyway?

Jake lifts his cellphone and snaps another picture.

Using their now-abandoned summer apartment as his ground
zero, he's spent the day methodically scouting the surrounding
streets for CCTV security cameras. He's made note of their street
addresses. Photographed their locations. And, as best as he could,
determined what precise frames their lenses were trained to cap-
ture.

He wants proof that William Crane was in Paris on the day of
his dad's murder. The more Jake thinks about it, the more convinced he is that Crane is responsible. *She chose us, you sick fuck.
And you just couldn't bear it.*

Jake is convinced Crane will show up somewhere on footage
from one of these cameras. He wonders if Crane's still here in the
city, wandering through the neighborhood, exulting arrogantly in
his crime. *Crimes.*

Jake will need evidence, concrete and tangible, if he has a hope
of getting the police to believe him. They had already checked area
CCTV footage (or so they said) and found nothing useful.

But they didn't know to look for Crane. And how can you find a
man you don't know you're looking for?

Jake won't let himself think about how many of these cameras
might be dummies. How certainly a number are broken. How even
if footage *was* taken on the day his dad was murdered, it's likely to
be erased or recorded over by now.

Whatever. Jake couldn't take another day in that hotel, watching Natalie wither before his eyes. He had to do something.

Thinking about Natalie twists at him. It was awful after Mom
disappeared, Natalie's rapid decline, followed by the thorny decision to put her into treatment. He feels guilty about his complicity
in the intervention, can't forget her beseeching eyes. How helpless
and conflicted he felt. And now it's starting all over again, she's
hurting herself. He *must* figure out what happened to their parents.

Jake pauses for just a moment by an oak wine barrel turned
planter, overflowing with scarlet geraniums. He smells the wet soil
and allows himself the still-rare luxury of remembering his mother.

For months after her disappearance, and then the letter taking credit for her death, thinking about her was agony.

They'd had a memorial service for her, well attended, replete with sadness over her loss and also joy in her remembrance. But Jake couldn't bear to imagine her rotting body abandoned somewhere unknown, denied a burial. He learned it was easier to pack up his memories and feelings. Put them away.

Tears sting his eyes. Mom. Cheering on the sidelines at his basketball games. Ruffling his hair as she passed him on the stairs. How understanding, no even better, how genuinely *nonchalant* she'd been when he came out to her.

He knows she wasn't some paragon of virtue, some idealized notion of a mother. She was sometimes hotheaded and flew off the handle, said things everyone regretted later. Sometimes she would retreat into her bedroom for days on end, watching crappy make-over shows or *Law & Order,* leaving Jake with the responsibility of fending for himself and Natalie if Dad was out of town.

But god, he misses her.

When he went back to school after she disappeared, when the creeping dread of "not-knowing" finally morphed into the horror and shock of loss, Jake dove equally hard into his studies and into partying. He couldn't think about his mother, he couldn't think about Natalie locked in that treatment center north of the city. He needed to occupy every minute of the day and night, so he burned the candle at both ends until he was burnt out.

But Nat got better and came home. Jake managed to kick ass with his grades (all A's that first semester back) but also realized he had to calm the fuck down, so he did. They all healed as best as they could. That's what their respective therapists encouraged. This summer in Europe was supposed to hit the reset button for all of them.

Look how that worked out, he thinks bitterly.

Jake shakes off his spiraling thoughts and concentrates on the task at hand. There's another camera, mounted above the entrance to an antiques store, lens trained on the street outside. Jake takes photos of the camera and its probable view and taps the name and address of the store onto his list.

His eyes are caught by the glimmering display in the antiques store window. Sun glints off silver picture frames, elegant cigarette cases, art deco jewelry. A collection of pocket watches, ivory figurines, a gold-embellished tea set. A selection of knives with ornately carved bone handles.

A shiver passes through him. He feels spooked suddenly, vulnerable. Is that a reflection of a man behind him in the glass of the store window?

Jake whirls around, heart thudding, arm raised, fist clenched, certain he will see the face of Will Crane behind him.

He startles a trio of pretty teenage girls who yelp and scatter. A hunchbacked old crone raps her cane against the pavement and spits at him as she passes by.

But Will Crane is nowhere to be seen.

CRASS

When Hank Scovell calls me, his eagerness to talk to "Hannah Potter" becomes an irresistible lure.

Brian Burrows's ambitious lieutenant invites me to meet him for a glass of wine at a restaurant on rue des Récollets in canal Saint-Martin called Les Enfants Perdus. "The Lost Children." How very apt.

Exposed brick in the square front room. Mahogany paneling lines the narrow room that extends behind it. The place is crowded despite the early hour. A blackboard announces the day's special in curlicues of pastel chalk. White-aproned waiters deliver plates of fresh vegetables and seared meats that look like paintings. At the small bar, there is room for only three stools. Two are empty. Hank Scovell occupies the third.

I've researched him, of course. I know he grew up in Michigan and studied architecture at Cornell. I've examined his bank accounts and credit card statements (he spends a little more than he ought). I know he is single and looking, and not above sending the occasional crass dick pic. (I personally find that predilection juvenile and silly, but will do my best not to hold it against him.)

I greet him, introduce myself as "Hannah Potter," thank him for meeting me. His eyes rake across my body in a way that makes me feel violated. I understand Ursine's distaste.

He's drinking Sancerre. I agree to join him in a glass.

"So you're a friend of Brian's?"

There's something about his tone, aggressive, slightly accusatory.

"Well," I reply cautiously, "*friend* might be too strong a word. We met at a grief group here in Paris shortly before he died."

He purses his lips and fixes me with a flinty stare. Scovell's features might be fine taken individually, but collected on his face they seem off—his eyes too small, his brow too heavy, his nose askew. There's no denying the intelligence in his eyes, though. Or the hunger.

"I didn't know Brian was attending any kind of a grief group," he challenges.

I shrug. "I guess it's not the kind of thing everyone wants to talk about." I fall silent, proving my point.

Scovell takes a sip of his wine. "Excellent, isn't it? So crisp and aromatic."

I take a sip myself. Flash a smile in agreement. "Delicious."

"So why exactly are you nosing around into Brian's murder?" There it is again, blunt aggression.

Is this just his manner?

Or does he have something to hide?

Perhaps something to gain?

I laugh lightly. Touch his arm. Play the coquette. "You make me sound like some kind of hard-boiled private eye when you put it like that, which is hardly the case. I just feel bad for his kids. He talked about them a lot. And so when I met Natalie and she asked, I said I'd talk to Lilja. She sent you to me. End of story."

Scovell's narrow eyes grow even smaller as he peers at me. His mouth opens as if he is going to say something, but then he pokes out a pink tongue and licks his fleshy lips. Takes another sip of wine.

"So what did you want to tell me?" I press.

Scovell slugs back the rest of his Sancerre and motions to the bartender for another glass. An American family piles into the restaurant, a couple in their fifties with three sullen teenagers. They uncomfortably crowd Scovell and me at the bar while waiting for their table.

I touch Scovell's shoulder, lean in close to his ear. "We all want to bring whoever did this to justice, don't we?"

Our eyes lock, but his defenses are up. I can see the reserve in his chilly gaze. The American family follows the maître d' as he gestures toward a table in the back. Scovell's eyes follow them. I gather up my jacket and bag.

"Look," I continue. "You're the one who asked to meet me. But, you're right. I should keep out of this. It's none of my business. If you know something, talk to the police."

One, two, three. I'm certain he'll stop me before "ten."

Four, five, six.

Scovell grabs for my wrist. "Wait. There's something I want to show you."

"Let go of me," I snap.

He pulls his hand off me as if scalded. "Sorry." His face turns pink.

I settle back down on the stool. Reach for my wineglass. "Okay. What have you got?"

CAKE

Uncle Frank's at the embassy *again*, and Jake's been gone for hours, god knows where. *Fuck it,* Natalie decides, *I'm going out.* Stupid really, that she's allowed herself to be constrained by Uncle Frank as it is. She's eighteen, a legal adult. Perfectly capable of walking around the streets of Paris unsupervised.

Natalie pushes away the annoying thought that his insistence on her staying in the hotel is for her own safety. She feels reckless. If there's a madman out there who killed her father and now is looking for her, bring him on! She may be small, but she's no one to mess with, the prick'll find that out soon enough. Whoever the fuck he is.

Armed with this bravado, Natalie slips out of the hotel, half-expecting someone to stop her. No one does.

She weaves through pedestrians, bicyclists, cars, and taxis. Idly, she window-shops boutiques, bookstores, ice cream stands, and *patisseries.* She pauses in front of one shop and admires the elegant formations of squared, crescent, and domed cakes, tipped with gold or ornamented with flowers made from icing.

She hasn't eaten all day. She darts into the *patisserie* and purchases the most fanciful cake in the case. She takes her time with the pastry, nibbling minute bites and letting them dissolve slowly on her tongue as she threads through the crowded streets.

Natalie checks her phone. Nothing from Jake. Nothing from Hannah Potter. Nothing from Uncle Frank.

She feels as if she might disappear into thin air, just like her mother did three years before. Unmoored and adrift, who or what could stop her?

Desolation sets in as she realizes she has no place to go.

Except back to that fucking hotel.

Natalie's tongue licks her fingers clean. She presses her damp finger pads into the wound on her wrist. The rush of pain is delicious, as sweet as the cake.

Catherine

LES PUCES

The Porte de Clignancourt metro station is the last stop on the 4 line, way up in the northernmost tip of the 18th arrondissement. I've been here hundreds of times, but even so, emerging from the station into the street above always causes a jolt of culture shock.

The sidewalks here are grimy. Garbage overflows from trashcans and blows across the pavement. Vivid, rude graffiti is splashed about indiscriminately.

Immigrants from many different countries cajole and catcall, pointing to the less-than-savory products heaped before them on ratty blankets.

Les Puces, the largest outdoor flea market in Paris and a popular tourist attraction, lies just a few short blocks away, but in order to get there, one must brave this teeming crowd selling T-shirts, knockoff sunglasses, counterfeit designer bags, African drums, illegal drugs, and sex on the cheap.

Also for sale here, and most essential to me, are cellphones.

I jostle my way through the aggressive hawkers with urgency. Earlier this morning, I detected an attempt to disable my firewall. I rapidly shut the worm down, but all the same it spooked me. Had I been sloppy? Does the Russian bastard know more about me than he should?

I immediately disabled and ditched the phone I've been using for all things related to Elena's kidnapping. Then I headed here, cursing myself. I should have switched out phones earlier. I should have been more careful.

Ten minutes later, money changes hands and I have five new phones at my disposal.

A fight breaks out between three angry Tunisians jostling for the same street corner. The gathering crowd eggs on the combatants, urging them to go for the kill, and placing bets on the outcome.

I tuck my purchases into my brown leather Chloe satchel, nestling them next to the Mace, stun gun, and leather pouch with loaded syringes (a girl needs to be prepared). Sirens howl in the distance. I hurry away from the commotion.

I enter "The Flea." Normally, I would take time to browse. I'm fascinated by the extensive variety of objects one can find here: antique bicycles, oil paintings, first-edition books, intricately woven rugs and tapestries, globes and compasses, clocks and watches, wooden tennis rackets in old-fashioned presses. China, crystal, and flatware. Vintage jewelry, handbags, dresses, hats, and gloves. Furniture of many eras, chairs with needlepoint seats and mirrors with ormolu frames. Military gear from both world wars, nautical equipment, telescopes. Copper cookware, steamer trunks, and charming, discarded shop signs, reading COIFFURE or BOUCHERIE.

I can spend hours here exploring, telling myself stories about the times and people who have left these artifacts behind. It may be the only hobby I have. Today, however, I hurry through as quickly as I can.

At the far end of the market, past a shop jumbled with sterling silver teapots, candlesticks, and pitchers, I cut into an alley. I stop in front of a metal roll-up door and rap sharply: two knocks, a pause, then three in rapid succession.

The door whines up and open. Delphine, protective goggles on her face and a blazing blowtorch in one hand, gestures me inside. She slams the roll-up door down behind us.

The space within is vast and dim, a disused warehouse. No windows. Dusty light filters in through a pair of filthy skylights. Cars line the perimeter of the space, older models, nondescript makes.

Delphine's latest sculpture, a gigantic humanoid figure shaped from harvested car parts, dwarfs the stepladder she has been using to reach the creature's "face," where the metal still glows red-hot.

Delphine shuts off the blowtorch and raises her goggles, rubbing the tips of her fingers gently over the ovals they have imprinted around her eyes.

"Looks good," I say admiringly, gesturing to her work.

Delphine shrugs. Compliments are meaningless to her. She does this work for her own process and pleasure and no one else's. Her fused-metal sculptures are all homages to her murdered younger brother. Over and over again she re-creates the boy she lost in steel and iron, copper and brass, first welding the pieces together and then blasting them apart when she is done.

"I need you," I begin. "Some of my Elena communications may have been compromised."

Delphine's eyes widen slightly. She knows better than anyone how careful I am. She sets down the blowtorch and goggles.

"Balint will bring her north to the safe house in Stockholm. I want you to meet him there. Stay with her until her transport out of Europe is finalized. It should only be a matter of days."

Delphine reaches back and pulls free the elastic that binds her long dark hair into a ponytail.

"When do you need me to leave?"

"Now."

Jake

STEAK FRITES

There's no doubt about it, this is the most uncomfortable family dinner in the entire history of family dinners. A record setter. And Jake ought to know because an inordinate number of *other* Burrows family dinners have also made the leaderboard.

There was the "which-take-out-place?" dinner the night after his mother disappeared (once the police had come with their questions and condescension and left trailing platitudes). Then there were the endless meals cooked from Uncle Frank's limited playbook: pasta Bolognese, steak on the grill, simple roast chicken, all served with a side of misery and a dollop of dread. And of course there was the infamous "last supper" just before they had Natalie committed (during which Jake, Brian, and Frank were so suffused with anticipatory tension they practically emitted sparks). Not to mention the take-out deli they'd consumed in silence the night after Mallory's memorial service, the salty meats, sour rye bread, and earthy mustards like glue in their mouths.

Tonight, Natalie's eaten maybe two French fries and sliced her steak into the thinnest of ribbons (Jake's caught her pushing them under the mound of potatoes). She doesn't look at all well; her face has a sallow cast; her eyes look empty.

And Uncle Frank. Packing in fat juicy morsels of bloody meat, gulping down swallows of rich red wine, dragging his fries through a mound of yellow mayonnaise before stuffing them into his mouth. Jake stares at Frank's furiously working jaws, trying to make sense of the information his uncle is trying to impart.

Frank's enraged about the embassy. Although Jake doesn't know what his uncle expected. Brian's death is an open murder investigation. Did Frank really expect they would all just be sent on their giddy way?

Besides, Jake isn't as desperate to leave Paris as Frank. He thinks he's genuinely on to something.

It makes sense. Dad would never have stopped looking for Crane. As much as Brian had spouted exhortations about "looking to the future," and how "*she* would have wanted all of us to move forward," Jake had always known these encouragements were for his and Natalie's benefit. After Mom died, Dad was broken. Jake didn't believe he'd ever let her go.

And then there were those reports Nat was so excited to share. That Dad's co-workers swore he'd been *afraid* in the days leading up to his death. Will Crane fit that too. Who else would Dad be afraid of?

Suddenly deeply sorry about all the loving things he'd never said to his father and all the awful things he had, Jake takes a hasty gulp of wine. He doesn't want to feel this sadness. His head starts to throb.

Uncle Frank's still yammering. Natalie's pushing food around her plate.

Jake catches her slipping the bone-handled steak knife into her purse. Their eyes meet, his mouth opens, he intends to speak but—

Please. Please let me have it, her eyes beg him. *Please don't bust me.*

Jake looks away from her. Takes a vicious stab at his filet with his own knife, imagining the blade is cutting into Will Crane's yielding flesh.

He doesn't bust Natalie. He lets her keep that weighty, greasy knife she tucked into her embroidered cotton bag.

He's not sure why.

Catherine

STAIRWELL

I've changed up all the electronics, shifted all of my plans, dispatched Delphine. I'm back in charge of the game. Natalie's been texting me with the relentless persistence unique to teenagers. When I finally replied, her eager relief was palpable.

The crush of press outside the hotel has largely dispersed, chasing fresher scandals, no doubt. Only three obvious members of the fourth estate still linger: a huge, lumpy man with an acne-scarred face, a hawk-nosed woman, whippet thin and bristling with energy, and a chain-smoking photographer, with a mane of silver hair and his camera at the ready.

I slip around to the hotel's back entrance.

I pass fifty euros into Nyura's receptive hands and enter. The bowels of the building smell rank, despite an overlying scent of bleach. The soles of my shoes squeak against the tile floors.

My chest tightens with a sticky pull of anxiety. I take the stairs slowly. What if Scovell's information is another dead end? What if I am only bringing false hope to a young woman who's already on the edge? This is not the time for these questions. But why do I feel so much dread?

At the third-floor landing, I stop.

I've ordered my life around choices that allow me to be in control. Of all things. At all times. Even my excesses are conducted under my rules and parameters.

But my life collided with the Burrowses' lives in a way that destroyed that imperative. My excesses caused their loss.

I can still turn around. It's not too late.

No. I owe them.

I owe Mallory.

I climb the last flight of stairs, itchy and uncomfortable in my own skin. Or should I say, "in Hannah Potter's skin"?

Natalie looks even paler than the last time I saw her, swimming in her long-sleeved shirt and jeans. Her face lights up when she sees me.

"I was afraid you weren't coming!"

"Here I am."

The door to the corridor swings open. I press a finger to my lips to urge Natalie to hush and pull us both back under the shadowy recesses of the stairs.

A man steps through the door. Mid-forties, attractive and fit, with salt-and-pepper hair and searching eyes. He blinks as he adjusts to the bright light of the stairwell.

"It's okay," Natalie assures me. "It's just my uncle Frank. I asked him to come."

Shit. I hadn't counted on this.

"Mrs. Potter?" Frank inquires. "Natalie says you have information about my brother?"

I step forward and Frank Burrows's eyes meet mine. Something about his intensity unnerves me. But I'm here. I have a question to ask. Surely I can handle a salesman from Connecticut along with this teenage girl?

I shake the hand he extends to me.

In for a penny, in for a pound, so I cut to the chase.

"You know Hank Scovell?"

Frank Burrows's face is blank, but Natalie chimes in. "Of course. He worked for my dad." She turns to her uncle. "Remember? He was Dad's second on the project here."

"Right. Well, Natalie, as you asked, I spoke to Lilja, the project manager. She suggested I speak to your dad's assistant, who confirmed Lilja's impression that your dad was afraid of something or someone."

"Who? Did she have any idea?" Frank Burrows's face twists in confusion.

"No. But Hank Scovell had something more to add. Brian also confided in him. He snapped a picture of a man he caught tailing him and he texted the photo to Scovell to see if he knew him. He wondered if it was somebody they had encountered in connection with the project. Someone that might have had a beef."

"Didn't Mr. Scovell turn the photo in to the police?" Natalie wants to know. Her face is alight with fresh hope.

"He says he did. But he also felt that the police had another agenda they were pursuing and so didn't pay him much mind."

"Did Scovell recognize the man in the picture?"

"He says not. Look, I have a copy. Will you look at it? Maybe you'll know who it is."

I extract a cellphone from my brown leather satchel. Open the photograph Scovell texted to me. The subject, a man I would gauge to be in his early thirties, has one hand raised to forestall the inevitable picture. His watery blue eyes are widened in alarm, but otherwise he's pleasant-looking, with a sweep of streaky blond hair that falls across his forehead.

I hand the cell to Natalie. She stares intently. Her face crumples. "I don't know him."

She passes the phone to Frank. He looks carefully at the picture, swiping his fingers across the screen to make the man's features larger.

"Not a clue," he says, handing the phone back to me. "Nat, why don't you go back to the room? Let me talk to Mrs. Potter alone for a second."

"Somebody must know who he is! He was stalking Daddy!" Natalie's desperation colors her cry.

"Come on, let me talk to Mrs. Potter alone," Frank repeats.

To my surprise, Natalie flings her thin arms around me. "Thank you for trying," she whispers before releasing me.

Frank Burrows waits until the stairwell door swings closed behind her. "Look, Mrs. Potter, I appreciate what you've tried to do. I'll follow up with the police and ask them to look deeper into that guy in the photo."

"Do you agree with Natalie that the police aren't investigating as thoroughly as they should?"

"How the hell do I know? They tell us jack shit! And the embassy's been useless. We all need this solved. For Brian to rest in peace." He groans. "We just need to go home."

"It must be very hard for you," I murmur. So often this is the only thing to say.

"You don't know the half of it!" And then the words spill from him in a torrent. I learn of his custody battle, how he feels he's betraying his own children by taking care of Brian's. His explosive fears about Natalie and Jake, the former reverting to old patterns of self-mutilation, the latter vacillating between withdrawal and rage, prone to what Frank believes is delusional thinking.

He speaks of their isolation in the hotel, his disgust with the press frenzy, how very badly he misses his daughters. He is overwhelmed. At a complete loss as to what to do next.

He swipes at his eyes with an impatient knuckle.

"It'll be all right," I mutter, offering the platitude but knowing all too well that nothing will be all right. Some things you can't recover from.

Frank fishes a crumpled tissue from his pocket. "Thank you for listening." He blows his nose. "I haven't really had anyone to talk to. And I try to be strong for the kids . . ." he falters.

"Of course." I give him an understanding nod. "But can I ask— did Brian confide in you? Do you know why he was so scared?"

He shoves the tissue in his pocket. "No. I wish he had. Look—

you seem like a nice person. I get you were trying to help. But I advise you to stay out of this from here on in. My brother was killed for a laptop. Whoever did this doesn't exactly value life."

"I can take care of myself."

"Yeah. That's what Brian thought too."

Jake

SUSPECT

Jake sits impatiently in the drab waiting room at the prefecture. With his right thumbnail he scrapes at the yellowing tape holding a flyer to the wall. She's kept him waiting for over forty fucking minutes. And after all that bullshit she put him through to begin with.

Aimee Martinet was polite to Jake the first time he called. Sympathetic even. But when he called again and asked to meet her, she put him off. Then she stopped taking his calls. So Jake changed tactics. Emailed her. Repeatedly. Finally she replied that he could make an appointment to come in with his guardian. So he had dutifully made the appointment. Except that he had never let Uncle Frank know.

At least he finally has an audience with the goddamn bitch.

Even as that last thought escapes, Jake kicks himself. If he wants Aimee Martinet to believe a thing he says, he can't afford anger. He's got to cool down. He clasps his hands tightly. Resolves to keep his temper in check.

There she is, swinging open the door to the inner sanctum. Her eyes alight on Jake, then dart about, searching for Frank. She click, click, clicks over to Jake in her pointy navy heels.

"Is your uncle with you?" She gets right to the point. Her point. Jake has to get her to listen.

"No, I—"

"You must go, then," Martinet says firmly. "Make another appointment. Come back with him."

"Just ten minutes of your time," Jake entreats. "How can it hurt to listen to what I have to say? Besides I'm twenty-one. He's my uncle, but he's not my guardian."

She cocks her head and studies Jake with frank appraisal. He meets her gaze confidently. The light shifts in her eyes. A decision has been made.

"Follow me."

Jake follows her down the corridor. She opens the door to the same meeting room they had been in the last time, the one with what Jake is pretty sure is a two-way mirror on the single red wall.

She gestures for him to sit. He does. Then he lays it all out for her. His theory about his mother's lover, Will Crane. His investigation of all the cameras in the vicinity of the apartment. His certainty that if they examined the footage from all of these cameras, they would see Crane.

She lets him talk without interruption. He keeps his voice calm and persuasive as he constructs a controlled argument based on logic and analysis. Jake knows he is right. Finally, he runs out of steam, his initial rush of words petering out into fumbled, half-formed phrases.

He's unsure how to read her expression.

Her lips tighten and release. She tucks a loose strand of hair behind her ear. "Quite a compelling presentation," she remarks.

Jake's heart leaps. Has he gotten through to her? He must have. She believes him. He's dizzy with relief.

"The only problem is that we've been pursuing a very different line of investigation. One that seems quite promising."

He can't hide his surprise. He didn't expect that. But she seems so sure, suddenly so primly disapproving of his story woven from strands of Crane.

"What line of investigation? What have you found out?"

She leans in toward him and touches his forearm lightly. Never breaking eye contact, she croons, "Well, for one thing, we know you came back to Paris earlier than you led us all to believe. In fact, you came back the day before your father's murder."

Catherine

WATCH

I kick off my shoes and close my front door behind me, firmly turning the lock.

My command center awaits; I have work to do. I press my thumbprint on the lock. Sink into my chair and roll between the two desks, firing up computers. I pull a bottle from a drawer and take just one healthy swig of tequila. I need to take the edge off, but can't afford to get stupid.

Punching Delphine's number into a phone, my stomach knots and twists. I've been trying to reach her unsuccessfully for hours.

I walk to the window and stare at the street below. The few people still out and about are raucously drunk. Or clinging furtively to the shadows. My call clicks over to a recorded message. Again.

Turning back to the monitors, I study the video feed from the exterior of the Stockholm safe house. The place is shrouded in darkness. Balint and Elena should've been there by now. So should Delphine.

My ears prick at the scratchy sound of a key entering a lock. I peer intently at the screens but see nothing. Was that the sound of a doorknob turning? My heart hammers in my chest as I realize the sound is not coming from any of my monitors.

Someone is in my apartment.

If it's an emissary of the Russian, the intruder will no doubt be armed. From the cache of supplies I keep under my desk, I pull a can of Mace.

Footsteps echo on the wide plank floors. The intruder is heading toward my bedroom, assuming no doubt that I am snugly asleep, an easy target. A chill judders through me. Have they been in here before? In and gone without me ever being the wiser? Searching and planning while I was oblivious? How could I have missed that?

I don't think the Russian will want to kill me just yet, not until he knows Elena's whereabouts, but I've seen firsthand evidence of his taste for torture. I remember the bastard's initials branded into Elena's flesh.

My bare feet pad silently as I sneak down the hallway, avoiding the creaky floorboard that could give my presence away. My fingers tighten around the can of Mace.

A dark figure is poised at the entrance to my bedroom. A man. He hesitates at the threshold; perhaps he's seen that the bed is empty. He turns. I cover the distance to him in three swift strides. As the Mace strikes him, he screams and drops to his knees.

Too late, I recognize the intruder. "*Merde!* What are you doing here?"

Gasping with pain, my lover Gerard grunts at me in French. "*I wanted to surprise you.*"

I curse myself for relenting to Gerard's entreaties that I give him a key. I should have known better. People close to me get hurt. Sometimes it's me that hurts them.

"Stay there," I command.

Returning moments later, I kneel next to him with a bowl of cool water and a clean dishtowel. He moans as I dab his eyes and face with the wet cloth.

"*Why would you do this to me?*" he whines plaintively in French. "*My wife is away visiting her* maman, *and we haven't seen each other—*"

"*You scared me half to death,*" I retort, also in French. "*Sneak-*

ing into my apartment in the middle of the night! A woman has the right to protect herself."

Twenty minutes later, I dispatch Gerard in a taxi, instructing him to go to the nearest emergency room. I convinced him he should claim he was mugged in the street by an unseen attacker. His wife may excuse his extramarital dalliances, but under pressure, Gerard understood my preference for keeping this incident on the down low.

I'd also surreptitiously removed my key from his ring.

Gerard doesn't know it yet, but I will never see him again.

Entering my command center, I see activity on one of the monitors displaying a feed from the Stockholm safe house. I draw closer and snatch up a phone.

On the screen, I watch as Delphine fits the key into the lock of the front door. Slings her backpack off and fishes in its depths for the ringing cell. She turns the key and muscles the door open with her shoulder, still floundering inside her backpack.

I shift my view to the next screen over. Delphine enters the vestibule, chucks the door closed with her hip. Flips on a light. Drops the backpack so she can rummage through it with both hands.

"Oui?" she finally answers.

"Why are you so late?" I snap.

"Delayed flight, boss. Some bullshit at the airport here. But B's on his way now with the package."

I exhale. Things are fine.

It's *all fine.*

Jake

RING

Jake rushes through the streets. He bumps into a woman with a baby stroller, reaches out a hand to steady them both, and ends up copping an inadvertent feel. The woman shrieks, swats him with her purse, and unleashes a volley of outraged obscenities.

Mumbling an apology, Jake backs away from her, turns the corner, starts to run. People brush past him in indistinct blurs of color. Voices and car horns and an unexpected refrain of classical violin compete with the roaring in his brain.

That bitch. The way she let him spell everything out for her, all the time just waiting. Baiting her trap and preparing to pounce. It's nobody's business but his own why he came back to Paris a day early.

His breath hitches in his chest. He slows. Drops his hands to his knees and gulps in air. Fuck.

The police suspect him. They think he killed his father.

A small girl holds a shiny gold ring up before Jake's watering eyes.

"You drop this, yes?" the child asks in heavily accented English, all big brown eyes and sweet, shy smile.

Jake feels the hand snake into the back pocket of his jeans. He spins around. A man backs away, early thirties, thin and wiry, with the same big brown eyes as the girl. He clutches Jake's wallet in one bony hand.

Fueled by outraged instinct and pent-up, bursting feelings, Jake lunges for the guy. Momentum crashes them both to the sidewalk.

Jake's fists slam into the wiry man's face. He welcomes the pop of cartilage and bone as the guy's nose splinters.

The skin on Jake's knuckles splits open. His blood mingles with the blood streaming from the guy's pulpy face.

The girl screams, "Papa, Papa, Papa!"

Jake rolls off the pickpocket. Staggers to his feet. Grabs his wallet from the pavement.

The girl drops down on her knees next to her father, tears running down her terrified little face.

"Sorry," Jake mutters to the girl as he gets to his feet. "I'm sorry. *Désolé.*"

A few people have gathered to stare, Jake realizes as he wheels about. A fat tourist with a fanny pack and socks under his sandals films Jake with his iPhone. Jake can't have that.

He's running down the street with his wallet in one bloody hand and the fat tourist's iPhone in the other before Fatso even has time to shout.

Catherine

SIMPLE

Mallory Burrows has haunted my thoughts over the past three years.

How could she not?

I've rewritten history so that I never had that first drink, or the next one, didn't miss that plane. Didn't fail Mallory. Fail myself. In this daydream, I get Mallory to safety while I ferret out and neutralize her stalker. It was a simple job.

It should've been a simple job.

I've imagined unraveling the clues her killer left behind and then locating Crane, forcing a confession, delivering him to the police and poor Mallory's body to the Burrows family for burial. For closure.

I know all too well the torture of *not knowing*.

Instead I fled to Paris, content to let the Burrows family suffer in ignorance. I am a coward as well as a failure.

Another favorite fantasy?

Mallory alive, living in happy exile with her lover, Will, her disappearance and Crane's letter taking credit for her death all an elaborate hoax executed by a desperate woman who needed to escape her old life and begin a new one. Who knows? It could be true. Haven't I done more or less the same for numerous clients?

Brian Burrows's murder made that pretty fairy tale less likely.

Now I can't shake the feel of Natalie Burrows's arms flung around me. Or the grief in her eyes, like looking into a mirror.

I cost that girl her mother. Her father too, if the murders are connected.

I study the photograph Scovell shared with me. Who *is* this man? Was he following Brian Burrows? Why? Did he kill him? And if he did, for what reason? Is he somehow connected to Mallory and her lover? Could it be that they are still alive and Brian was their victim?

How can I find this man before he kills again?

I reach for the tequila bottle.

I don't like today. I don't like delays. I don't like mistakes. I don't like near misses.

I don't like unanswered questions. I like to *know*.

Most of all, I don't like to care.

Bad things happen when I care.

KNUCKLES

The narrow floor lamp with its wide woven shade casts a lonely circle of light over the hotel room. It's otherwise hushed and dim, the thick orange curtains drawn tightly against the glitter of the Parisian night. Natalie slumps in a shadowy corner, knees drawn up to her chin.

What *did* Hannah and Uncle Frank discuss after she left them? What does he know that he isn't telling her?

Natalie could worry this bone all day.

They don't keep secrets from each other, she and Uncle Frank. They *share* secrets. Have done since Natalie was a little girl. So why's he hiding shit from her now?

She inhales her brother's scent from the T-shirt she's pulled from his messy pile. Blood from her nibbled cuticles dots the white cotton.

Where is Jake?

When Jake hadn't come back in time for dinner, Uncle Frank called Aimee Martinet. Uncle Frank's face turned white as he listened. Then he disappeared into his bedroom, banging the door shut behind him.

Natalie tried to eavesdrop, but could only make out a low rumble. When Uncle Frank finally emerged, she badgered him. What had Martinet told him? Where was her brother?

"All I did was report that I was concerned because Jake was late coming home."

"That's not true! I saw your face."

"I don't know what you're talking about."

"Why are you lying to me?"

"Natalie! That's enough. I know you're upset. I am too. But you know your brother. More than likely he's just blowing off some steam.

"Please don't worry, Natalie," Uncle Frank had added.

Oh, yeah. Don't worry. That's a fucking excellent piece of advice.

And why did Hannah Potter seem to make Uncle Frank so *anxious*? What the hell was that about?

Natalie's dazzled by confusion. How can she be suspicious of Uncle Frank? And suspicious of what, exactly? That he's worried? Who the fuck *isn't* worried?

Why can't I turn my fucking brain off?

Natalie yearns for sweet, aching relief. For numbing the pain the world throws at her by controlling the pain she inflicts on herself.

But Uncle Frank is on high alert, watching her every move. And Natalie wants to go to *college*, not back into treatment.

Dr. Bloom's voice floats through her thoughts like a cloud. *"Worry is interest paid on trouble not yet due, Natalie. Be grateful. Life is a gift. Be grateful for every day."*

Natalie grips Jake's T-shirt so tightly her knuckles turn as white as the fabric.

How many fucking times did Bloom say that to her? *Loser fool bitch. What if you have every right to be worried? And anyway, just what part of my fucking life is a fucking gift?*

With a jolt Natalie realizes that RISD may be in jeopardy. She knows nothing about her family's finances. What if she can't afford the tuition now that Dad's dead? Will Jake know?

Where the fuck is he?

Natalie bangs on Uncle Frank's door.

His reply is a muffled groan.

Natalie shoves open the door to find Frank instantly alert, pulling back his covers, clad in a T-shirt and boxers. "What is it?"

"Tell me," she demands. "What did Martinet say about Jake?"

Uncle Frank sinks back down onto the edge of his bed.

"All right. She said Jake wasn't in Amsterdam when your dad was killed. He was right here, in Paris. He lied, Natalie. To the police. And to both of us."

Catherine

SPIRAL

I am drunk.

Wasted.

Not proud. Just stating facts.

The last time I was this drunk . . .

I stagger toward my bed, bottle in hand. Stub my big toe against the night table, painfully.

Fuck!

I slug tequila, not caring that it slops down my face and onto my shoulder, leaving a pungent snail trail of liquor.

Tears puddle and drip messily down my cheeks. My nose is leaking. My head pounds. I feel like hell.

I catch a glimpse of myself in the mirror hung over my dresser as I collapse onto a mound of pillows. I look like hell too.

The last time I was this drunk . . .

The last time was when I missed my rendezvous with Mallory Burrows.

I never actually met Mallory, but the widely circulated image of her face is burned into my brain. Those gray eyes. Eyes that are mirrored in the pale, drawn face of her daughter.

I yank my soft chenille blanket up over my face. Breathe in the faint mingled scents of sweat and sex and my favorite lavender body lotion.

I groan. I press my palms against my streaming eyes. I beg for oblivion.

It finally comes.

I have no idea how long I'm out.

Dragged into consciousness by a mechanical roar of sound, my eyes still closed, I struggle to make sense of where I am.

My body is folded and tucked into a tight space, a seatbelt fastened across my lap.

A seatbelt?

The sound washing over me is that of jet engines. My eyes pop open. I'm strapped into an airplane seat, but suspended midair, no plane, no pilot, just this overwhelming rush of sound, and my rigid body in a single seat, aloft in a cloudless sky.

My mouth opens. I scream into the wind.

And wake. Soaked with sweat, heaving with terror.

I remember: I've had this dream before.

Harsh sun streams in through the window. My mouth is ashy, my throat parched. I lurch into the bathroom. Gulp cold water from the faucet. Release a stream of pee into the toilet. It smells like tequila, as does my sweat. I need a shower, but it seems like too much effort.

I'd been in an airport bar about to board a flight to New York when it happened. I'd been contacted by Mallory, determined her fears of a stalker were legitimate, was on my way to help. But there it was, every news channel exploding with coverage about the Farm, my former home.

The FBI had raided the Farm.

Have I mentioned the Farm? Probably not. There are some places and times it's best to leave forgotten if one can. The Farm is a part of my story that I would rewrite if I could.

Nobody loves you, Catherine, except all of us.

———

My father and I had left the Farm when I was only eight, and so much had happened to us both since our time there. As I sat waiting for a flight in an overlit airport bar, my years at the Farm felt foreign and distant, definitely not of this world, *my* world.

Nobody loves you, Catherine, except all of us.

Funny how that's always in my head. Or not funny at all.

Now, as I was supposed to be heading to Mallory, a spotlight was shining on the Farm, news vans and hungry reporters circled, it was of our world, my world, after all. I missed my flight. Stayed glued to the live coverage like millions of other Americans, drawn to the tantalizing thrill of a cult of fathers' rights activists in an armed standoff with the Feds. I drank and drank, pushing the rising tide of memories down and away.

Let's go, Cathy. Let's go.

After over nine hours of waiting, each minute breathlessly spun and dissected by a bevy of pundits, a hothead inside Father Karl's compound fired the first shot. The Feds blasted the Farm to the ground. Father Karl watched twelve of his people die, including two of his own three children, before jamming his shotgun in his mouth and blowing his brains out.

Nobody loves you, Catherine, except all of us.

By the time I was sober, Mallory Burrows was missing and presumed dead.

STOMP

The music is rough and loud, *"nouveau punk,"* the shifty-eyed barker outside had squawked. The club is packed with skinheads in leather. Blood thrums through Jake's veins.

Jake hears a glass shatter somewhere across the room. Pushing and shoving and shouts erupt in its wake. The violence rolls through the crowd like a wave.

Jake's sucked into the writhing mass on the dance floor. It's claustrophobic. He brings his elbow up sharply, struggling to find a space to breathe. He feels the point of his elbow connect with someone's jaw. There's a torrent of curses in a language Jake doesn't recognize. Then he's hauled into the air and tossed across the room like a rag doll.

Good, Jake thinks, as he lands hard and a boot smashes into his head, *this is good.*

Catherine

HUSH

"*Cathy.*" The whisper is soft in my ear. "*Let's go, Cathy. Let's go.*"

I struggle toward consciousness from deep slumber. Mama stands over my bed.

"*We're having an adventure,*" she whispers, gathering me up in her arms, huffing to settle me on her hip. I am five, a big girl now; Mama can hardly carry me.

Mama hurries to pull open the front door. Daddy looms in the threshold.

He swings me in the air. He laughs. His big hand curls around my small one.

A squeeze. A jerk so hard it rockets pain through my shoulder. A flash. A bang.

Something splatters. Pink and red and gray.

"*Hush,*" Daddy commands, clamping his hand over my lips. "*Be quiet, Cathy. Hush.*"

It's only then I realize I'm screaming.

I wake in my apartment, roused by my own shrill keening. It takes me too long to remember where I am.

Paris.

Home. I'm safe.
It was a nightmare. Just a nightmare.
I will my hammering heart to slow.
Lift the tequila bottle to my lips.
"Let's go, Cathy. Let's go."

Frank

_____

DEAD OF MORNING

The tantalizing scent of freshly brewed coffee invades the breakfast room. Frank sniffs deeply. Pours a cup from the carafe on the sideboard.

The interior courtyard the breakfast room faces is muffled in darkness, only the faintest streaks of early light paint the sky. A few waxy green plants press their broad leaves up against the glass. A waiter nods a greeting and gestures that Frank should sit anywhere he likes. Frank surveys the room. He's the sole patron at this hour.

Frank chooses a table right next to the window, pops his laptop open. Asks the waiter for *jus de pamplemousse* and croissants. As his computer warms to life, Frank thinks uneasily about Hannah Potter. He doesn't like this stranger nosing around in their business; her clandestine communications with Natalie annoy him.

Thinking about Hannah gives his loins a tug. He shifts in his seat to accommodate his erection.

Frank checks his phone's display. It's too early to call Aimee Martinet. Besides, if she had news of Jake, wouldn't she call him?

He opens CNN on his laptop and scrolls through the news. Bombings. Shootings. Chemical spills. Corruption. A feel-good story about the love between a dog and an otter. Same old crap.

This morning Frank had found Natalie dead asleep on the floor, her head pillowed on Jake's overflowing duffel bag, one of his T-shirts clutched like a teddy bear in her arms.

He'd lifted her and tucked her into her bed. She was lighter than his much younger girls. Deep purple shadows pressed in below her eyes, she hardly stirred as he moved her. He expects she will sleep for hours. He suspects she was up all night.

Frank cringes as he remembers her reaction to Aimee Martinet's revelations about Jake. But what did he expect?

The waiter brings him the grapefruit juice, a basket of croissants, a pot of creamy butter, and a white tray with three kinds of jam. Frank splits open a flaky pastry and watches the steam waft from its moist center. He slathers one half with butter and strawberry jam and crams the whole delicious bite into his mouth.

There's no other option, he decides grimly, Natalie must go back into treatment. He moves the cursor over to his search history. He'd called the center Natalie had been in three years ago only to learn that Dr. Bloom, the former director, had tragically died in a car accident this past year. The new doctor in charge told Frank there were no available beds, but had kindly emailed a list of referrals. Frank had started to investigate the alternatives when Natalie had walked in on him mid-search. He'd slammed his laptop closed, flustered at being found out.

He needs to have a plan in place for her before anything is discussed. And with Jake missing . . . *Damn it, where is that fucking boy?*

Frank doesn't know if he's more worried or furious. He shoves another hunk of buttery, jam-laden croissant into his mouth and checks his email.

A billing question from his mother's assisted living. An infuriating email from his lawyer about the custody case. Jesus. He needs to get back to the States! He's put his whole life on hold. He drains the last of his coffee. Whatever it takes, he is getting hold of those two kids and getting the hell out of Paris.

Frank's urgent steps propel him back into their suite. A quick glance reveals Jake has not yet returned. He flings open the door to Natalie's bedroom, expecting to find her curled on the bed where he'd left her.

But the bed is empty. A quick check of the bathroom reveals it's empty too.

Both kids are gone.

Catherine

ROUSE

A sharp tap. The tinkle of broken glass. My gluey eyes reluctantly peel open.

Darkness. Night? I'm on the floor of my bedroom, head uncomfortably pillowed on a fringed Burberry bootie. No recollection of how I got here.

An ankle crosses my line of vision.

I snap a hand out. Seize my intruder's leg. A sharp *"Merde!"* explodes into the shadowy room as he (she?) face plants.

Wait. I recognize the voice.

"Jumah? Is that you?" I inquire in French.

His reply in French is heated, a stream of irritated, curse-laden words: *"Who else comes up here to help your drunken ass? I think you broke my nose. Shit. Fuck. That hurts. Motherfucker."*

Jumah goes on to explain that he was knocking on my door for ten long minutes before he finally scaled the spiral fire escape that crawls up the side of my building. He was worried because he could hear me inside, even though I wouldn't answer.

"Hear me?" I blurt.

"Yes. Yelling. As if someone was hurting you. But I guess you were dreaming?" Jumah looks away, embarrassed by the intimacy of this, his inadvertent spying on my troubled sleep.

After rustling around in the bathroom, Jumah comes back with a cool, damp washcloth, a glass of water, and a handful of Prontalgine tablets (that miraculous French over-the-counter cocktail of aspirin and codeine).

Do you remember my young friend Jumah? The teenage son of my spice-selling neighbor, the young man I enlisted to drop Elena's ransom note onto Boris's broad lap?

Jumah was our local juvenile delinquent when we met, engaged in the rewarding business of finding the vulnerabilities in the many apartments in the Marais that were now renting as vacation stays. He'd take cash, computers, or jewelry, whatever he could carry out easily. The tourists would file a police report and then head home to wherever they came from with a few less possessions (but a dramatic vacation horror story).

Until he made the mistake of hitting my place. Details aside, let me just say that I set Jumah on a new path, putting his particular skill set to use in what I like to think is the service of good. I pay him well too. In return he's picked my sorry ass up from more than one bender.

If that's not friendship, what is?

I take the proffered pills and water. Lay the damp cloth on my clammy forehead. Close my eyes.

Maybe I fall asleep? I'm not sure. But then there's the aroma of coffee teasing at my nose. Bless that boy.

"*I'm going out to get you some food,*" Jumah says in French. "*You have nothing here. And you're going to need to get your shit together. I have news on that photo you gave me.*"

He slips from my bedroom.

"*Wait,*" I cry after him. "*You actually got something on that guy?*"

"*À bientôt,*" Jumah calls. "*Food first.*"

I hear the clink and jingle as he lifts my keys from their bowl.

Then the sound of the door opening and closing softly behind him.

LOOK

Wandering through the blush of a Paris dawn, Natalie runs her hands through her snarled hair. Worries her thumb and index finger along the shaft of one strand, right down to the root. Tugs the hair out with one quick yank. The pull elicits a tiny pop of pure euphoria.

"Body-focus repetitive behaviors," Dr. Bloom had called them, but Natalie disliked the term. The thrill of charring, the calculated pleasure of cutting, the joyous release of hair tugged clean from the scalp, the easy flow of blood from nails and cuticles bitten to the quick. Char, Scar, Trich, Bit. They were *hers*, private and gratifying; she resented their clinical naming.

As she twists the plucked strand of hair into her palm, the usual post-release shame consumes her. She pushes up her sleeves and stares at the scars on her arms, welting, scabbing, healed over.

She has to stop this.

A familiar chorus rises in her head.

You stupid, hateful, ugly freak. You're grotesque. No wonder Uncle Frank doesn't want to let you out into the streets. You should be locked up like the animal you are.

Maybe true, goddamn it, but first she needs to find her brother.

Natalie thinks she will literally break clean in half if something bad happens to Jake.

Just make Jake be safe. I promise I'll stop everything if he is.

Catching the pitying glance of a passing tight-suited business-woman, she wrenches her sleeves down over her arms.

"None of your fucking business!" Natalie screeches as the woman scurries away.

It feels good to be loud.

Catherine

LIES

I'm bringing the information that Jumah sourced to Frank and Natalie Burrows. Maybe I *can* bring them some measure of peace. A step back toward the light, away from the darkness. Does that sound grandiose? I mean it sincerely nonetheless.

I enter their hotel through the main entrance, blowing past the sole lingering member of the press, a fat paparazzo slung with cameras.

Frank Burrows is waiting for me in the lobby. He steps forward, hand outstretched, and steers me into the hotel bar.

"Thank you for coming, Hannah."

I'd been surprised he'd agreed to see me so readily after warning me away from his family's business the last time we met. Now, looking at his haggard face, I suspect it's not that he's receptive to *my* agenda, it's that he has one of his own.

"What's up?" I ask, as we settle onto a pair of chrome and leather barstools.

He shoots me a glance. "Okay. I'm going to get right to it. Jake and Natalie, both kids, they're gone."

"What do you mean *gone*?"

Furrows deepen on the bridge of his nose. "Jake's been AWOL

since yesterday. Natalie took off sometime this morning, early, while I was at breakfast. Neither of them is answering their phones."

"And you have no idea where they are?"

"Not a clue."

"Have you called the police?"

He vigorously shakes his head.

"Why not? What's going on, Frank?"

He beats a nervous tattoo on the meat of his thigh with two fingers.

"The policewoman, our liaison, she told me Jake lied about when he got back to Paris. He was here when his father was killed and now he won't account for his whereabouts during the time of the murder. She had him at the prefecture, but had to release him. And now he's disappeared."

Does he really believe his nephew, that lean, morose string bean of a boy, is a vicious killer? I examine Frank's eyes. I see fear. Uncertainty.

"And Natalie? Where is she?"

"I told you! I have no idea! Except I'm sure she went searching for her brother. And if the police are right about Jake . . ." He trails off.

A prickle of warning creeps up my spine.

"Okay, look, that picture, the one Brian snapped of the guy following him? I gave it to a friend of mine and he found the guy in the photo. He's an actor. An American living here in Paris. He told my friend he was hired to follow Brian as a prank."

"A prank? Who the hell would do something like that?" Frank's face flushes red.

"The actor, his name is Victor Wyatt. That name mean anything to you?"

"No."

"Well, Wyatt claims he was hired through a service that sometimes employs him. As a male escort. It's the kind of business that typically doesn't ask too many questions and Wyatt didn't either. But it's a place to start."

Frank summons the bartender and orders a whiskey despite the early hour. Offers to buy me a drink. I decline even though I'm tempted by the hair of the dog. Frank knocks his own drink back in one greedy swallow.

Then he miserably volunteers, "I found a bunch of postcards and flyers for male escorts in Jake's things. At the time, I didn't think anything of it. After all, he's over twenty-one. . . ."

There's nothing left but to be blunt. "Do you believe Jake killed his father?"

There is a long, painful silence before he replies.

"I don't know. I don't know anything anymore."

Natalie

SPIKE

Les Halles had been a bust. Natalie had been sure she would find Jake emerging from one of the after-hours gay bars in the neighborhood that he'd told her he'd frequented on his nocturnal outings. But she must have been at the wrong place at the wrong time.

Why am I so fucking stupid? Why would I ever even think I could track Jake down in a city as vast as Paris? What an idiot I am.

She's wandered for hours, welcoming the increasingly brutal heat of the day, her deep abiding thirst, the way her head feels like a balloon, loosely moored to her head, at risk of floating away into the clouds at any instant.

The Champs-Élysées is flooded with tourists. Natalie trudges along, licking her dry lips, ignoring the vendors with their carts full of icy cold bottles of water. She needs to punish herself. For being so stupid.

Natalie finds herself at the Arc de Triomphe. She mounts the stairs that take her to the top. Panting, she ascends the final set of steps and emerges into glaring sun; sweat trickles down her spine and temples, between her breasts.

The city lies beneath her, arrayed like the spokes of a wagon wheel. She can see the Eiffel Tower down one long tree-lined avenue; one distant skyscraper anchors another.

A spiked fence encircles the perimeter of the viewing platform. *Erected to discourage jumpers,* Natalie realizes wryly. She wasn't thinking about jumping when she came up here, but now the fence rouses the thought. She wonders if it's done the same for others.

Natalie presses her face up between two spikes and peers out. *You're out there somewhere, Jake.*

She checks her phone. No reply from her brother despite her numerous texts. She knows she should contact Uncle Frank, but she's sick of him, always thinking he knows best.

I miss Mom. The ache is sharp and sudden. As a rule, Natalie tries not to think about her mother. Part of the past Dr. Bloom encouraged her to tuck away. But how do you just *forget* your mother? Even if she cheated on your dad, disappointed you, misjudged you, *abandoned* you?

Dr. Bloom had told her to be more forgiving, to remember Mallory had just been a person, a human being with strengths and failings like anyone else. And also, sadly, a *victim.* Her mother hadn't abandoned Natalie; she'd been *murdered.* Like Natalie needed to be reminded.

Natalie sinks down onto her haunches and buries her face in her hands to shut out the memories crowding her. Dr. Bloom had been right.

What was the point of remembering?

All it did was hurt.

Catherine

ARTIST

While I don't know where I expected Lilja Koskinen to live, it certainly wasn't this old brick factory converted to artists' lofts in Belleville. But in the grimy vestibule, next to an ancient hand-operated elevator with a creaky metal gate, there is a list of tenants. *Koskinen/Fouquet* is among them. Fourth floor.

As I ascend in the rickety elevator, I square my story. I hope this is simple, that Natalie is here, that I can return her to her uncle and get back to my business with the Russian.

I reach the fourth floor and push open the whining door into a spectacular space, flooded with light. The entire top floor of this old building, with windows running from casement to ceiling on all four sides, the loft is open plan, with hanging dividers on runners that can be configured to redefine the space at will.

One side of the loft is devoted to Fouquet's canvases, enormous abstracts in muted tones of sand and beige and cream. The other side is a long narrow kitchen, kitted out with expensive appliances, anchored by a steel-and-stone table that could easily seat a dozen. One of the hanging dividers partially blocks the sleeping area, where I can see an unmade bed heaped with snowy pillows. Another reveals half of a large enameled claw-footed tub.

Lilja welcomes me and introduces me to her husband, a tall, whippet-thin artist by the name of Pierre Fouquet.

Tantalizing scents of garlic and spices rise from a simmering pot on the stove, competing with an undercurrent of paint and turpentine. The couple sips white wine from chilled stemless glasses. Lilja offers me a glass and I accept.

"How can I help?" she asks, settling into the sleek cream-colored leather sofa and tucking her bare feet up and under her hip. Fouquet stays by the stove, stirring the contents of the steaming saucepan.

"I don't want to alarm you, of course." I register with calculated pleasure the flicker of alarm that instantly crosses Lilja's face. She's already invested. "It's just that Natalie took off from the hotel where she's staying with her family and her uncle is worried sick. I thought she might have come to you."

"No!" Lilja exclaims. "I haven't heard from her."

"Or Jake?"

"Neither one. Is Jake missing too?"

"This has got to be an awful time for them both. I'm sure they're just acting out."

Fouquet tops off his wife's wine and addresses me in heavily accented English. "Neither of them has been here. And if they were to come, I would send them away."

There is a pointed and rapid exchange between Fouquet and Lilja in French. I crease my brow as if I can't understand, although I comprehend every word.

Fouquet's worried about his wife. He insists she have nothing more to do with the Burrows family. I get the sense the artist was bothered by Lilja's admiration and respect for Brian Burrows when he was alive, even as Lilja dismisses his jealousy as unfounded. And ever since Brian's murder he's been afraid for her. Their argument grows heated as Fouquet urges his wife to quit her job at the power plant renovation.

As if suddenly realizing I am there, Lilja silences her husband with a wave and turns back to me.

"Of course we wouldn't turn either of those children away. But if they come, or we hear from them, what should we do?"

"Call their uncle." I give her a piece of the Burrowses' hotel stationery on which Frank's cellphone number is scrawled. "And let me know too. Just for my own peace of mind."

I leave the couple to their meal. As I ride down the elevator, I'm stabbed with poison green envy of the simplicity of their domestic routine. To be loved so passionately, worried about, cared for, the way Fouquet so obviously cares for Lilja.

That's never been possible in my life.

And it never will be.

Jake

MANDARIN

Ache. That's Jake's first thought. *Everything aches.*

His cheek presses into rough concrete, his nose is probably bro-ken. The caked blood rimming his nostrils makes it difficult to breathe. One eye is swollen shut, his lower lip swells and bursts.

He rolls from a fetal position onto his back. Groans at the sharp pain in his chest. He suspects he's broken a couple of ribs. His one open eye is crusty. He swipes away the mix of tears and sleep and dirt.

A black silhouette looms over him, an outstretched arm holding a red umbrella that shelters a black cat. The cat, in turn, intently, expectantly, observes a red fishing pole. It's a painting, Jake realizes queasily. The quaint blue-and-white enameled street sign affixed next to the mural reads RUE DE LA CHAT QUI PÊCHE.

Jake tries to pull himself up to a sitting position. Grunts in pain. Eases back down. He needs to be still. Just for a little longer . . .

Maybe if he pushes from the other side . . .

He realizes he's lying in an alley, or more accurately half-in and half-out of it, his long legs stretched across the sidewalk. People stream past, deftly skirting his limbs, averting their eyes.

The night returns to him in flashes. The girl with the gold ring and the beatdown of her thieving father ignited a bloodlust in Jake.

He'd gone looking for trouble and he'd found it, welcoming every punch and every kick, both landed and received.

He understands Natalie a little better now. There is a perverse pleasure in his physical pain and the temporary escape it provides.

Shit. Natalie must be worried sick about him. How is he going to explain coming back in this state?

Bells peal and Jake counts along, curious to know the time, even as the chimes bruise his throbbing headache. Five o'clock in the evening. He's lost an entire day.

Jake takes a shaky breath. Yelps as pain ricochets once more across his chest. But he grits his teeth and pushes through it, maneuvering himself upright, his back pressed against the painting of the hopeful black cat.

A mugging. He'll tell Natalie it was just a random mugging. He was jumped coming out of a bar. That'll have to do for now.

Christ knows what he'll say when that bitch Martinet shows up to tell Natalie she thinks Jake murdered their dad.

Struggling to his feet, Jake staggers into the pedestrian flow. He keeps his battered head lowered to avoid the curious glances of passersby. He catches the comet's tail of a glittery pack of young socialites as they shoot off rue Saint-Honoré and into the Mandarin Oriental hotel. Keeping one arm raised to shield his broken face, he trails them through the lobby and into the woodsy Bar 8, before cutting away to the bank of elevators going up to the guest floors.

Jake fishes out his wallet. There's the key card, pressed between his driver's license and his NYU student ID. He pulls the key card out.

A pair of elevator doors whooshes open. A couple stumbles out, laughing, hanging on to one another, she tripping out of her stiletto heels, his hand snaking inside her flimsy dress. Jake steps past them. He punches the button for the fifth floor.

Jake's certain he can make his pitch about coming clean with success. The last time they'd been alone together (which admittedly had also been the *first* time they'd been alone together) had been in this very hotel, Room 517. Everything about that night had magic dust sprinkled on it. Why shouldn't there be more of the same?

But as the elevator rises, so does his anxiety.

What if he's not in the room alone?

Oh god.

What if this is all a terrible mistake?

The elevator stops. The doors open. Jake hesitates. Steps out onto padded carpet. The elevator doors whoosh shut behind him.

Walking down the hallway, Jake runs his key card along the flocked wallpaper. Thup, thup, thup goes the plastic card flicking against the paper's raised pattern.

Room 517. Jake inserts the key card into the door handle. The sensor blinks green.

He swings the door open.

"Honey, I'm home," he attempts feebly, to both announce his arrival and make light of it.

"My god. What happened to you?"

Anger and worry crease Hank Scovell's face in equal measure as he looks up from his sprawl on the room's maroon sofa.

Jake blinks. *Whoa. Fuck, I'm dizzy.* He puts a steadying hand to the wall.

"I got mugged. Jumped. Coming out of a club." There, it's done. The first time he's told the lie. Keep it clean. That's the trick to lying well.

"Come with me." Hank directs him into the bathroom. Gestures that Jake should take a seat on the edge of the white porcelain tub. Hank soaks a washcloth, twists it out, and dabs a smidgen of the hotel's fig-scented Diptyque soap onto one corner.

"This is going to hurt," he warns.

He cleans Jake's face of blood and dirt, extracting a couple of glass splinters from his left cheekbone along the way. Jake winces.

"I even have Band-Aids," Hank promises. "Lucky you."

"Yeah. Lucky me."

Hank leans in closer to clear the crusted blood from Jake's right eye. Jake snakes a hand up and cups Hank's jaw. Rises up to kiss him hungrily, despite his busted lip. Hank responds with urgency.

But then Hank pulls away. Places his hands solidly on Jake's shoulders and eases him back to sitting on the tub's edge. "We can't."

"Why not?"

"Come on. Your father was my boss, my mentor, my friend—"

"I'm your friend."

"Yes. You are. But don't be naïve. You're twenty-one, I'm thirty-nine. We both know how it'll play. Older man corrupts young innocent, betraying the trust of his boss in the process . . ."

"We both know I turned you, Hank. Not the other way around."

"I'm talking about perception! I have way more on the line here than you do. And for Christ's sake it was bad enough before your father was—"

"You have *more* on the line?" Anger rips through Jake. "The cops found out that I came back to Paris a day earlier than I said. They want to know why. They think I *killed* my father! But I couldn't have, could I? Because I was here *fucking* you!"

"Did you admit we were together? What have you told them? Dammit, Jake—"

"*That's* what worries you? What is it, 1950? Do you think anyone actually *cares* if you're gay?"

"That's not the point! Our . . . thing . . . it could be construed as motive."

"What the hell are you talking about? We're each other's alibis."

"Or co-conspirators to murder if the cops want to spin it that way."

"But we didn't do anything!"

"That's why we don't have to worry."

"So we're just supposed to say nothing? They think I did it, Hank! They came right out and said so!"

Hank extends an index finger to Jake's jaw. Tilts his head so he can look into his eyes. "We will if we have to, if it comes to that, of course. We're just not there yet, is all I'm saying."

Jake pushes his hand away. "I'm out of here—"

"Okay. But don't be so harsh on me, Jake. You know who you are. You're lucky that way. I'm . . . I'm just not so sure yet."

Catherine

UNRELIABLE

Ursine Fournier's tiny apartment in the 5th had revealed three Siamese cats, a cleverly arranged collection of Japanese fans, and the hot waiter from the Indian restaurant, bare-chested and pleased with himself.

But no sign of Natalie.

If the girl sought out help and comfort, it wasn't from either of the only two women she knew in Paris. That I knew of. I try to put myself inside Natalie's head. I understand all too well the hardship of *not knowing*. How it twists at your guts and leaks poisons into your mind. How filling in the blanks allows one to create an endless loop of catastrophic outcomes, each one more horrible than the last.

Poor girl. Poor Natalie.

I stop that thought dead as soon as it floats. Neither of us can afford sentimentality.

The brutal heat is fading as the day turns to evening and the sky glows cobalt. A welcome breeze caresses my face.

As with any missing persons case, I'm starting with known associates. I'll fan out wider based on any gleaned information. I'm applying a cold-eyed assessment to each person I encounter: psychologies and quirks, soft spots and hard shells, the nature of their relationship to truth, the self-interest that powers their actions.

The social engineering aspect of any endeavor is always paramount. There's always a human being who can be worked.

I've dispatched Jumah as my advance man to the Mandarin Oriental. He's confirmed that Hank Scovell returned to the hotel. Jumah has kept to his post across from the main entrance, and as far as he can tell, Scovell hasn't left.

As I turn the corner onto rue Saint-Honoré, Jumah sees me and straightens, squares his shoulders. I join him. Thank him. Tell him I'll take it from here. He gives me a sharp little salute and goes on his way.

A pair of smartly clad doormen flanks the hotel entrance. Its simple façade, golden rectangles of light forming orderly rows five wide windows across and seven stories high, doesn't do justice to the sleek, austere beauty I know lies within. The hotel appears deceptively small, when in fact it runs a full block, cradling a courtyard with a pool and lush greenery. The guest rooms are gorgeous, both aggressive in their modernity and boldly spare in color, touched with Asian accents. I stayed here once, in a happier, long ago time.

I'm about to cross the street when I see Jake Burrows exiting from the hotel.

Quelle surprise.

He hesitates, glancing first right and then left, before turning sharply and striding down the avenue. I follow him.

Jake's agitated. Muttering to himself, tugging his hands through his hair, his back curled into a protective hunch.

I calculate my approach. I don't know what Natalie or Frank has said about me to Jake, if anything. Still, Hannah Potter seems my best alternative. Keep it simple.

Hurrying my steps, I catch up to him. His long legs take big easy bites out of the pavement; I have to double step to keep pace.

"Jake? Jake Burrows?"

He wheels to face me, eyes wild, barely contained violence bristling through his lanky limbs. I get a good look at his face, bruised and battered, see the stiff and halting way he's moving to protect his ribs.

"Are you okay, Jake? Do you need a doctor?"

"Who the fuck are you?'

"My name's Hannah Potter. I know your uncle. And your sister."

"How did you find me?"

"I was looking for Natalie, actually. I thought she might have gone to see Hank Scovell."

"Why would Natalie go to see *Hank*?" Jake is incredulous. His face contorts with confusion. He towers over me.

"Jake. I'm trying to help you. Calm down."

He laughs then. A wild, unrestrained chortle. From deep in his belly. He bursts away from me and down the sidewalk. Dashes across the street.

An irate driver in a red Peugeot has to slam on his brakes to avoid hitting him and lays on the horn.

I cross the street as the horn blasts, Jake staggering ahead of me. I make a grab for him. Get only a handful of his bloodied T-shirt. He whirls. Hauls back to punch me.

I duck. As the momentum of his futile swing arcs the nape of his neck into my easy reach, I jab a syringe upward.

Jake shoots me a bewildered glance before folding in half and swaying toward the ground.

I catch him under his arms and haul him to his feet. He's surprisingly light. Parchment over dry bones.

One or two passersby give curious glances, but in French I angrily berate the unconscious young man for drinking too much yet *again*.

Scanning the street for a taxi, I'm surprised and pleased to see a dinky white van pull up.

"*Get in*," Jumah insists urgently in French. "*We have a problem.*"

Like I need another problem.

Frank

GRAVE

He needed to get away from that fucking hotel. He's furious with both Jake and Natalie. Scared shitless about them. And terrified of the face and the name that Hannah Potter has put to the man who had been stalking Brian. *Victor Wyatt*. Funny how a photograph and four syllables can lead to an onslaught of emotion.

Frank longs for action, but has no idea of what to actually *do*. He walked for blocks without a destination. Then one occurred to him. A place he knew would provide both peace and perspective.

Here at last.

Striding through the wrought-iron gates of Père Lachaise gives Frank a profound sense of relief. A sigh escapes him.

He's always liked cemeteries.. The tangible monuments to love and respect. The sense that honor can endure after death.

And Père Lachaise is extraordinary, housing as it does the remains of French presidents and poets, scientists and novelists, opera singers and painters, statesmen and foreign generals. Hundreds of years of history are concealed under its softly rolling hills.

Forbidding mausoleums with names carved into stone flank his walkway: *Famille* Arman, Gueretor, or Ricard. Ponsat, Bourdieu, or Demonjay.

Many are simple gray slabs, others fantastically carved and

adorned with swooning women, spritely cherubs, or musical instruments so realistic they look as if they could be played. Some of the tombs are lovingly tended, with blooming flower boxes or potted trees. Others are neglected, leaf-strewn, moss-ridden, crumbling stone.

The last time he had come to this cemetery, it had been 2011. Frank happened to visit the day *after* July 3, the fortieth anniversary of Jim Morrison's death. Hundreds of emo-looking kids had poured in to visit Morrison's grave in macabre celebration on the third, leaving behind offerings of wine, record albums, flowers, posters adorned with lipstick kisses. A handful still lingered when Frank was there on the fourth, burning candles and singing along as a soulful-eyed teenager strummed Doors songs on his guitar.

Today, Morrison's grave is quieter, still a highlight of the cemetery tour, but with no traces of the frenzy from Frank's prior visit. The Oscar Wilde tomb has changed too. Then, it had been covered in scrawled graffiti: hearts and lips and penises. Lovers' initials and exhortations such as "give in," or "reach for the stars." Now Wilde's final resting place is scrubbed clean and barricaded behind protective plate glass.

The cobblestone path is painful under the thin leather soles of Frank's shoes. His back is aching and tight. He suspects a blister has risen on his left heel.

He settles down on a curb and sags back against a tree just across from Edith Piaf's grave. Heavy black marble with etched gold lettering and a carved depiction of Christ on the cross. Earthenware pots filled with blood-red begonias surround the monument.

The wind picks up. Frank tilts his head and watches cotton-candy clouds scud across the sky. Shielded behind his sunglasses, he closes his eyes, enjoying the feel of the cool air on his face.

Everything changes, Frank reflects. He wishes he could roll back time, just put it in reverse like film through a projector.

For a moment he pretends his brother is still alive, his nephew and niece in the safe arms of his paternal care. Then he allows himself a deeper flight of fancy: Mallory—vibrant, beautiful Mallory—resurrected. Their whole golden family intact, an inspiration of enduring love for all, frozen in perfection forever, in that magical time *before*.

Catherine

HIDEOUT

Jumah pilots the van expertly through the narrow streets and alleys of the Marais.

He pulls into an open, empty garage, wooden pallets piled along the sides. His father, Akili, waits for us, stepping in after the van and pulling the roll-up door firmly down behind us.

Silently, the three of us move into action, hoisting Jake Burrows from the van and up a narrow flight of stairs. Finally, we haul his long, lean body into the attic of this stone-and-timber building.

Weathered rafters span cathedral-style across the plastered ceiling. Green velvet curtains are drawn tight against a pair of vaulted windows. An enormous antique trunk overflows with discarded costumes, a jumble of sequins and feathers. The rough-hewn floor planks vibrate with the provocative music thundering up from the cabaret below.

We dump Jake on the narrow cot in the corner. I examine his face. Someone cleaned and bandaged the worst of it. Still, the kid looks like hell. I pull up his shirt to examine him further and then wince at the bruises. The best thing for him in this state is unconsciousness. This must hurt as bad as it looks.

He should be out for hours, but I can't take any chances. I loosely fit a hood over his head; I want him to breathe, after all. I bind his wrists with plastic ties. I murmur thanks to Jumah and Akili and quietly they slip away.

I pull open the rope attached to the attic crawl space and lower the ladder to the floor. Take a last look at Jake's inert form before scrambling up the ladder, lifting the hatch and clambering onto the roof. I pay an exorbitant amount of rent each month for this threadbare little attic precisely for this view: a place of pure obscurity from which I can observe my apartment cleanly.

Down below, lurking on the sidewalk a few meters from my front door, I see two shadows, one boxy and jittery, the other lanky and languid. Both smoke cigarettes, the glowing tips arcing from hand to mouth. They would seem benign, two friends shooting the shit, if it were not for the forbidding bulges in their waistbands. Akili had spotted them. Called Jumah to warn me.

I spy Jumah, moving as elegantly as a cat along the rooftop of the apartment building adjacent to my own.

Jumah leaps over to my roof. Shimmies down the spiral fire escape and slips into my apartment through a window. Slides out the same window moments later and skims back up to the roof with my emergency backpack strapped to his shoulders.

If mine was that kind of company, I'd give the kid a promotion.

In a matter of minutes, Jumah ascends the stairs and emerges to join me on my rooftop perch. He hands over my emergency pack. I rummage through it, confirming all is in order. Passports granting me three different identities, each one based on a dead double from a different country: U.S., Canada, France. Credit cards that match. Ten thousand euros in cash. Ten thousand American dollars too. Half a dozen prepaid cellphones. A laptop. A modem extender/scrambler. A night-vision camera. A stun gun. A packed medical case which holds, among other things, three more syringes loaded with the powerful sedative fentanyl.

I train the night-vision camera on my two visitors. The bulky guy looms green through the scope. Something about him is vaguely familiar, but I can't place him. I draw a blank on the lanky kid, but take several pictures of them both before clambering back down the hatch and into the attic.

I thank Jumah for an excellent day's work. Send him home. Pop open the laptop and get to work.

Natalie

CERTAIN

Natalie clatters down the Arc de Triomphe's stairs. They're closing up; she's one of the last of the tourists the security guards chased down. For the hundredth time she checks her phone. Calls and texts from Hannah and Uncle Frank. Nothing from Jake.

Natalie hasn't been certain of much in her life, but she's certain that her brother isn't a killer. She longs to talk to him, to just flat-out ask why he came back to Paris early, who he was with, why he lied. She's sure that if she could only talk to him, all would be clear.

She's afraid to speak to anyone *but* him; what other horrible aspersions might they cast?

The sun slants now, although the heat of the day looks like it will linger into the evening, moist and sticky.

Natalie catches sight of her reflection in a store window. Automatically, she picks apart her appearance with derision and scorn. *You fat ugly freak. You stupid, hateful, grotesque monster.* She whirls away from the window, sickened and ashamed.

She has to find Jake, has to prove he couldn't have killed their father. She needs to confess her own sins to him as well.

She's a monster, a freak. But Jake is good. She knows this in every cell of her being. His goodness will be her redemption.

TALISMAN

I speak to Frank Burrows around midnight. He hasn't heard from either his niece or his nephew. He confesses he is going to knock himself out with an Ambien and face everything fresh in the morning. Can't say I blame him.

Of course I don't mention I'm in possession of Jake, trussed and drugged unconscious. I have too much work to do; the entire subject has to stay on mute.

The rest of the night is busy. I check in on Elena's safety, the progress in securing her new papers. Periodically call Natalie's cellphone, to no avail. Hack deeper and deeper into the layers of Boris's criminal enterprises until I am able to expose connections to a handful of prominent politicians and several captains of legitimate industry.

Using just the photos from the night-vision camera, I hadn't gotten a fix on the men lurking outside of my apartment. Now that it's morning, I'm itching to get back on the roof for another look. I check on Jake. Still out cold, which suits my purposes just fine.

I sneak back up to the cabaret roof, camera in hand. The men are there, still smoking, leaning against a dark blue Renault Talisman that is parked about ten meters from my door. I don't know if it's their car, but I take a shot of the license plate all the same.

I climb down the ladder and back into the attic. Run a trace on the license plate number. The Renault is registered to one Patrice Duszu. I run a search on the name. Transfer the new photos of my stalkers into my computer. Hack into Europol's facial recognition search engine and let the program do its job.

I try Natalie's cell again, for what seems like the millionth time. Right to voicemail. Where can that girl be?

Stop it. My attention must be on these two strangers lurking outside my apartment. Who sent them? What do they want?

Jumah returns to the attic laden with pastries and *café au lait*. I thank him and give him his instructions. He'll work at his father's spice shop today, an unobtrusive second pair of eyes keeping watch on my front door.

I check my computer as I finish off a flaky *pain au chocolat*. Bingo. The Europol face recognition software has identified the bulky man outside my apartment as Arpad Lazar, a Hungarian national (aka Patrice Duszu, aka Anton Liszt, aka Jacques Tamas). Arpad is a thoroughly delightful fellow if your idea of charming is human trafficking, extortion, assault, armed robbery, and murder.

Hungary. That night in Budapest will haunt me forever, but now it seems it's come back to *hunt* me as well.

I rescued Z from a human trafficking ring after her brother, Balint, sought my help. Freed a dozen other starving, abused girls along with her. After I got the women to safety, their keeper tracked me that rainy night in Budapest. He tried to cut my throat. So I killed him. I had no choice.

Remember those commemorative shoes on the banks of the Danube marking murders committed by the Arrow Cross? X marks the spot.

He was a monster of a man, but still his death weights me. He's the only person I've ever intentionally killed. Odi Lazar. Arpad's big brother. I don't know how they found me, but it's time to turn the tables. With a few quick keystrokes, I launch my plan. Sit back satisfied.

For the hell of it, I try Natalie's cellphone one more time.

MERMAID

All the avenues of Paris seemed so beautiful from the top of the Arc de Triomphe: broad, tree-lined, the very definition of elegant French order. But the longer Natalie walks, the more the character of the streets shifts. That sense of neat, contained beauty dissipates as fancy shops and restaurants give way first to discreet and tony homes, then dingy townhouses, then graffiti-strewn apartment blocks.

Things get sketchier, the streets grimier, the shadows more menacing. Natalie hastily passes a homeless encampment, avoiding the stares of the blank-eyed children, the supplicating hands of their mothers.

She decides to circle back toward the more commercial areas. She doesn't know where she's headed, but she doesn't care. She has no idea what time it is and she doesn't care about that either. She doesn't know where she's going to sleep. She doesn't know if she'll ever sleep again.

Where is Jake? I need Jake.

Light-headed, Natalie feels disconnected, like an alien clinically inspecting this strange place called earth. Passersby seem so carefree; laughter and affectionate banter drift past her. *Who are these people? What fucking right do they have to be so happy?*

The enticing aroma of grilling sausage assaults her nostrils. She follows the scent, drawn as though by the Pied Piper himself, suddenly flooded with memories of Sunday afternoon barbecues back home in Westport. Mom's tart, fresh lemonade; Dad manning the Weber.

She turns a street corner and finds herself in the middle of a lively little square. Late-night cafés sparkling with light spill their patrons out onto the sidewalk. The café tables are crowded with people sipping cocktails, smoking, chatting, gesticulating.

The source of the delicious-smelling food is a restaurant in the center of the square, if you can call it a restaurant, as it's really no more than a door through which cardboard trays heaped with steaming-hot food are passed.

Natalie's mouth fills with saliva. She purchases a sausage loaded with onions and wedged into a fresh baguette slathered with mustard. Wolfs it down. Chases it with a frigid beer. Orders another sausage and finishes that one too.

She fights against the wave of nausea that comes from the gobbled food and her shameful, *shameful,* loss of control.

She buys two cold bottles of water and wanders into a nearby pocket park. It's a triangular scrap, barely able to hold its handful of benches and a gurgling fountain, formed like a little boy gleefully riding a dolphin. She sits down on the first bench she sees. Chugs the two waters back-to-back.

Patting down her bag from the outside, she confirms the presence of her cellphone, wallet, that steak knife she lifted under the plain view of her brother's anguished eyes. She's mulled that moment often in her mind, feeling both grateful for her brother and understood by him. Oddly enough, the fact that he let her steal the knife has allowed her to avoid its use. It's stayed wrapped in a napkin, dangerous ridges muffled and tucked away from her tender skin.

Now she's grateful she has the knife for protection, here in this anonymous little park, here in the dark.

I'll stop everything if you bring Jake to me. Everything. I prom-ise. I've lost everyone. I can't lose him too.

She doesn't know with whom she's bargaining. If God exists, She abandoned Natalie long ago, of this Natalie is certain.

Hands over her roiling stomach, she leans her head back and tries to find some level of comfort on the unforgiving stone-and-metal bench. She burns with that oh-so-familiar rising tide of anx-iety, those feelings that can only be dealt with by a pinch or a cut or a burn or a bite. But she's made a promise. She has to try and keep it.

Please, Jake.

Natalie's eyes drift closed. She nestles into the bench sideways, a protective fetal curl, restlessly plucking fingers finally falling still.

She sleeps. And dreams.

She dreams her mother is a mermaid, living peacefully in the depths of the silent sea. Natalie's buoyed with happiness to see Mallory smiling in the ocean blue, hair floating in extravagant ten-drils around her lovely face. Natalie swims toward her. They face each other, daughter and mother, underwater, treading water, mi-raculously both able to breathe. Natalie reaches out to touch Mal-lory's face.

She's so deep in her dream that at first she thinks it's her moth-er's hand, tucking a lucky shell into Natalie's pocket. But some-thing about the hand's insistent, stealthy searching corrupts this sweet belief.

Natalie bats away the last vestiges of ocean and peace and Mama.

Her eyes pop open. Night. The park. A filthy man of indetermi-nate age stands over her, bearded, hair matted, skin dark with dirt and sweat. His stink is so rancid Natalie gags.

She realizes it is *his* grubby hand on her hip.

"Get off me, creep!" She smacks at his hand with her own.

She doesn't know if he's trying to rob her, molest her, or *what,* but whatever it is, Natalie's not having it.

He yanks his hand away but stays where he is, swaying, staring at her with red eyes.

"Get the fuck away!" Natalie tries to yell, but it comes out strangled.

She remembers being taught in her self-defense class to shout as loud as possible. No one mentioned how fear closed your throat.

Her eyes dart right and then left. Which is the best way to get past him?

The guy mumbles some crazy gibberish. Rises up on his tiptoes. Raises his arms as if performing an incantation. She's about to break left when he lunges at her.

"I said, get away!" she shrieks.

You don't want to fuck with Natalie Burrows.

Natalie crosses her arms protectively over her chest, squares her shoulders, and charges, ramming her head into her assailant's gut with every ounce of power she possesses.

He stumbles backward. Lands on his ass, letting loose a furious string of curses.

Natalie grabs her bag and runs. She pounds out of the park and into the streets, turning her head only once to see if she's being followed.

Finally she pulls up short several blocks away, winded, drenched in sweat. She struggles to catch her breath. Her shaking fingers scramble for the bone-handled knife in the depths of her bag. She plants her feet and braces herself, unrolling the blade from its napkin, welcoming its heft in her hand.

She scans the street. She seems to be alone, her attacker lost. All she can hear is the distant pulsing heartbeat of a big city in deep night. The streets around her are empty. Shuttered.

Her foot hits a soda can. It rolls away down the street, unnaturally loud, jarring. She spins, whirls to a stop, disoriented. Crap. Where the fuck is she? What time is it?

Her cellphone vibrates. Wary prickles raise the hairs on the back of Natalie's neck.

She pulls the phone from her bag: 5:23 A.M.

"What?" she blurts into the phone, knowing even as the word comes out of her mouth that she sounds belligerent and childish.

"It's me. Hannah," says the voice on the other end.

"Duh. I know that. Caller ID. What do you want?" Natalie doesn't know why she's being so nasty to Hannah. She just knows she's sick of everything. Of loss. Of grief. Of being scared. Of needing her brother so very badly. Of needing anyone.

Why does everybody leave me?

And for fuck's sake, she slept on a park bench, was practically raped by a homeless creep, she's thirsty and scared and helpless and angry. Why should she be *nice*? Fuck nice. Natalie's sick of the brave face, the secret wounds, her own hollow heart.

If Hannah's irritated by Natalie's belligerence, she shows no sign. Calmly, she tells Natalie that she's found Jake; that he's fine, sleeping now or Hannah would put him on the phone.

Instantly Natalie feels awful about having been such a bitch. "Where are you? Back at our hotel?" Her voice wobbles with relief.

Jake's at her place, Hannah informs Natalie. But Natalie should head back to the hotel, her uncle is terribly worried about her. Hannah will bring Jake when he wakes.

The thought of returning to the prison of their hotel to sit in strained silence with her uncle is unbearable. Uncle Frank is yet another thing Natalie is fucking sick of. "I can't," she blurts. "I don't want to go back yet. Not without Jake."

"Where are you, Natalie?" Hannah wants to know. "Do you want me to come get you?"

Natalie hesitates. "I've got to go," she says firmly.

"Wait," Hannah implores. "Natalie, I have information about the man who was stalking your father."

Natalie is silent.

"Natalie? Are you there?"

"Yes," Natalie whispers.

"Let me come get you. I'll tell you what I know," Hannah promises.

"Tell me what you know and I'll let you come get me," Natalie counters.

There's a pause.

"His name is Victor Wyatt. He was hired through an escort service called Le Boy Bleu. Now, where are you?"

Natalie disconnects the phone.

Catherine

GRAB

The air is sour with the stink of recent revelry—spilled alcohol, vomit, urine, and sweat.

Tucked into a shadowy vestibule, I watch. Dawn reveals shuttered bars and restaurants and damp, trash-littered cobblestones: a single cobalt-blue stiletto, a confetti spill of cigarette butts.

It looks like it will be another steamy day; a trickle of sweat already runs down the back of my black tank top.

The stench and the heat further darken my mood. When juggling a hooded, bound, and drugged Jake Burrows with the launch of my counterattack on the Hungarians, it had felt a reasonably calculated risk to give up Wyatt's information.

I won't underestimate Natalie again.

When I finally see her crest the horizon, a tiny, unsteady figure coming over the rise of the street, I'm shocked by her appearance. She's the thinnest I've seen her. Her cheekbones are sharp, her eyes sunken.

What does this child think she's going to do? Storm into the escort service at the crack of dawn and demand to speak to Wyatt? Now that she's shown up, I'm almost amused by her misguided spunk.

She checks the buzzer panel at one doorway and then the next. I hurry out of my hiding place and onto the street, my rubber-soled sneakers padding soundlessly. She's reached the right address now. Her finger is poised over the button marked for Le Boy Bleu.

"Hello, Natalie."

She whirls. "How did you find me?" she spits angrily.

"I get it," I say gently. "How badly you just want to *do* something, but you have to let the police handle this. Come on. Let me take you back to your hotel. Anyway, don't you want to be there when Jake gets back?"

"He never, *ever* could've killed Daddy," Natalie shrills.

"No, of course not," I reassure.

Her eyes flicker to mine, relieved to find agreement. "Why isn't Jake back at our hotel already too?"

"When I found Jake he wasn't in the best shape. He'd been on the losing end of a fight, maybe more than one."

Natalie's eyes widen in alarm.

"I helped clean him up and then let him sleep it off. He's fine, though, Natalie. He really is. And so are you. So let's get you back to the hotel and keep you both that way."

I put an arm around her narrow shoulders and she lets me lead her away.

Jake

RUST

He opens his eyes and sees only blackness. Blinks. Still dark. He gasps for air. Cloth flaps against his open lips. He's going to suffocate. He realizes he is hooded.

All he wants to do is run. But he can barely move. His limbs feel heavy. He realizes his wrists are bound.

What the fuck's happened to him? Hank. Oh god. That woman on the street. Did she *drug* him? Has she kidnapped him? Where is he?

He licks his lips, tastes blood. His tongue feels like it's coated in rust. He tries to speak: All that emerges is a garbled moan.

When the black wave washes over him, sucking him back into unconsciousness, Jake feels only relief.

Catherine

WAKE

I've delivered Natalie to a somber and exhausted-looking Frank. Both seemed completely spent.

They've promised to nap. I've promised to bring Jake when he is up and able to travel.

My breath quickens in my chest as I turn the corner onto rue des Archives. The street bustles with activity as usual; its crowded, transient mix is one of the reasons I chose to live here. My apartment's rented in the name of Mario Paone, a specialty tile manufacturer based in Milan. Mario's practically unknown to his neighbors in the building. He travels a lot. Lends his apartment out to a succession of young women.

They've all been me, of course. But except for Jumah and Akili, no one's gotten close enough to my apartment to know that.

I can be anonymous here. Have been. Until now.

Carrying a festive spray of flowers to shield my face, I stroll right past Arpad and his young associate, both still positioned a few meters from my front door, smoking.

My heart pounds at my audacity in crossing so close; these men are vicious. My life would be worthless in their hands.

Other than perfunctory swings of their heads to assess my rear view, the men seem utterly uninterested in me. This, and the scrutiny they apply to each passing male confirms my hope that they have a location on me but no other pertinent details about who I am. So often my enemies assume I'm a man. So often I play that to my advantage.

I duck into Chacun à Son Gôut. The cabaret's blessedly cool but unnervingly dark after the sun-drenched street.

This is a place that exists for the night. In daylight it's robbed of its vitality, as hushed as a morgue, shabby and spent. The owner, Michelle, perches on a barstool, her glasses sliding down her aquiline nose as she reconciles receipts.

"*For you, my friend,*" I say in French, handing over the bouquet.

"*Merci,*" Michelle replies, surprised and pleased. "*What's the occasion?*"

"*Landlady appreciation day,*" I call as I hurry through the cigarette-smoke-infused velvet and satin of the cabaret seating area.

"*Oh, honey, you know I'm no lady,*" Michelle banters back, in a voice suddenly more baritone than soprano.

I reward her with a chuckle as I wend my way through the cramped backstage.

In the attic, Jake lies just where I left him. I check his breathing: shallow, even, steady. I stride over to the pair of dormered windows. Inch one of the velvet curtains open.

Arpad and his scrawny pal are still on the street below. Smoking. Talking. I watch. The minutes tick by.

Four unmarked cars converge on rue des Archives slowly, with no fanfare or alarm. The street is packed with pedestrians, the cars must patiently nudge themselves into position in order to block off the Hungarians' possible escape routes.

Two suit-clad men emerge from each vehicle. They descend on Arpad and his confederate before the pair have even registered the threat.

The Hungarians are cuffed. Whisked into separate cars. Driven away. It's all done with an efficiency and restraint that I admire.

The crowd on the street scarcely reacts. A handful of officers remain behind as a tow truck arrives and hoists up the Renault Talisman.

There may not have been anything illegal in the car when Arpad
arrived in it, but there's a satchel full of plastic explosives in it now,
thanks to Jumah's sleight of hand.

A well-timed anonymous tip can accomplish so much.

Natalie

FLYER

Uncle Frank had been *awful* tonight after Hannah brought her back. Told her to *sit her ass down* for a talk. He ranted on about himself, the fucking narcissist, as if he was the only one in the world! *His* anxieties. *His* divorce. *His* children. *His* burdens and obligations and sacrifices on her behalf.

Natalie pulled into her little snail shell and let him hammer away at her while deep inside she burned. *What about me?*

Where was the sympathy? The concern for her health? Where were the desperately needed reassurances: No, Jake *couldn't* have killed your father, of course not!

Why was Uncle Frank so angry? Why did he seem so *unhinged*?

After the tirade flowed and ebbed and finally petered out, they'd shared a pot of chamomile tea in perfect silence and then Natalie retreated to her room.

Huddled there now, pretending to sleep (Uncle Frank presumably doing the same—sleeping or pretending), Natalie restlessly turns things over in her mind.

They've always shared secrets, she and Uncle Frank. Ever since Natalie was a little girl. Ever since he caught her at age five, with her fingers plunged in the chocolate icing swirled on Jake's birthday cake.

Uncle Frank had put his index finger to his lips, signaling Natalie to be quiet. Called to her mother to stay put, that he would bring the cake into the dining room. He told Natalie to lick her fingers clean. Then pulled out a butter knife, smoothed the cake so all looked perfect, and with a wink went about the business of candles and matches.

After that they had other "little secrets." Uncle Frank slipped her ten bucks. Or let her have a soda when they went out to lunch. In turn, Natalie solemnly offered "big girl advice" about Ana and Addy, what birthday presents the twins might like, for example, gleaned by casual interrogations of her cousins and then whispered in her uncle's ear.

When Natalie was thirteen, she caught Uncle Frank kissing her friend Melissa's mother at the family New Year's Eve party. "Blame the mistletoe," Frank had shouted jovially as Sunny had giggled and escaped into the kitchen. Then he'd leaned down to whisper in Natalie's ear, "Just *our* little secret. Right?"

Natalie was thrilled. She felt "in" on some exotic grown-up intrigue, and excited to see how it progressed. She nobly decided it would be wrong, cruel even, to tell Melissa what she had seen until things developed further. So she kept her mouth shut while she waited for the next chapter to unfold. But she vowed she would be the best damn friend *possible* to Melissa as her parents' marriage tragically collapsed and Sunny ran away with Uncle Frank. And hell, then they'd be best friends *and* first cousins, sort of, so *there* was an upside!

Unfortunately, Uncle Frank stayed with that bitch Della. And Sunny stayed with boring old Benton.

But Natalie discovered having a secret gave you a kind of power. She could make Sunny blush with merely an intense stare and a meaningfully cocked eyebrow. Natalie exploited this delicious trick until the novelty waned. It was the least she deserved for her chivalrous silence.

She'd developed a taste, so Natalie expanded her craft, collecting salacious tidbits about her schoolmates or teachers. Sometimes she simply gloried in the *knowing* power of these secrets and held them close. Other times she played them like a hand of cards.

Until now, Natalie had believed that the *particular* pool of secrets she shared with her uncle formed the building blocks of an essential trust; they were *bound* after all. He was a nag sometimes, sure, but wasn't their well-being linked? Wouldn't he always look out for her? Hadn't he proved that?

Would he still?

Or will he abandon me like everybody else?

Natalie's thoughts twitch to the knife in her bag.

Char. Scar. Trich. Bit. Always reliable. Unlike so much else in Natalie's life.

Jake will be here soon. I'll feel better then. I can resist, I promise. I'll be grateful for every day.

Something tickles at the edge of her memory, tantalizing, irritating.

Le Boy Bleu. The address in Bastille had been easy enough to find when Hannah mentioned the name of the place, God bless the Internet. But Natalie had seen a flyer for Le Boy Bleu before, hadn't she? Or an ad? Something, anyway.

She closes her eyes and tries to remember. A white and red background, jaunty blue script, a picture of a half-naked man, chest and abs rock solid and glistening with oil, crotch captured in skin-tight pants. The man's image was cropped at the chin, leaving him faceless, the same kind of objectification to which women were usually subjected. Natalie remembers thinking that when she saw the flyer.

But where had she seen it?

Memory swims into focus.

A stack of flyers in Jake's duffel bag.

Is that right?

Her eyes open.

Natalie steals out of her bedroom and into the living area.

There's Jake's duffel in the corner, clothes erupting from its jumbled midst and spilling onto the carpeted floor.

She searches efficiently, folding Jake's belongings as she goes, welcoming the sense that in doing so she is in some way caring for her brother.

There are the brochures and flyers. Natalie sorts through the stack. Sure enough, Le Boy Bleu, just like she remembered it.

Jake had asked her if she'd put them there. She hadn't known what he was talking about. But if she hadn't put them there, and Jake hadn't, there is only one other possible choice.

Uncle Frank.

Catherine

STEW

With a scissors I cut away the bindings around Jake's wrists. I lift the hood from his face and pull it off his head. Tuck the bindings and hood deep into one of my bags. Insert a quick hypodermic into a pale blue vein in the crook of his elbow. Grab a bottle of water to have at the ready and sit down on a stool, facing Jake on the cot.

Jake's eyes peel open. He pulls himself up to a sitting position, groggily.

Fear fills his eyes. "Who are you?" he croaks. "What do you want?"

"Here." I offer Jake the bottle. He eyes it suspiciously. Then snatches it away from me, closely examining the seal to make sure it's unbroken. Satisfied, he twists the bottle top off and gulps the water down gratefully. His wary eyes never leave mine.

"Did you *drug* me?" he sputters, once the water bottle is drained.

"Of course not. You passed out. I *helped* you."

He rubs his wrists, urging circulation back into the reddened, pressed flesh. His eyes skitter down to his hands. "What about my wrists?"

"What about them?"

"I was tied up."

"Don't be absurd." I say it authoritatively. "You must have slept on them funny."

The kid was a mess when I found him, physically beaten, emotionally destroyed. If I'm canny, it won't be too difficult to persuade him around to my version of events, PTSD being what it is.

I briskly introduce myself as Hannah Potter. Show American ID that gives truth to the lie. Use the same fiction I've told everyone about how I knew Brian. I clock that Jake gives a quick jerk of the head at the mention of the "grief group."

I explain I came across Jake accidentally while trying to find his sister, who their uncle believed was in turn out looking for *him*.

At least that much is true.

"I was just going into the Mandarin to see Hank Scovell when you came out and collapsed." My tone is uninviting of dispute.

"Why would Natalie go to see *Hank?*" Jake asks with a crack in his voice. Some emotion here is running hot.

"I don't know." I shrug. "I was checking every logical place, everyone she knew in Paris. Your uncle has been worried sick about both of you," I add reproachfully.

"Why are you doing any of this?"

Isn't that always the question?

"I like to be of help where I can," I reply.

That much is true as well.

Jake goes silent then. I can't tell what he's thinking, but I just need enough plausible deniability to deliver him safely back to his uncle. I can't work if I'm babysitting.

I let us stew in silence for a while. It's often the best way to invite conversation, even confession. Most people feel compelled to fill in the space.

"I'm not surprised Dad was going to a group. I knew something was stirring shit up for him," Jake offers up finally, no exception to the rule.

"How do you mean?"

His eyes flicker around the attic, taking in the sparse furniture, the piles of discarded, glittering cabaret costumes, the folding table with my laptop and emergency pack. "Where are we?"

"A friend's place," I tell him. "It was convenient."

Wary confusion plays across his face. It's not the first time I've been grateful for my nonthreatening appearance. As I'm currently dressed, black tank top, jeans, high-tops, I could be a suburban kindergarten teacher on her summer vacation.

And surely better to believe one was rescued by a friendly face than drugged and bound by an unknown enemy? Maybe, *just maybe*, he hallucinated the hood, the plastic digging into his wrists, the barely remembered prick of a hypodermic needle?

"You would have seen it too if you knew how Dad *usually* was," he finally blurts.

"Seen what?"

"How agitated he was. Ever since my mother died, well, it was like he had this hard shell on all the time, and then, one day, right before we left for Paris, it cracked. Got worse once we were here."

Jake levels his eyes with mine as if daring me to believe him. "He was scared of something."

I nod, careful to keep my face impassive. "You're not the only one who thought that, Jake. A couple of his co-workers said the same. I believe you."

Jake pulls a deep breath into his lungs. He rises and stretches, unsteady on his feet. He shambles about the attic. Fingers a length of sequin-laden satin. Takes a peek out the window.

Natalie's anguished cry rings in my ears: *"He never, ever could've killed Daddy."* I want to believe she's right. I want to know more about where Jake was the night Brian's throat was cut.

I offer up the lost-my-family Hannah Potter details, speaking with somber urgency about the horrific deaths of my little boy and husband. I'm not even a decade older than Jake, but this is a boy who's lost his mother and his father and I pull ruthlessly on the string of grief.

Gradually, he opens up to me like a budding flower in the warm spring sunshine.

He broaches his Will Crane suspicions. I remember the name, of course—the killer who claimed Jake's mother, his lover, as his victim before vanishing into thin air. The bastard I didn't stop in time. I settle my face like a mask over the ricochet of complex and painful emotions brought on by hearing Crane's name.

"Tell me more," I encourage Jake, thinking about the gaping wound in Brian Burrows's neck. It suggested that Brian knew his attacker, allowed his killer to get close enough to seize his head from behind and drive his bloody point home.

Jake has two theories. The first is that Crane, still bitter about Mallory's defection back to her family, tracked Brian to Paris and killed him. The second is that Brian had found Crane, maybe even took the job in Paris because he knew Crane was here.

Jake *could* be right. Maybe Crane did emerge from hiding to torment and kill Brian Burrows. Or maybe Brian had hunted Crane and met him willingly, looking for closure. Or vengeance. Before it all went wrong.

Jake elaborates, his young face lit with excitement. He details his study of the security cameras around their former apartment. I'm impressed with his initiative.

Jake confesses that when he went to the police to report his suspicions, they in turn told him they knew he'd lied about when he returned to Paris. That they suspect *him* in his father's murder.

He looks at me with tortured defiance. I feign both surprise and shock. Murmur another "That must be so hard for you." Followed by, "And it's absurd, of course."

A palpable wash of relief passes over Jake's face. He's so grateful to be *listened to, believed,* that all reticence fades. Words tumble from his lips.

Jake tells me about his agreement of silence regarding his whereabouts the day he returned to Paris in order to protect another's reputation. How torn he is about holding this secret tight. I sense that a bit of heartbreak, or at least a painful rejection, lies underneath the tale. I think about Hank Scovell and his overt sexual aggression toward women, about Jake's distraught state upon leaving the Mandarin hotel. I wonder if it was Scovell who patched up Jake's face.

I find I like Jake Burrows. Quite a lot. He's smart. Emotionally intelligent too, self-deprecating about his anger issues, trying hard to do right in a world that's frequently done him wrong. I realize with a bit of shock that our empathy isn't faked.

It occurs to me that Jake is the one member of the Burrows family that I haven't yet asked about Victor Wyatt. I fish the phone with the actor's picture on it out of my pack.

"Do you recognize this man?"

Jake peers intently at the image. "No, I don't think so. Should I?"

"His name is Victor Wyatt. Someone hired him to follow your father in the days before he was killed."

"I don't know him."

"Are you sure? He works for an escort service, Le Boy Bleu?"

"Well, that's a little weird."

"Why?"

"I found a bunch of brochures and postcards for gay clubs and stuff inside my duffel bag. One was for Le Boy Bleu. I asked Natalie, but she said she didn't know anything about them, so I thought it must have been my uncle. At the time I thought he was, you know, trying too hard to be cool, but . . ." Jake trails off with a shrug.

Caution's siren wails in my gut, call it instinct. This *could* be meaningless. But somehow I don't think so.

CREEP

Natalie tiptoes out of her room and down the hallway. She knocks softly at Uncle Frank's door. No answer. She taps again, a little harder this time.

A muffled groan. Natalie takes this as a "yes." Opens the door. Peers in from the hallway.

The blinds and curtains are drawn. Indistinct shapes hulk in the gloom. As Natalie's eyes adjust she sees clothes piled on the armchair, a fan of papers on the desk pinned under an open laptop, Uncle Frank huddled under the blankets, lying on his side, his back to Natalie.

Frigid air-conditioning blasts into the room from the unit under the window.

"I can't sleep," she confesses softly. "Can we talk?"

Frank lifts his head and trains bleary eyes on Natalie. Hands clasped behind her back, swimming in oversized sweats, hair hanging across her downcast eyes; Natalie knows she looks a pathetic sight.

Frank pats the bed. "Come. Sit down."

Meeting her uncle's eyes fills her with panic. *Maybe this is a bad idea.*

Frank beckons to her. Pulls himself up to a sitting position. Natalie hangs back in the doorway.

"Come on, Nat, what's on your mind, honey? I know things got a little rough between us earlier, but—"

"Have you heard of transitive doorway effect?" she interrupts.

"What?"

"Transitive doorway effect. It's a real thing. It's when you cross through a doorway and forget why you entered the room in the first place. It's because the act of entering a new physical environment makes the brain sort of, like, clear itself for new information." She knows she's babbling but she can't stop.

"That's very interesting, Natalie, but I can't believe you woke me up in the middle of the night just to tell me that." Frank laughs, pulls off his covers, and rises from the bed. Walks toward her.

She backs away from him. He comes closer.

Natalie's heart flutters in her chest.

"And I don't believe you've forgotten why you came in here either, for that matter. So what is it that's on your mind?"

Natalie's mind spins with questions, but her words are stuck in her throat.

Frank's eyes are pooled in shadows, his jaw rigid and set. He shifts into the rectangle of light cast by the open door and their eyes meet.

His eyes are bloodshot, red-rimmed. There's a glint of anger.

And a hint of something else: a cold desperation that chills Natalie to the core.

Catherine

FLY

I pound across the cobblestones, my eyes frantically raking the snarled traffic for a free taxicab on the rue de Rivoli. I glance behind me to see Jake racing to keep up, one hand protectively clasped against his battered ribs. He's wheezing. Red-faced. Confused.

"What's going on?" he heaves.

"We need to get to your hotel."

There. An open cab. I wrench open the door and urge Jake inside. I settle into the cracked leather seat and give the address to the driver.

Something is wrong. I feel it in my bones.

Natalie

READY

She deserves to die.

That much she knows with deep, abiding certainty. Spots swim against her closed eyelids, yellow and red, looping, trailing, rising, fading. Will they be the last things she ever sees?

Natalie longs for Jake. If only she could see him one last time before she goes.

Stupid freak. Do you think he'd still love you if he knew who you really are?

Maybe it's better this way. She'll die and he'll never have to know.

She presses her palms into the bleeding wound in her belly. Warm, sticky liquid pools around her fingers.

Natalie feels giddy and dizzy, unexpectedly lighthearted. Her body feels light too, as if the flesh, bones, blood, and organs that have been her enemies for so long are finally at peace, freeing her from their oppression.

So this is death, she thinks. *I'm ready.*

Catherine

RESCUE

Jake is one step behind me as I hurry down the hotel hallway. We reach the Burrowses' suite.

"You have your key card?"

Jake pulls his wallet from his pocket. Slips the key card into the slot.

The hum of the air-conditioning is loud in the stillness, the room dark, the curtains drawn. I flick on a light as we enter. The dining table is littered with empty chip packets and old newspapers. An overripe banana fills the air with a cloying sweetness.

"Natalie?" I call. "Frank?"

The door to Natalie's room is ajar. I push it all the way open.

Empty, the bedsheets twisted. Jake crowds behind me, treads on my heel.

"Sorry! Sorry."

I race to Frank's room. This door is also half-open. I peer inside. Flick the light on.

Blood. That's the first thing I see. Too much blood.

I slam the door closed. "Call an ambulance, Jake," I command. "And stay here."

"Is it Natalie? What's happened? What's wrong?"

"I don't know yet. Just *call*!"

I race back into the bedroom, locking the door behind me.

Two bodies on the king-sized bed. Blood pools downward from Frank Burrows's slit throat, an eerie, ugly parallel to my discovery of his brother mere weeks before. Frank's open eyes stare blankly.

Natalie lies curled next to him. A red, sticky puddle blooms through her abdomen and soaks her baggy sweats. But her chest rises and falls, a shallow promise. She's alive.

I check her pulse. Weak but steady. I apply pressure to the bubbling wound in her belly.

In the hallway Jake cries out: *"What's happening? What's happening?"* He pounds on the door.

"Stay there!" I shout. "Natalie needs an ambulance, but I think she'll be okay."

I have no idea if she'll be okay. But for fuck's sake I need to keep Jake out of this carnage.

Natalie's cold hand clutches at mine. I look down to see her trying to speak.

"Shhh. It's okay," I reassure. "We've called for help. You'll be okay."

Natalie rasps something out, too low for me to hear. I lean in closer.

"Is he dead? I think he's dead," she whispers. "But I had . . . no choice. He killed Daddy. . . . He's killed me too."

I study her beseeching eyes.

"Protect Jake. Please." Natalie falls back on her pillows.

I reapply pressure to her wounded stomach with both hands.

In the distance sirens wail.

Jake

WITHOUT A TRACE

He's been in the hospital waiting room for endless hours, Aimee Martinet unsympathetically slumped in a chair across the aisle. Jake can't bear to even look at her. What a horror show: the ambulance, the police, the ER, Natalie rushed away into surgery.

Jake tries not to think about his uncle. The blood. The corpse. The betrayal.

Jake wraps his arms around himself. He's trembling and doesn't want Martinet to see. He's still trying to sort out what happened. What exactly did Hannah Potter say Natalie had whispered? That Uncle Frank confessed to killing their father before trying to kill Natalie too?

But why? This is insane.

Jake suspects he's in shock. Eventually it'll make sense, won't it? *Whatever.* Who cares? As long as Natalie survives.

Please don't die, Nat.

Jake rises and pours himself a cup of decaf coffee from the freshly filled carafe on a side table. There's a tray of *madeleines* too. Jake eyes them, their pleasing formal curves, but has no appetite. He sips his black coffee. Studies the other people who have found their day poisoned by tragedy.

Six children cluster close to their white-faced mother, murmuring reassurances in both French and Hebrew: an orthodox Jewish family waiting for their patriarch to emerge from surgery. A sudden heart attack no one saw coming, followed by an emergency quadruple bypass.

The parents of a toddler who'd mouthed a shard of broken glass clasp hands as the mother silently prays.

A young French-Asian woman in bicycle shorts collapses into the arms of her sister. She'd been out biking with her boyfriend when a car hit him.

Jake has no one to reassure him, he reflects, perversely pleased to be picking at his own misery. Both of his parents are dead, his uncle a murdering monster, his sister probably dying. . . . He's all alone in this world, except for that awful gimlet-eyed Aimee Martinet, keeping watch, *judging* him.

A police officer Jake recognizes from the frenetic scene at the hotel draws Martinet over to one side of the waiting room. A hushed and hurried conversation ensues.

Jake watches with wary interest. Martinet glances over at Jake with a flash of agitation before thanking her colleague and escorting him to the door.

She comes over to the side table and pours herself a coffee. Stirs in a single packet of sugar. Leans against the wall and takes a sip with a studied casualness that puts Jake instantly on edge.

"Jake, we need to talk about Hannah Potter. Do you know where she is?"

"No, how should I? We got Natalie in an ambulance and she stayed behind to talk to your people."

"Is that what she told you she was doing? Staying behind?"

"Giving her statement. Right. What's this about?"

"How well do you know Madame Potter?"

"I told you. I only met her last night."

"But she knew your sister and your uncle?"

"A little, I think. I don't know that much about her, really." Jake fights a rush of panic as he flashes on a hood, a hypodermic, bound wrists, the things he'd allowed himself to believe—no, *convinced* himself to believe—were a hallucination. "What the hell is going on? Why are you asking?"

"Hannah Potter doesn't exist."

"What? Don't be stupid. I met her."

"I don't know who you met, but whoever it was slipped away from the hotel while the paramedics were seeing to your sister. She didn't identify herself to any of the officers on the scene. And it seems she's vanished without a trace."

"I don't understand." And he doesn't.

There's actually a glint of sympathy in Martinet's eyes. "The only Hannah Potter we can come up with whose age and nationality even roughly match up with what you've told us? She died at the age of four, twenty-three years ago, in a town called Council Grove, Kansas."

Catherine

PAST TENSE

I'd made a true home for myself here in this apartment in the Marais.

I filled the comfortable rooms with eclectic items of furniture and quirky knickknacks I picked up on my many excursions to Les Puces. The rugs are soft underfoot. The closets are heaped with designer clothes and accessories. If one is going to live in Paris, one might as well be chic.

My command center had been a work of great beauty too. Past tense. I'd wiped all digital traces clean before dousing my hardware with an acid bath. The apartment still reeks of its burn through metal and plastic and wire.

Walking through the rooms for one last time, my eyes rake over this version of a life, pressing the memories into my mind like flowers into a scrapbook.

I knew this day would arrive eventually. Although I'm sorry it's come so soon.

Jumah will sell most of what I've left, the rest he'll trash.

I'll be traveling light.

I pop on a dark brown wig with heavy bangs. A little kohl on my eyebrows and I'm virtually a different person. Actually, I *am* a different person. I'm Sydney Fletcher, from Indianapolis, Indiana, thank you very much; at least that's what my passport and credit cards say.

I take one last look around my sweet apartment. Drop my keys into their usual bowl by the door. Step through the doorway into the dimly lit hallway.

Adieu, Paris.

I just have one or two stops before I go.

SOUNDS AND SIGNS

Sound comes in first.

Natalie's eyelids are too heavy to lift. She stays sunk deep beneath their comforting black shroud. Her limbs seem disconnected from her body. And her mind.

She couldn't move them if she tried.

She does try. Fails.

But she can *hear*.

Hisses and thumps and beeps.

Muffled voices. *In another room,* she thinks.

The distant squeal of rubber wheels on linoleum.

Her mouth is dry.

Hisses and thumps and beeps.

She hurts in a lot of places. Her arms. Her belly. Her head is *pounding*.

All this pain must mean she's alive, right? Surely you don't feel things when you're *dead*.

Natalie's eyelids flutter open, but the sting of bright fluorescent light hits her dilated pupils and she promptly squints her eyes closed again.

Hospital. She's seen enough to know she's in the hospital.

Sound comes in: the swoosh of a door opening.

Padding footsteps generated by sensible, rubber-soled shoes.

Natalie forces herself to open her eyes. The face looking down at her is coal black, with huge dark eyes and a dawning, hopeful smile.

"*I see you're awake! That is excellent. I will let the doctor know,*" the woman says in French. The nurse's smile grows wider. She repeats herself in English, adding "Here, *ma chère,* here is the button to push for the morphine. For the pain?" She wraps Natalie's fingers around the pain pump before scurrying from the room.

Natalie hesitates. The pain is excruciating. It's so tempting to think she can relieve it at will.

But doesn't she *deserve* the pain? Shouldn't she feel every place she was cut apart and every inch she was stitched back together again? Hasn't that been the cycle of her life to date? Crime and punishment. Crime and punishment. All of it self-inflicted. Most of it, anyway.

But maybe the fact that she lived through this *ordeal* is a *sign.*

Natalie turns this notion over. Maybe, just maybe, she's been punished enough? Perhaps she's been forgiven for her sins? Has *sacrificed* enough? Maybe she can actually carry on with her life from this point forward with a clean slate.

The more Natalie dwells on this idea, the more concretely it aligns beneath her, a sturdy plank; the first solid step in a new direction. It must be so. A fresh start. She deserves that more than anyone, doesn't she?

She has a *larger purpose,* she is certain of it. This is it: her chance to truly be *grateful every day.*

The punishment can stop.

The *pain* can stop.

Natalie's finger depresses the button on the morphine pump. Her savaged body floods with a euphoric cloud of blissful relief.

Catherine

VANITY

I've reserved a room at one of my favorite hotels.

To get there, I thread through a crowd, dodging families sweaty and sticky-sweet from cotton candy, shrieking teenagers and squealing kids, giddy young lovers with arms entwined. The Fête.

The Fête springs up in the shadow of the Louvre every summer; this one is no exception. A Ferris wheel, its spokes picked out in white neon that glows against the night sky, anchors one end of the nonstop party. Food stalls line either side of the avenue. I'm tempted by the scents of grilling meats and frying dough. There are games of chance. Bumper cars. A King Kong ride. A pendulum swing that lifts its screaming riders high into the air for a breathless view of the city of lights.

I love the pure, old-fashioned whimsy of the Fête and am glad to have a chance to walk through one last time. I have no idea when I'll be back in Paris.

Buoyed by the hoots and clamor of the crowd, I turn a corner and enter my destination, the Grand Hôtel du Palais Royal on rue de Valois.

The hotel's gracious reception area is designed to create an atmosphere of soothing luxury. Cream-colored walls offset chocolate-brown paneling. Muted Oriental rugs tastefully cover marble floors. Crystal vases overflow with pale green flowers that perfectly match the cushions on the nubby ecru sofas.

I register as Sydney Fletcher, handing over my identification and a credit card, making small talk about the warm weather. The desk clerk slides over a folder with two key cards. I remove one and slide it back.

"A gentleman will ask for me in about an hour. When he does, please give him the key and send him to my room."

The clerk doesn't bat an eye.

My room is exquisite. White furniture. A frothy bunch of hydrangeas in a vase on the glass-topped coffee table. The space is dominated by the bed at its center: crisp white sheets and a lush mauve blanket. The pair of windows overlook a perfect Parisian rooftop landscape of water towers and fire escapes.

I settle down into the mauve armchair tucked into one corner of the room.

Right on time, the hotel room door swings open. Victor Wyatt enters, his smooth, handsome features contorting in surprise when he sees "Sydney Fletcher" is a woman. It's why I chose "Sydney" in the first place. He recovers quickly as I invite him in.

He gets right down to business, confirming I know his hourly rate, surreptitiously popping a little blue pill that I assume is Viagra. He shouldn't have bothered.

Handing over convincing press credentials for the international edition of *The New York Times,* I tell him I'm covering Brian Burrows's murder. That I know he's connected. Wyatt tugs at his streaky blond hair. Glances at the door as if he just might run.

"I shouldn't talk to you . . . I don't really know anything anyway."

I remind Wyatt that the police will be talking to him soon enough; I know for a fact they have his photograph and name. That they know he was stalking Brian Burrows in the days before he was killed.

I hand Wyatt a wad of euros, four times his hourly rate. There's hesitation in his eyes but the lure of the money is too great for him to resist. He pockets the cash. Perches on the edge of the bed.

"Like I said, I don't know much. . . ."

"It doesn't look so good for you, Victor. Following a man just before he was murdered. But I'm offering you an opportunity here. You can get your story out in the media ahead of the game. Before you're brought in for questioning."

Wyatt starts whining then. There's no other word for it. Kind of disgusting coming from a full-grown man. He had nothing to do with Brian Burrows's murder! He was hired to follow the guy for a few days and report back. That was it!

"Report what?"

"What his schedule was like. What time he got back to his apartment from work each day. His routine. Stuff like that."

"And who were you reporting to?"

"I don't know." He's a bad liar. "I just was given an email address."

"Bullshit. Look, Wyatt, you have a choice here. I can position this story so it's clear you were an innocent dupe manipulated by a killer. I can generate sympathy for you, get your name and your face out there as a brave citizen who came forward to help solve a heinous crime. That's a narrative you can make work for you. Outside of the investigation too, if you're smart about it. But only if you're straight with me."

The opportunity for reinvention flowers in Wyatt's hungry eyes.

I learn Wyatt was hired and paid by someone called Larry Finley. When pressed, Wyatt insists he hadn't even heard of Frank Burrows until he was killed and he saw the news, learned he was Brian's brother.

He swears up and down that he was told he was following Brian to help arrange a birthday prank. It was easy money for an easy service; he never imagined anything *like this* would happen.

Fear, cowardice, and avarice render Wyatt's handsome face quite ugly.

"You'll help, right? Like you said? I didn't do anything *illegal*. I didn't *know*."

I offer Wyatt my assurances. Tell him I'll be back in touch before my article runs in order to "fact check." I like that detail; it gives my lies the ring of authenticity.

I tell Wyatt to stay on in this room as long as he likes. It's paid for until checkout the next morning. I leave him there, slumped on the bed, tugging at his hair, hopeful Sydney Fletcher will be his redemption. I can only imagine his disappointment when this story never runs.

But who the hell is Larry Finley?

The pieces don't all add up yet. I can't stop asking questions until they do.

REVELATION

Natalie's propped in her hospital bed, frail and wan, pierced by IVs, but alive, breathing, finally talking. Jake's consumed with relief. And a newfound respect for his little sister.

"You're tougher than anyone I know, Nat." He grins at her and she smiles back.

If only I hadn't left Natalie alone with Frank. It's a miracle she's alive. And how could I not have suspected him? Not known he was a killer? Am I too self-absorbed? Too stupid?

Jake knows this self-excoriation is pointless, but he's compelled to do it just the same.

"What happened to Uncle Frank?" Natalie asks.

Before answering, Jake's eyes dart around the hospital room, shades of mint green and peach. *Who in their right mind picked that revolting combination?*

"He didn't make it," he finally replies.

Natalie gives a mute nod. She's very pale. She gestures for the cup of water sitting on her bedside tray. Jake lifts it so she can sip through the straw.

"We don't have to talk about it, Nat." *God knows if I never even think about any of this again, it would be just fine.*

Her fingers pluck at his arm. "I need you to understand what happened," she implores.

Jake feels something shifting, a fissure cracking open. He wants to avoid its slippery edge at all costs. He shifts uneasily in his uncomfortable institutional chair. The scent of hospitals—disinfectant, urine, blood, and suffering—fills his nostrils, makes him feel queasy. He's not sure he can bear to hear the details, but doesn't he at least owe that much to Natalie?

"Okay," he relents.

In low tones, Natalie recounts the thought process that led to her suspicions.

"I couldn't really *believe* it, you know? But I knew *you* couldn't have killed Dad, like they kept saying. And I never believed the idea it was a random mugging. So I pushed Uncle Frank . . ." Natalie's wide gray eyes fill with tears as she continues. "About Le Boy Bleu, about that man hired to *stalk* Daddy . . ."

Jake takes her small hand in his large one.

"And, Jake, he just *snapped*. I wasn't even scared of him, not at first. He was pathetic, whimpering about how Daddy never appreciated all the things he'd done for him." Natalie's hand grips Jake's tightly. "And then . . . then . . . he admitted he killed Will Crane! He said it was yet another thing Daddy didn't understand."

For a moment the heady whoosh of blood in Jake's ears obliterates all other sound. He had been *so sure* Crane had killed their father. So sure that the man who had stolen their mother was walking the earth free, mocking them.

"What? When?" he finally chokes out.

"Back then. Right after Mom . . ."

"But why? Why would Uncle Frank *kill* Crane?"

"He said he went to confront him about Mom. That Crane admitted killing her! But mocked him, said he'd never be caught. Uncle Frank said . . . that he lost his shit. Killed him. Dumped his body. But that he did it to 'claim justice' for our family. And that I should be thanking him. That we all should."

Jake's head is swimming. "But that letter Crane sent . . ."

"Uncle Frank wrote it. To cover his tracks. Jake, it was like a *stranger* was talking to me. The *crazy* in his eyes . . ."

Jake has to look away from her. "But why did he kill Dad?"

"He admitted killing Crane to Daddy. He wanted him to know what he had done for him. He was *proud* of it. But Daddy was going to turn him in. Of course he was. Daddy wanted to do the *right* thing. So Uncle Frank killed him!" Natalie's voice breaks. "When he started talking about Dad, I started crying, Jake. And Uncle Frank got so mad! He kept saying I should be *grateful*. To him. That Dad should have been *grateful*."

She gestures for another sip of water. Jake obeys.

"I had the knife in my pocket, you know, the one you let me keep that night at dinner?"

Jake nods. He remembers all too well.

"I wasn't going to *use* it or anything." Natalie looks at him with imploring eyes. "I just thought it might make me feel *safer,* you know. . . . But he kept yelling at me to *shut up*! He grabbed me, hurt me. I just tried to back him away from me, but then he grabbed for the knife and . . ."

Natalie dissolves in tears. Jake stands and wraps his arms around her birdlike body. He stares down at her bandaged forearms.

Defensive cuts, the doctor had said. Sustained in fighting off their uncle. Before the fucker succeeded in plunging the knife just below her rib cage, lacerating her liver.

It was a miracle she'd had the strength to pull the knife out and retaliate. Luck (if you can call it that) that she'd severed an artery in Frank's neck before he could wrest hold of the knife and stab her again.

"It's okay, Nat," he soothes. "It's all over now. You're going to be all right."

"I *killed* him, Jake. I'm a *killer* now." Natalie stares at him with stormy gray eyes, daring him to still love her.

Guilt and gratitude war inside Jake. He allowed Natalie to slip *that knife* into her bag.

The knife that saved her life.

The knife that made her a killer.

Part Six

ORIGINS

There's always something hidden.
Layers we can't see.
Isn't that why we spin stories?
To fill in the gaps?
Answer the questions?
And still our anxious hearts.
Let's go back in time, just a little bit.

Mallory

MISSED CHANCES

She was pissed. Fucking over it. Her hands shook as she inserted the key into the ignition. How infuriating to be treated like a child by Brian. Dismissed. Ignored.

I'm getting out of here.

Unexpected tears spilled hotly down her cheeks; a throbbing headache took root in the center of her forehead. She shook her pill bottle from her bag onto the passenger seat, unscrewed the cap, and popped one dry.

She couldn't wait to see Will. To feel his hands on her body. His mouth on her mouth. Wrapped in his arms, she knew she'd feel safe. She never thought she would fall in love again. She couldn't believe she had.

A flirtation that turned into conversation that turned into a stolen kiss. A solemn first fumble, and then pure joy—laughter and connection and fucking awesome sex. Mallory was giddy with it all. Glowing. Alive like she hadn't been in years.

It wasn't without cost. What pleasure is? Betraying her husband, keeping secrets from him, all of that didn't sit lightly on Mallory, even though surely they would both acknowledge the marriage had been over for years.

And anyway, even Steven, right? She was certain Brian had

strayed at some point, what with all his travel. Of course he had. But that was hardly the point. It was more that the two of them would always be linked through Jake and Natalie. It would be better if they could remain friends. Mallory felt magnanimous in the bloom of her new romance. There was enough love for all.

The only question was timing.

Jake was off at NYU already, his own life started. Mallory worried more about Natalie, still in high school and always more *delicate;* it had been a big point of discussion with Will, regarding any kind of *official announcement.*

But it wasn't like either Natalie or Jake would be loved any less.

Love begets love. There was enough love for all. Mallory fervently believed this.

Something pulpy and bloodied reared up suddenly in the glare of her headlights. Mallory swerved to avoid hitting it. Too big to be a squirrel. She hoped it wasn't a cat.

There was enough love for all, but someone was angry at Mallory. At least it felt that way. First there was the bouquet of dead roses left on her windshield. Mallory shrugged that one off. But next, her car was viciously keyed while she was at the movies. Six days later, she awoke, padded to the front door to bring in the newspaper, and found it and the front stoop splattered with what appeared to be *blood,* the word *bitch* drawn in thick, sticky, red capital letters. Mallory quickly disposed of the sodden paper and washed away the blood with furious blasts from the hose before Natalie was even awake.

The incidents pointed to someone who knew her schedule, who was lurking somewhere just on the periphery, waiting. Watching.

Her anxiety over it all had made her sick, vaguely nauseous all the time, exhausted.

After the blood-splashed doorway, she'd confided in her friends at the shelter. To her unease, they took it all very seriously. Mallory realized she'd secretly hoped for dismissiveness as a form of reassurance.

Instead, Ivy gave Mallory a darknet contact for someone who might be able to help, for the first time confiding in her how the organization used certain shadowy channels to help women and children reinvent their lives.

Mallory had reached out. Received a brief, anonymous reply stating her case was under review. Yesterday a second email arrived. It instructed her to come to the gift shop in the Westport Historical Society tomorrow at noon; her contact would find her there.

It had been over a week since the blood. Nothing had happened since then. Maybe it was over. Maybe the blood and the withered roses and the keyed car weren't even connected. Maybe all of Mallory's terrible speculation about the possible culprit could be put to rest. She felt a little silly about having put the whole thing in motion.

Anyway, she could decide if she would go tomorrow. In a matter of minutes, she'd be at Will's house. Mallory's heart thrummed with possibilities.

Not only was she in love, her volunteer work at the shelter had really stimulated something within her. She was going to go back to school, work part-time while she did. She was practically done raising Jake and Natalie and she'd done that more or less single-handedly. Wasn't it her time?

New love. New career. New chances. She deserved that, didn't she?

I'll go home before the kids wake up, be there for breakfast, she promised herself. *I'll talk civilly to Brian, I'll work it all out.*

Enough love for all.

Part Seven

CONVERGENCE

Here's the thing, you see, I'm not some kind of saint or savior.

I only wanted to save myself.

EXCLAMATION

Sydney Fletcher arrived in New York, only to promptly be put in storage again. I'm burning any trails that might link me back to Paris. Too many people looking for me there.

I'm glad to be back in Manhattan. I like the easy anonymity. But I find myself thinking in French and having to work to speak in English. It made me feel a half-step behind, at a disadvantage, except when I successfully used my *"Parisian* charm" on the gruff Israeli guy from whom I bought two off-market laptops this morning.

I can't stay in New York for long, though. It's another place with too many ragged endings. But likewise, I can't move on anywhere until I *know.* From my midtown hotel it's an easy ninety-minute drive to Westport, Connecticut.

In the cool hush of my air-conditioned hotel room, I surf the Internet, combing for any and every scrap of information I can find about the Burrows murders.

The story has been covered internationally, of course. How could the press resist? It was a family tragedy so salacious it made even the most fucked-up among us feel a little bit better about our own miserable lives.

There's a rehash of the details of Brian Burrows's murder in Paris alongside an appreciation of his architectural career (including a sidebar profile of the "troubled" canal Saint-Martin renovation, repeating most of the dark history Lilja had given me about the site).

There's an interview with Victor Wyatt, finally milking his fifteen minutes of fame as the "dupe" who unwittingly followed Brian in furtherance of Frank Burrows's murderous ends.

There's a profile of Frank's self-righteous ex-wife, Della, regretful that her daughters would from here on in be branded and shamed by the "vicious actions of that horrible man" (even as she shops her side of the story for a TV deal).

Mallory Burrows's disappearance is resurrected and rehashed too, of course, the linked tragedies charted and dissected.

I've read everything available. Straight news coverage. The accolades and memories from Brian Burrows's colleagues and peers. The pundits and psychologists. The specialists on family violence. The experts on international law.

The Burrows children, Jake and Natalie, declined all interviews after releasing a prepared statement through a lawyer, although that hasn't stopped wild speculation about the impact of the tragic series of events on these two young people, the poisoned fruit of a deadly family tree.

It'd been simple enough to find out that one Lawrence Finley worked with Frank Burrows at Good Hair!! Easy too to learn that Finley had also attended the trade show in London that had brought Frank overseas.

An old friend of mine in New York, Paco Rodriguez, was good enough to do a little legwork for me. Paco informed me that since the story broke, Finley has been basking in the tarnished reflection of notoriety: happy to tell his tale of unwitting participation in a homicide to anyone willing to buy him a scotch.

I enter a sports bar on West Forty-seventh Street, around the corner from the offices of Good Hair!! It's the place in which Larry Finley has been dining out, or should I say drinking out, on his peripheral involvement in the Burrows family tragedy.

The bar is as expected. Banks of television screens. Neon signs advertising beer and liquor. Jerseys and pennants flaunting New York team insignias. I spot Finley immediately. He's redder and fatter in the face than he is in the pictures of him I found online; the drinking and boasting are taking their toll.

I sidle onto a barstool a couple of seats down. Finley pulls off his thick-framed black glasses and gives me an appreciative glance.

I've dyed my hair blond. Finley likes blondes, I know (but I was also ready for a change for a whole host of reasons). I'm wearing tight jeans and a low-cut blouse, an opal necklace with an ornate setting nestled provocatively right above my cleavage, drawing the eye.

Finley is happy to preen and puff for me. He always knew something was *off* about Frank Burrows, he says, with the cockily brilliant hindsight of a man who never actually thought any such thing. He never would have suspected Frankie was a *murderer*, not that, but *peculiar*, yes, that he always knew.

It turns out Frank had done more than use Finley's credit card and name to book Victor Wyatt. He had also swiped Finley's passport and used it to travel to Paris and back the day he killed his own brother. Finley had no idea, of course! Frank had lifted the passport, used it, and slipped it back into Finley's hotel room without him even noticing. But of course after, well, *everything* came to light.

Finley's story seems to confirm Natalie's: Frank Burrows murdered his brother in a premeditated act of violence, having finally confessed to murdering Mallory's lover, Will Crane, three years prior in revenge for her death. The chances were old Frankie had been madly in love with poor Mallory.

But something doesn't sit right with me. It all feels so *convenient*, a dead man's confession tidily wrapping up this whole grisly chapter.

In my experience, things are rarely that neat.

MYSTERY

Yesterday is history. Tomorrow is a mystery. All we have is right now.

Amara, Natalie's day nurse, had offered up this affirmation in her sweet West African singsong on a daily basis, encouraging Natalie to stay focused on her recovery.

She's a very kind woman, Amara. She's washed Natalie and changed her bandages, helped her to the bathroom, brought her things to read and treats to eat. Natalie feels a great deal of warmth for Amara.

Yesterday is history.

When the worst has happened, things have to get better, right? Right.

Tomorrow is a mystery.

When Natalie confided in Amara that she was experiencing a sense of reinvention, Amara nodded understandingly. The next day she brought in a small stack of biographies in English: Mata Hari, Coco Chanel, Marie Curie.

Natalie devoured the book about Mata Hari. Talk about reinvention! Pampered daughter, unloved wife, heartbroken and heartless mother, exotic dancer, lover, celebrity, and possibly a spy! The controversy fascinates Natalie. Was Mata Hari a wily seductress who used her charms for betrayal? Or was she railroaded by the government to cover up high-level collusion and corruption?

The book about Coco Chanel also resonated. Natalie thrilled to the words depicting a woman of iron determination and impeccable standards, far ahead of her time and steeped in controversy. Many lovers. Nazi collaboration. Ruthless in business. An artist, just like Natalie. And also a survivor. A survivor at all costs.

Natalie had dutifully studied Marie Curie in elementary school, but this new biography opened her eyes. After Marie's first husband died, she not only won a second Nobel Prize, but she also embarked on an affair with a married physicist that sent the gossips' tongues wagging.

All of these women made history. All of their lives involved scandal. Natalie is grateful. Amara has been so very perceptive in her choices.

Natalie closes her suitcase and zips it shut. She looks around the peach-and-mint room that has been her home these past few weeks.

She *lived*. There must be a reason.

She's ready to begin writing a new story of her own.

Catherine

SHELTER

If you weren't looking for Haven, you'd never find it.

In fact, it's designed so that if you *are* looking for Haven, you'll never find it.

There's no sign on the door. No phone company listings. All bills relating to the property are issued to and paid by an off-site company called A-One Detail Work, no mention of Haven anywhere. Payroll is issued from behind the same blind.

The staff is trained to be completely discreet. Referral is passed along a tattered trail of abused spouses, furtive and stealthy. All of this secrecy is necessary. So often it could mean the difference between life and death.

Haven is a way station. A short-term solution for women and children who need to disappear. I've called ahead to the shelter's director, Ivy Phillips, knowing all too well how the appearance of any stranger can affect the women and children housed there. When you've lived your life in fear, anything can make you flinch.

Ivy's possessed of broad shoulders and broader hips; she looks substantial, comforting, no-nonsense. She ushers me into her cluttered office and sweeps a basket of knitting off the guest chair, looks about for a clear place to put it, finds none, and then resignedly balances it atop the mountain of papers on her desk. She gestures to the now open seat, then plants herself in the swivel chair that tilts precariously behind the desk. She shifts the knitting basket slightly so she can see me clearly.

"I've never met someone before, you know, from . . ." she begins, her tone surprisingly thin and tentative given her solid persona.

"Well, the boss says that's best, of course. The less we know, the less we can let slip."

"Who exactly *is* the boss?" The question bursts out of her and I can see she's thrilled at her daring, while also slightly appalled she had the nerve to ask.

I shrug. "I was given an assignment and I'm here to do it, that's all I know. No more than you do."

Her bulk deflates into her chair, the frisson of daring evaporating just as fast as it had ballooned. "I just hope that you'll relay, you know, that we're really grateful here at Haven for the times the Burial Society has been able to help. If you get a chance, would you communicate that to . . . whomever?"

I assure her I will. And truth is, I'm pleased by the compliment. Invisibility is so much my hallmark that I rarely get to hear words of gratitude directly.

I raise the subject of the Burrows family and Ivy's face remains impassive save for a sudden twitch in her right eye. She blinks it away. Years of working with women burdened by tortured pasts and possessed of uncertain futures has taught this woman the value of listening while appearing neutral.

"Did you know any of them?" she asks me. "The Burrowses?"

I shake my head.

She releases a heavy gust of a sigh. "Mallory I knew best, of course. She volunteered here. And really came alive! A wonderful, sweet woman. I think she got as much from being here as we got from her help. Maybe more. She'd even talked about going back to school to get her master's in social work."

My heart twists. I cost Mallory that chance. I denied Mallory *and* all the women she could have helped in the course of her life. My transgression is worse than I knew. I force my attention back to Ivy.

"Brian, I only met once, after she disappeared. A condolence call. Her kids, I met a couple of times. Never the uncle." Ivy shudders thinking about Frank; she's read all those articles too. She reaches into her knitting basket and extracts a pair of needles. Starts clicking away at a length of pale blue yarn.

"It all looked so normal, you know?" she continues. "No, not even normal, so *perfect*. They were all healthy, attractive, had financial comfort and success, the kids were growing up, starting their own lives. . . . So shocking, all of it. You never know, right?"

We never do.

I ask Ivy what she knew about Will Crane.

"Well, that was the first shocker. That Mallory was having an affair with him. I'm not judging. It's just that it blew the lid off that pretty family portrait. But I never believed Crane killed her, I'll tell you that."

I lean forward in my chair. "Why's that?"

"I saw them together. Ran into them one night at a restaurant. They were seated already when my friend and I came in and didn't see us at first. The way those two looked at each other? God knows, I'm no romantic, but that was as close to pure love as I've ever seen."

Or lust. Or infatuation, I think cynically.

"But it was more than that," Ivy continues. "Do you know about the creepy things that started to happen to Mallory?"

I do, of course, but I ask her to tell me.

It started with a bouquet of dead roses left on her car's windshield. Shortly after that, Mallory found her car keyed when she returned to the parking lot after a movie. Mallory had told Ivy she'd felt watched as she surveyed the damage, nothing she could pinpoint, no one she could see, just an uneasy sense that sent a prickle down her spine.

The final straw was the blood she'd found splashed on her doorstep. The word *bitch* scrawled. That's when Mallory finally had confided in Ivy.

"That's when we, you know, linked her up with TBS," Ivy says. "It was escalating. Creepy shit."

"Did Mallory report these incidents to the police?"

"I don't know. I advised her to. I know she told Crane about them."

"How do you know that?"

"We keep our location a strict secret, of course."

I nod.

"He insisted she give him a nearby cross street. That's why she confided in me. Mallory wanted to make sure I would be okay with her giving him even a hint of our location. They designated a different spot every day and he met her after she left here. I escorted her to the meet-up point. Crane followed her home to make sure she was safe, every single day. That man loved her, I'm sure."

"Plenty of us hurt the ones we love."

Ivy's knitting needles still. "All too true."

A baby's cries pierce the thin walls, followed by a softly sung lullaby. The baby's howls grow louder.

"But after all the years I've spent doing this"—Ivy gestures with her needles at the rooms surrounding us—"I trust my instincts. And they tell me Will Crane never would have touched a hair on poor Mallory's head."

"You must have suspected someone when Mallory disappeared," I coax.

Ivy is silent for a moment. "I always thought it was some random nut job who just got fixated on her. I knew her husband was away when the dead roses and all that started, so even though I know some people thought he might have hurt her, I never did."

"Why are you so sure the disappearance and the 'creepy shit' were the work of the same person?"

"Well, it makes sense, right? Wouldn't it be too random otherwise?" A faraway look enters Ivy's eyes as she remembers. "She was a beautiful woman, you know. And charismatic, in a way that went beyond her looks."

Ivy lays down her knitting and fixes me with her warm brown eyes.

"And then Crane disappeared and sent that confession." Ivy shrugs. "I didn't really buy it, but the cops strongly encouraged me to take it at face value. So I did."

BODIES

An international funeral shipping provider. Jake sits opposite the woman bearing that title, wondering, *How the hell does this end up being someone's job?* She's got frizzy gray hair and angular gray-framed glasses. Pinned to one lapel of her neat charcoal suit is an old-fashioned enameled pin shaped like a vase containing a bunch of flowers.

Her unlikely name is Maria O'Donahue-Keyes. It feels like marbles in Jake's mouth.

Her office in the funeral home is appropriately sober. Nondescript, solid furnishings in neutral colors, a couple of framed inspirational quotes on the wall, a big vase filled with lilies. *Kind of a cliché, the lilies,* Jake thinks.

They'd decided to bury Brian here in Connecticut, in Westport, the town both he and Natalie still thought of as home.

Maria O'Donahue-Keyes has been talking and talking and Jake has given the appearance of listening. But he's distracted by Miss Marbles's unlikely career path, by the very surreal nature of the task before him, by Natalie, slumped in the chair next to him.

The words Marbles has been spewing, *acte de décès* (death certificate), *permis d'inhumer* (burial permit), as well as all the details of the procedure for repatriation of the body, have floated on the air before Jake but escaped into the ether before he could really grasp them.

Isn't this why we've hired old Miss Maria O'Donahue-Keyes anyway? So that she can handle all this shit?

He glances at Natalie. She looks dazed, as if she too is overwhelmed by the torrent of words coming their way. She's gnawing the side of her thumb bloody, and he longs to reach out, pull her hand away from her nimble teeth.

Somehow it seems too intimate an act in front of a stranger.

Jake's gaze turns to one of the framed pictures on the wall. A golden sunset turns a smooth, sandy beach luminous. A silhouetted woman faces the horizon, her flowing black hair lifted in a breeze that whips her long dress around lean bare legs. The text reads:

The only people who think there is a time limit for grief have never lost a piece of their heart. Take all the time you need.

Sure. Great advice. But what if new grief keeps getting tossed on the old, incendiary kindling stoking an already raging fire?

What if my grief will never end?

Jake glances back at Maria O'Donahue-Keyes, who is looking at him with an expectant air. He realizes she's asked a question.

"What? I'm sorry," he mutters, his color rising.

"I asked if you also wanted to make arrangements to bring your uncle's body home."

Natalie pulls her thumb away from her mouth. Stares at Jake with panic-stricken eyes.

"No. I don't think we do."

He grasps Natalie's hand and runs his index finger along her thumb, leaving bloody smears on both of their hands.

Catherine

THE HUSBAND

The Westport, Connecticut, police station is a plain, two-story russet brick affair. It projects solid, affluent, suburban American values, set back behind a white-striped asphalt parking area.

I pull my rented Ford Escort into one of the empty parking spaces. In the visor mirror, I give myself a last check. Dark hair streaked with gray is pulled into a chignon at the base of my neck. I practice pulling the furrow between my brows. I look serious, a bit severe.

Exiting the Escort, I tug my fitted navy skirt suit into place. Adjust my crisp white collar. With four-inch heels on my simple black pumps and a black leather envelope bag clutched under one arm, I exude stylish French efficiency.

Aimee Martinet from the 8th arrondissement, Annexe Madeleine, is coming to have a casual chat with the detectives who handled the Mallory Burrows disappearance. Professional courtesy between law enforcement officers on opposite sides of the Atlantic.

I can't shake Ivy Phillips's certainty about Will Crane's innocence. Ivy is a woman trained to expect the worst of people, yet she was certain Crane would never have hurt Mallory. And if Crane *hadn't* killed Mallory, who had? Could it have been Brian after all?

Someone else altogether? And if Crane hadn't killed Mallory, why would Frank have killed *Crane*?

I remind myself Frank's confessions have come to me only repeated through Natalie's filter. The girl was attacked, fighting for her life. Could she have misunderstood? Is it possible Frank murdered Mallory too? And then every other man Mallory loved? Had Frank been in love with her? Is that where this whole twisted story began?

The more questions I ask, the more I seem to have.

Detective Benson is pleasant enough, but pointedly dismissive, as Detective Karen Cooke sits silently beside him. As far as Benson is concerned, their case is open only to the extent that William Crane is considered their prime suspect and still at large. He sees no connection between what happened in Paris and what is old news here. The Burrowses are certainly a tragic family, but he can't understand why I'm even asking questions. No bodies have been found. No new evidence has been offered. He fixes me with piercing black eyes.

I wave off his intensity with a laugh and a fluttering hand. I can see he will give me nothing. In French-accented English, I make a collegial joke about "we police," who can't help being "on" even when "on vacation." I thank them both for their time and ask Cooke if she can direct me to the ladies' room before I head back to New York. I have tickets for a Broadway show, I tell Benson happily, as Cooke escorts me from the room.

Once in the hallway, I put my hand on Cooke's elbow and draw her toward the front entrance. She doesn't resist. Nor does she seem surprised. She may have been silent in our meeting, but her compressed lips and shifting body told me she had things on her mind. As we step outside, I suddenly regret my heels. I loom over the petite detective in her flat shoes. She squints up against the sun to see me.

"I can tell," I plunge right in, "that your partner is taking the official position. But maybe you have other thoughts?"

The detective shifts her weight back and forth like a fighter getting ready to feint. She shoots a glance back inside the station. "You understand, in an affluent community like this, an unsolved disappearance, well, it didn't sit well," she says quietly. "But there were always things I questioned. For one thing, why did Crane hang around so long after Mallory disappeared? We weren't looking in his direction for like three weeks, didn't even know about their affair. Why didn't he take off then?"

I nod, encouraging her to continue.

"Plus, when we did learn about them . . . I interviewed him. He admitted to their relationship right away, even that he had seen her the night she disappeared. And that man was *crushed*. His anguish felt totally real to me. And he completely cooperated with us. It just didn't hit my gut right that he did it."

That's two people who believed Will Crane wouldn't have hurt his lover, Mallory Burrows.

"Then there was the confession letter itself. No drafts of it were found on either Crane's office or home computers."

"Maybe he used another computer?"

"Okay, but why, when he had two readily available? And why use a different computer if he was claiming responsibility anyway? Also the letter had no fingerprints on it. Why bother to sign a confession, but be so careful not to leave fingerprints?"

"Plus"—Cooke leans in closer—"Crane left all his bank accounts open, he's never used his credit cards. The man simply vanished."

She makes eye contact affirming I register the significance of these details. I do.

"We looked into the whole family, of course, at the time," the detective continues. "Two of Jake's friends confirmed he was with them. Natalie was at her friend Melissa Masterson's. We looked into Frank, but he was at a fundraiser for his kids' school, seen by dozens of people. But Brian had no alibi for the night Mallory was killed; he insisted he was home, alone. And you know, with the affair . . ." She shrugs. "It's usually the husband, right? I always thought Brian did both of them, if you must know. Jealousy."

"What about when Crane disappeared? Did Brian have an alibi then?"

"That's the thing. We don't know exactly when Crane left. Or was killed, if that's what happened. He was seen at a local market on a Tuesday, but had told his employees he was taking Wednesday and Thursday off. No one was really looking for him until that Friday."

I regard Cooke sympathetically. "You seem to have all of this information, how do you say in English? Right at the tips of your toes?"

She smiles faintly. "At my fingertips. Yes. Well, you know how it is, some cases just stay with you."

Indeed I do.

"And now what do you think? After Frank Burrows?"

"I don't know. I keep wondering what exactly went down in Paris." She shrugs. "Something keeps itching at me."

A kindred spirit.

As Aimee, I express my own reservations about the tragic events in Paris. We commiserate on the topics of gut instinct, sexism in our respective forces, and the administrative pressure to close cases, or at least not stir the pot.

Before I get back into my Ford Escort, I extract Detective Cooke's promise to email me her case notes on Mallory Burrows.

Jake

CUSP

Jake's had enough.

Funeral arrangements, lawyers, taxes, wills and trusts, partnership valuations, settlements and outstanding bills. Making sure Natalie's school fees and logistics are sorted. Deciding what to do with the apartment on the Upper West Side. The mess that is Uncle Frank, his dead body abandoned in France, no one willing to bring it home, his muddled, unfinished, convoluted affairs.

After getting off the phone with crazy Aunt Della, Jake feels like he might just explode right out of his skin.

He'd had a very different notion of what his life would be like after the Paris trip. With the lease signed on his new place in Brooklyn, and a job lined up bartending at a local restaurant, he'd planned to work nights and devote the days to figuring out his next steps. He didn't necessarily know what he wanted to do with his life, but he could support himself while he figured it out. That was enough.

He was on the cusp of the beginning of *everything*.

But death is everywhere. He doesn't want to feel sorry for himself, yet he can't help it. How many of his recently graduated peers are dealing with this kind of bullshit? They're coming back from European backpacking trips or cross-country drives. They spent the summer having a last taste of freedom before facing new jobs. None of them buried a parent, lost an uncle, became responsible for a sister. Probably none of them learned all too fast the necessity of *growing the fuck up*.

Jake thinks about calling Rami and seeing if he wants to go out. Get blotto. But Natalie is home, tucked up in her room, and he worries about leaving her alone.

God, he can't wait until she starts school. It'll be easier to worry from afar than to be on constant *watch*, worried she'll start to hurt herself again.

He reminds himself to ask Natalie if she's followed up on finding a therapist in Providence. Someone with training and skills needs to be looking after her. There's only so much he can do.

Maybe when Natalie starts school, Jake thinks. *Maybe my life can begin then.*

Catherine

BFFS

The homes in Westport are massive. Set back behind scrupulously maintained topiary, emerald green lawns, flowering trees, and sturdy stone-crafted walls, these palatial estates exude wealth, privilege, security, safety.

This story started here. And it always makes sense to start at the beginning.

I've circled the neighborhood a few times. I've cruised past the site of the former Burrows home (razed to the ground and rebuilt by its purchaser), passed Crane's former place of business (still a bustling nursery but under new ownership), saw Crane's neat little colonial home on the less affluent side of town. I buzzed by the high school that Natalie and Jake Burrows attended. With a few weeks to go before the school year, the building was deserted, its brick and glass façade closed, the parking lot empty.

The home where Melissa Masterson was raised is one of the more impressive in this cavalcade of veritable castles. It's located in an exclusive waterfront enclave, nestled on the river's edge, where it opens to the Long Island Sound. The house is designed to meld artfully with its environment, with soaring windows that bring light and nature in harmony with traditional post-and-beam craftsmanship. Or so says the architect's tony description.

I park my car in the circular driveway. I already know that behind the seven-bedroom, eight-bath manse itself there's a boathouse and a dock with deep-water mooring. Also a full outdoor kitchen, and a movie projection system with theater-style seating for fourteen, used for entertaining on summer nights.

Judging from the catering truck parked in front of my car, and the bustle of white-clad workers unloading rolling carts filled with prepped foods, I gather this is one of those nights.

This suits my purposes. I didn't specifically ask Melissa Masterson *not* to tell her parents I was coming, but I did lean heavily on an eighteen-year-old girl's proclivity for drama and secrecy when I asked if we could talk.

I slip unnoticed around the side of the house and head toward the poolside "cabana." It's a miniature of the grand house, like a child-giant's toy, able to sleep six. Catering staff mills about the lavishly landscaped backyard, placing floating candles atop the pool, lighting Tiki torches, setting up bar stations. The door to the pool house is unlocked and I slip inside.

Melissa's waiting for me curled into the corner of a plaid sofa, bare, freckled legs tucked up under a sleek citron dress, one index finger twirling a lock of strawberry blond hair. She's polished to a sheen, her elegant WASPy attire and composure a stark contrast to Natalie's worried face and uniform of baggy sweats and disheveled hair.

"My going-away party," she explains, gesturing toward the hubbub outside. "I'm leaving to start at Vassar."

"Congratulations," I offer in the lilting tones of Aimee Martinet. I'm keeping my story a simple and consistent one in Westport.

"Yeah, well, whatever, it's mostly my parents' friends. They just want to show off. I, on the other hand, can't wait to get the fuck out of here." She graces me with a radiant smile intended to undermine the coarseness of her words. "So. How can I help you?"

"You were Natalie Burrows's best friend?"

"Yeah. Till, you know, everything with her mom. And then they moved, so." Melissa shrugs.

"Can you tell me about that night? When her *maman* disappeared?"

Melissa's eyes shift rapidly around the room searching for a safe place to land.

"Haven't you talked to the police here in town? Because I gave them my statement a whole bunch of times."

"Yes. And that's why I wanted to ask you, mademoiselle, because I saw a discrepancy in the reports. When first interviewed, you said Natalie left here before ten. But later you said it was closer to midnight."

I let the statement hang in the air between us.

Melissa gets up abruptly, long lithe limbs honed from what I would hazard has been a lifetime of sailing and tennis lessons, horseback riding and Pilates, suddenly restless and agitated.

"How can it matter? It's like a hundred years ago. And that creeper from the nursery confessed, right? I mean I'm not even *friends* with Natalie anymore. And I'm leaving for college *tomorrow*."

"Nothing should interfere with that, Melissa," I reassure. "I'm not even here *officially*. It'll stay between us, I promise. I'm just trying to get everything clear for my own sake."

I offer her my silence once again. She wouldn't have agreed to see me if she didn't have something she wanted to get off her chest.

"Okay. Well, here's the truth. She left here at nine-thirty or so." She looks at me defiantly, daring me to chide her for lying. I don't say a word.

"She was being weird. She'd been acting weird for a while. She wasn't *fun* to be around. She wasn't even *nice*. And that night, well, we had a stupid fight. But we were having fights all the time then, so when she asked me to say she left closer to twelve because she had left here and hooked up with Adam Nash and didn't want her dad to know, I said sure. I mean, what was the big deal?"

"I understand. That's the kind of harmless lie anyone would tell for a friend."

Melissa nods assertively, pleased. "Right. Like I said, not a big deal. Especially with everything else that was going on."

"Why did you stop being friends, Melissa? Was it more than just that the Burrowses moved away?"

Melissa's eyes flick to the built-in cabinets surrounding the sixty-inch flat-screen TV. This girl should never play poker; she's transparent as plastic wrap.

"Is there something you want to show me?" I ask.

Melissa hesitates, but only briefly. "Okay. Yeah. I might as well."

She strides to one of the cabinets and pulls the door open. She pushes aside a stack of board games: Monopoly, Clue, Candy Land, Boggle, Chutes and Ladders, Operation. "My little brother's," she explains derisively.

Finally she extracts a sealed manila envelope from behind the pile of games.

"Here. These are why we stopped being friends. I took them because I saw she needed help, and they were a big part of how we convinced her dad to, you know, put her into treatment. But to be honest? They scared the shit out of me."

Melissa gives her shoulders a shake, as if she's brushing off a memory as sticky as a spider's web. "I should have gotten rid of them long ago. So take them. Do whatever you want with them."

She proffers the envelope. I take it.

Suddenly morphing into a poised swan of a girl, Melissa arches her neck and extends a thin, elegant hand for me to shake. I get the sense that perhaps she's channeling her mother.

"And now," she says, "I need to get ready for my guests."

I've been dismissed.

NEVER HOME

Their Manhattan apartment is full of dust and ghosts.

Has it only been a matter of weeks since they left it for their family adventure in Paris? It seems impossible.

It never really did feel like home here, Natalie reflects. Mom never lived here. Jake was a fleeting presence. Dad tried his best, but it was never *home*.

Natalie's caught herself a few times since her epiphany in the hospital. Gnawing her thumb, for example, at the funeral home. But for the most part she's embraced her faith in a *fresh start*.

She contemplates her full-length reflection in the mirror inset into her closet door. The pageboy haircut she got this morning suits her sharp features and frames her eyes beautifully. She's wearing a simple black shift and black chunky booties. She's pleased with how she looks; it's as if a little French gleam and polish rubbed off on her this summer. Warmth spreads through her with the realization she is being *kind* to herself. Surely this is another sign of her *redemption*. Isn't that what Dr. Bloom used to say? *Compassion starts with self-compassion.*

Natalie pulls her box of treasures from its deep hiding place in the closet. Jake's asked her to think about writing something to read aloud at Dad's funeral. She wants—no, *needs*—the comfort of the talismans inside, the reminders of happier times. She lifts the lid.

Immediately she knows something is wrong.

The box is half-empty. All her sketchbooks are gone; that much is apparent immediately. Quickly, she rummages through the rest of the contents. Her Menehune doll is here. Mallory's rosy pink lipstick. Ticket stubs and that funny sketch she did of Jake on a paper napkin. Her heart-shaped lapis lazuli. The program for Cabaret Night is still there, but the half-joint is missing.

Natalie sits back on her haunches, heart pounding. Who'd been inside her room? Who'd *messed* with her things? Jake? *Daddy?*

She can faintly hear Jake, talking on the phone in another room, using that "grown-up" voice that he's pressed into service when dealing with the awful *formalities*. That's what he calls all the responsibilities that seem to have fallen on his shoulders, the *formalities*. The word leaves Natalie with images of businessmen in tuxedos and bow ties, bowing and scraping as Jake navigates their politely treacherous paths.

Creeping from her bedroom, Natalie heads down the hallway. Jake's voice is coming from the kitchen. Okay. She'll take a look in Brian's office first.

Daddy's office smells like him. A mix of his favorite aftershave, pepper, a faint lemony overtone from the wood polish, a hint of coffee. The scent makes tears spring to her eyes, but she wipes them away impatiently.

She searches with furtive urgency. It seems *wrong* to sort through Daddy's private papers. He's *dead,* Natalie understands this, but still this feels sneaky, a violation.

The same violation he perpetrated on her if he rummaged through *her* room and took *her* things, she thinks angrily.

If Jake comes in, she will tell him she is looking for mementos to put aside before they pack up Daddy's belongings to donate to charity. He'll like that. It's totally plausible. Completely reasonable.

She finds the sketchbooks stuffed into a plain brown paper bag on the top shelf of the closet, underneath a stack of old issues of *Architectural Digest*. She sinks into Brian's desk chair and flips the pages of the top book of the stack.

Her fingers find the rough edges of the handful of drawings that were ripped from the center of this sketchbook three years ago. All this time, and she still *feels* in her *physical body* the violation and betrayal represented by those torn and exposed pages.

She flips through the next book in the stack and then the one below that.

The sense of exposure is overwhelming. These are her *private* sketchbooks. Daddy had no right! What did he think when he saw them? Oh god, what must have he thought? Why didn't he talk to her about them? She could have *explained*. She could have explained *everything*.

Natalie gathers up the stack of books and shoves them back into their brown paper bag.

These are hers. No one else needs to see them. In fact, Natalie's decided.

She's going to destroy them all, the very first chance she gets.

Catherine

FRESH

Back in my Manhattan hotel room, I toss the manila envelope Melissa Masterson gave me down on the bed. I haven't yet looked inside.

I strip off the guise of Aimee Martinet and pad into the shower, washing off the perfumed, chilled-air affluence of Westport as much as the grimy heat of Manhattan.

Clean hair toweled dry, wrapped in a luxurious hotel-supplied robe, I open the twist-off bottle of chardonnay in the mini bar and chug half of it before settling onto the crisply made bed. I slide a fingernail under the manila envelope's seal.

Pull out a sheaf of drawings.

The one right on top is a portrait of Natalie, her face scrunched with concentration as she flays a delicate slice of flesh from her torso. She is nude.

The second one is even more disturbing: Natalie crouched on her haunches and grinning wickedly while cutting off her own baby toe. Blood spurts in exaggerated plumes.

Natalie's flamboyant signature graces the bottom right-hand corner of both drawings.

Riffling queasily through the other pages in the stack I understand why Melissa was happy to be rid of them. Why she held on to them too.

I put the drawings aside and boot up one of the computers I purchased yesterday. Log in to the hotel WiFi.

I run a check on Elena, now traveling under the dead-double identity of Irina Sherkov (born and died 1989 in Kiev). Irina's safely en route to Sydney, Australia; although with her chopped, dyed hair and baggy clothes she looks nothing like the elegant international model she once was, more like an underfed charwoman.

An apartment has been purchased for her in Sydney, a three-bedroom luxury unit on fashionable Gloucester Street. Bank accounts have been opened and filled with a hefty portion of Boris's illegal gains. She'll have the quiet life there that she craves.

As for her pig of a husband, I drained most of his accounts. Some of his wealth went to Elena, some to me. I left enough behind to give the authorities a solid trail of money, guns, and blood. But before I turned him over, I had a little fun.

A hot blonde paid a hundred euros to saunter past him, a quickly stuck syringe, and he was mine. Jumah rolled up in his dinky white van and we were off the street before anyone blinked. Boris was delivered the next morning, stark naked, cellophane-wrapped to a streetlight in the middle of Saint-Germain-des-Prés. His head was bald, shaved of the mane of which he was so proud. A flash drive with details of his operations and proof he paid kidnappers to abduct his wife was taped over one bare nipple.

I was safely in a plane over the Atlantic by the time he was discovered.

Maybe it was childish of me, but I didn't have much of a childhood. I take my pleasures where I can find them.

With Elena happily resolved, I am free to focus on the Burrowses.

I may have more and more questions, but I also have ideas about how to get some answers.

FUNERAL

The ceremony in the church had been unbearable. First the minister spoke. Then Jake. Natalie got through her own remarks and cried only once. Jake put his arm around her when she came back to the pew, and she nestled into his side.

But then all those teary faces, all those endless testimonials.

Not that there was anything *wrong* with people saying nice things about Brian, of course not. It was the having to stay *composed,* face frozen, while all these *virtual strangers* droned interminably on about Daddy.

Jake had organized the service. Natalie had been happy to let him. Now she wishes she had looked at the list of speakers. Insisted on a few changes.

She's grateful a smaller crowd has followed them to the cemetery, reducing the number of former friends and acquaintances collected for another greedy glimpse of scandal.

Natalie loathes them all. She knows they use the misfortunes of her family as a kind of protective talisman. *So awful, what happened to the Burrowses. But so close to home, that kind of horror, it couldn't possibly strike us too.* She's sure that's what they all silently hope as they cross their fingers and say their stupid prayers.

Here in the verdant, softly rolling hills of the cemetery are a

small assortment of people from Dad's office, including Hank Scovell, Mr. and Mrs. Masterson (although Melissa's already left for
Vassar, Sunny told her proudly, offering up Melissa's condolences
in proxy), a few of Jake's friends from school.

Grandma Sue is here of course, with an aide to manage her
wheelchair, but Natalie is not at all convinced that Grandma has a
clue what's going on.

Maybe that's better. Maybe she's lucky.

The coffin is lowered into the earth and Natalie looks away. She
doesn't want to think about earth and worms and maggots and rot,
Daddy's body turning to fetid carrion. When she dies, she'll be cremated, she decides. Burnt to ash and cinder. Maybe she'll purchase
one of those urns she saw advertised that takes cremated remains
and converts them into trees. She'd like to be a tree.

Out of the corner of her eye she catches a glimpse of a figure,
somehow familiar, but also oddly out of place, tucked behind the
large oak tree down the path. It's a woman, her face obscured by
enormous sunglasses, her hair wrapped in a patterned scarf in
shades of gray. She wears well-cut black trousers and a steel-gray
silk blouse.

Natalie glances at Jake. He's beside her, staring fixedly at the
sight of Brian's coffin nestling into the dirt.

Who is she?

Natalie goes very still as realization hits her.

It's the mysterious Hannah Potter. A woman who does not exist.

Come to pay her respects to the living and the dead.

Catherine

STORAGE

Natalie looks different. Her long hair has been chopped into a short angular bob. It suits her. With a simply cut black wrap dress taut on her thin frame and high-heeled strappy shoes, she looks downright chic. She looks older too. Not surprising, really. Tragedy takes its toll.

But there's something else about her that I can't quite put my finger on. A *lightness* that seems at odds with the somber burial service unfolding in front of us.

Jake Burrows looks terrible. Haggard. Deep dark circles rim his eyes. He greets mourners' condolences with a weary stoicism. Hank Scovell wraps an arm around Jake's hunched shoulders and whispers briefly in his ear before departing.

A couple approaches the siblings; the wife looks like a tanner, ropier version of Melissa Masterson. Wifey bends to kiss Natalie. She flinches, visibly.

Finally the mourners drift away, leaving just Brian's kids by the open graveside. Jake crouches down on his haunches, and Natalie places a hand on the top of his head. He shakes her off, then shoots her an apologetic smile.

Natalie looks over at me. I step out from behind the tree. Natalie leaves Jake to his thoughts and heads toward me.

"Hello," I offer when she's close enough to hear me.

"Why are you here?" she snaps. "And just who the hell are you *really*, *'Hannah Potter'*?" She's very pale.

In reply, I extract the envelope Melissa gave me and hand it over to Natalie. She opens it and pages through the contents.

On top are the drawings of Natalie injuring herself.

Beneath them is another series of images with a different star: Will Crane.

Will Crane stabbed. Will Crane hung. Will Crane impaled on a spike, Will Crane burning at the stake, Will Crane buried alive, one clawlike hand grasping at nothingness from under the pile of mounded earth pouring into his gaping mouth.

Alongside the grotesque drawings of Crane are notations. Natalie had apparently stalked Crane; notes lining the margins of each artwork include detailed accountings of street addresses and drive times, people met and meals eaten.

Natalie looks at me with stony eyes. "So? You have some of my old drawings. So what?"

"I have questions—"

She interrupts. "You offered to *help* me. I thought you *gave a shit* about me. But everything you've ever said to me is a lie and I would like to know *why*. Who are you? Why are you all up in our business?"

I glance over at Jake, kneeling by his father's grave, oblivious to our conversation.

"Tell me about the drawings, Natalie. Were you following Will Crane?"

"So what if I was?"

"What did you hope to accomplish?"

"He took my mother from me! I had a right!"

"A right to what, Natalie?"

She crosses her arms over her chest and juts out her chin. "I'm done talking to you, whatever your name is. I'm *mourning*. I don't have to put up with this." She spins away from me and walks away briskly.

"I found your uncle's storage unit," I call after her retreating form.

She freezes. Turns to face me. "What are you talking about?"

"Your uncle had a unit in a storage facility in Trumbull. He rented it the week Will Crane disappeared, which I thought was an odd coincidence. I've been there. There's a body inside. I believe it's Crane's."

Natalie doesn't blink.

"I'm going to have to call it in to the police, Natalie. An anonymous tip. Is there anything you want to share before I do?"

"I don't know what you're talking about. So take your fake name and fake-ass bullshit and get the fuck away from me."

Well, that went well.

Jake

PRIVACY

Some things should remain private. Jake had never been one to splash every precious morsel of his life on social media, for example. He's discreet about his sexual liaisons, cautious in his romantic ones. He respects others' right to privacy. He's never nosy (although he likes to think he is a good and reflective listener). He doesn't gossip. He doesn't meddle.

Strange then to be picking and poking through the most intimate private details of his father's life, to be *charged* with this task. It was triage at first: location of the will, identification of the trusts in his and his sister's names, the deed of sale on the apartment, access to bank accounts; a thunderous train of legalese delivered by properly composed, sadly serious faces.

Now, with provisional money available to both of them and Natalie's school fees settled, Jake has to dive deeper into the archaeological dig that was the life of Brian Burrows. It feels unnatural. Uncomfortable. It feels surreal.

Jake pulls open the top drawer of his dad's night table.

Condoms right on top. Okay, that's something he didn't need to know about. He tosses them aside. A flashlight. A tube of dry-skin lotion. A nail file. A Swiss army knife. Post-it notes and a loose bundle of pens. A set of keys, small ones that look like they would fit padlocks, say, or safe deposit boxes, as opposed to doors or a car. Jake pockets the keys.

Buried underneath all the clutter is a zipped portfolio.

He slides it out from the drawer and lays the portfolio on the bed. Opens it.

Inside is a stack of childhood artwork: one carefully preserved, proudly signed artistic effort of both Jake's and Natalie's for every school year, grades K–8. Jake fans out the pieces, examining their paintings and drawings. Even in kindergarten Natalie's artistic talent was evident. Her family drawing of the four of them actually has an *essence* about it that makes Jake's heart surge with sudden, painful longing for his mother, who he suspects curated this collection.

Jake replaces the stack in the portfolio and zips it shut.

In the next drawer down, a pair of furry cuffs. Yuck. More shit he doesn't want to think about. He slams that drawer shut without digging any further.

He'd seen Natalie talking to Hannah Potter at the cemetery; he'd swear it. But Natalie denied that the woman he'd seen her with was their mysterious disappearing friend, so Jake let it go. Particularly since he's thought he glimpsed Hannah any number of times since they've been home. Maybe he's going crazy.

Questions about Hannah Potter's true identity and why she abducted him from a street in Paris loop through Jake's thoughts. The more he thinks about it, the more certain he is that she *drugged* him, *bound* him, *gagged* him. But she also probably saved Natalie's life with the first aid she administered before the EMTs' arrival. So who is she? What does she want with them? He's teased out a thousand different explanations in his head.

His questions about Hannah are entangled with the motives and murders that will forever mark the pathways of his life.

His mother killed by her lover, who hid her body. Why? Now Jake may never know. He prefers to believe Mallory did choose Brian and Jake and Natalie in the end. That was the story, after all.

Uncle Frank's actions disturb on a whole other level. Jake shares

DNA with a man callous enough to kill at least two men in cold blood, one of them his own brother.

And his motives! Jake remembers how very chuffed Uncle Frank became when Mom disappeared. How he bloomed into his role as the pillar of stability in their disintegrating midst. Frank killed Crane for his own ego, more or less, that's how Jake figures it. To prove something, fill some stupid, gaping hole in his psyche. And then he murdered Brian out of fear of receiving justice for that killing. What a coward. What a creep. A crazy.

A shiver passes through Jake as he recollects how very close he came to losing Natalie. Followed by a rush of guilt about how very anxious he is to be free of her, how very badly he wants Natalie safely in school. She's too much responsibility for him. Is he awful to feel this way? Yeah, he is.

Jake moves over to the other bedside table. Opens the top drawer. Bundles of letters.

Actual letters is Jake's first thought as he recognizes his mother's handwriting. He runs the tip of his index finger gently over her spidery scratches before opening the letter on top. He starts to read and feels the blush rise through his throat and cheeks.

Love letters from Mallory to Brian. More intimacy Jake never should have shared. He stuffs the letter back into the envelope and tosses the stack back like it was radioactive.

He peers deeper into the drawer. Other letters. One in particular catches his eye. Addressed to his dad and from Dr. Bloom, Natalie's shrink at the treatment center.

What catches Jake's attention is the postmark: April of this year. Jake hadn't known Natalie had anything to do with the doctor since she'd been released from the treatment center over two and a half years ago. Not that it would necessarily have been Jake's business, but still.

Jake pulls the letter from the envelope. Starts to read. The words leap up off the page and swim before his eyes.

Maybe I really am going nuts. After all, it runs in the family, doesn't it?

Catherine

HOOK

I arrive in the dead of night. Park my rental car, cut the lights, and wait, slumped down on the seat, a hat pulled low over my eyes. The parking lot is nearly empty: two white vans with the storage facility's logo; a rusty old Dodge Dart that looks like it might have taken up permanent residence in a corner.

A pair of headlights sweeps into view, casting sharp beams into deep shadows. There's enough light for me to see the slight figure emerge from the car and open the trunk.

On sneakered feet, I pad across the asphalt of the lot. The figure is listing to one side, straining to lug a heavy can. As I get closer I can smell the can's contents: gasoline.

"Where's the fire, Natalie?"

The heavy can drops, hitting the asphalt with an echoing clang.

"Oh, that's right," I persist. "You were going to set one, weren't you? Isn't that what the gas is for?"

She turns to face me.

"Is there a reason you'd want to burn Crane's body, Natalie?"

"Who are you?" Her voice is tightly controlled. "What is it you really want?"

"I'm someone who wants to help you, Natalie. Talk to me."

The polished young woman I had seen at the funeral dissolves back into the frightened girl I knew better.

"Why should I trust you? I don't even know who you are."

"Haven't I helped you so far? I found your brother when you couldn't. I found your dad's stalker. I saved your *life*."

She tears away a shred of cuticle from her thumb with her teeth. "*Why?*"

"It doesn't matter why. Just trust that I'm on your side."

"Okay," she concedes in a hoarse whisper. "I was there that night. The night Crane died."

Eyes cast downward, bloody thumb lodged in the corner of her mouth, Natalie tells me her story.

Will Crane had welcomed her in when she'd showed up unannounced at his kitchen door. She wanted the truth! Answers! She burned for a confrontation. He seemed surprised but pleased to see her. Which made her perversely angry. As did his offer of tea and cookies.

Crane poured the boiling water over strainers and into a matched pair of blue earthenware mugs. Natalie wondered if Crane and her mother had sipped from these mugs together.

They perched on stools set by the kitchen's center island.

Crane was kind. He knew things about her, things he could only have learned from her mom. The nicer he was, the more confused Natalie got. Angrier too.

Finally, he admitted killing Mallory. It was a lovers' quarrel gone terribly wrong. He loved Mallory, just wanted her to *stay*. He never meant to hurt her. He was so *matter of fact* about it all. That was the creepiest thing.

Natalie lifts her eyes to meet mine as she continues.

"I watched as he lifted his tea to his lips. I kept talking . . . asking him questions. I was trying to stay calm even though I was reeling. And . . . and . . . not just from his confession."

Natalie casts her gaze back down at the asphalt. Continues in a hesitant mumble, speaking so softly I can barely hear her.

She'd seen him slip something into her cup. But she'd been smart. She'd swapped their mugs when he went to the pantry to comply with her request for sugar.

Panic flooded Crane's eyes as pain and paralysis took hold. He gasped like a beached fish, clutched uselessly at his throat. Wracked with fear and loathing, Natalie watched until he slumped across the stainless steel table. He was dead.

It was meant to be her. He'd tried to kill her.

A sharp rap on the kitchen door made her jump.

She had no idea what Uncle Frank was doing there but she could see his silhouette through the frosted glass pane, hear him calling her name. She ran over to let him in.

He'd found her sketchbook, he told her. With the drawings and notations. Guessed where she was.

He spotted Crane's lifeless body and stopped in his tracks.

Natalie's voice breaks as she continues. "I told him, like I just told you, about the tea, the switched mugs. I wanted to call the police. But Uncle Frank said no. He said he wanted to spare me, all of us really, a trial, all the awful press. He said we'd been through enough. He said Crane deserved what he got. That it was *justice*. That he would take care of everything."

Natalie buries her face in her hands. "I still can't believe that Uncle Frank killed Daddy over this!" she cries. "Don't you see why I said Uncle Frank admitted to killing Crane? Who would believe me? Uncle Frank is the only one who was there that night who could confirm everything and now he's dead. *I killed him.*"

Pure anguish contorts her voice. "*And technically I killed Crane too.* What happens if my DNA is on that body?"

She gestures to the storage facility. "Please—if you really want to help, you'll let me burn this place down.

"You have to understand," she continues earnestly, "I'm on a new path. Everything in my life is going to be different now. Yesterday is *history*."

"There's no body inside, Natalie," I reveal. "I've got no idea where Will Crane's corpse is. I just needed to know."

Her face shifts as she processes this information. "So now you know," she says hesitantly. "What are you going to do?"

Her wide eyes are fearful. Her palms splay open, beseeching me.

"Go home, Natalie," I order her. "Start your life. Not everyone gets a second chance. Don't blow yours."

She nods. Ducks her head shyly. "Thank you," she whispers.

And she is gone in a flash, leaving behind the reeking can of gasoline.

PROVIDENCE

Natalie loves being at RISD. She loves the architecture of New England, the crisp autumn air, being a part of a community of artists. She's milked the notoriety of her family too, a disappearance and two deaths, leaving her free of the typical freshman insecurity about where she fits in. With a tragic and heroic past, about which she only lets escape the occasional tantalizing detail, as well as pockets full of cash, she was popular almost instantly. It was silly, she now reflects, that she ever worried.

Natalie feels healthier than she has in years.

A pile of dead leaves materializes in front of her, and Natalie kicks through it with abandon, laughing when a pair of old ladies cross themselves as they swerve to avoid her.

It's all behind me now.

Maybe one day she'll be able to explain it all to Jake. What it was like after he left home to start college. How *lonely* she was with only Mallory in the house. Mom became more depressed and withdrawn, retreating to her bedroom to watch stupid police procedurals and makeover shows. Natalie had to take on the maternal role, making dinner, doing most of the shopping, the laundry.

Then Mom *lit up*. There was just no other way to describe it. Natalie was excited. She suspected it had to do with the volunteer work Mom was doing at the women's shelter, but she didn't care about the *why*, she was just glad to have her mother back.

Of course she did care about the *why* when she realized the reason was that slick Mr. Crane with his nice hair and big laugh. Natalie started following her mother, obsessed with their movie dates, intimate dinners, quick coffees, and long, lingering talks at Crane's nursery. It was there she got the idea to use a pinch of pesticide in Mallory's food. Natalie decided to give her just enough to keep her *sick,* keep her home.

Natalie never *wanted* to *kill* her mother. Of course not.

The night she did was tragic, in that circumstances left her *no choice*.

She'd been just zipping along home from Melissa's when Mallory tore out of their driveway, nearly knocking Natalie off her bike! Mom didn't even see her! Natalie could've been killed! Where the fuck was she going in such a hurry? Dad and Jake were both just back, Mom going out tonight made no sense. Unless . . .

Natalie followed her mother to Will Crane's house. Waited outside for over two hours. When Mallory emerged, Natalie was waiting. *That* put a hitch in Mom's lighthearted step.

Natalie confronted her. It got loud. A light snapped on in a neighbor's house. Mom suggested they take their conversation to her car. Natalie petulantly suggested they go over to their boat, *The Happy Daze.*

"Our *family* boat. Remember us? Your family?"

They sat in silence as Mallory drove them over to the yacht club.

Once on board the boat, Mom tried to explain about her *feelings* for Crane. It was pathetic. She thought *she* was in charge. Natalie set her straight about *that*. When they argued, Mallory asked about the dead roses, her keyed car, the bloody message on their front doorstep. Natalie shrugged. She had to do *something* to keep Mallory at home. Her mother gave Natalie a look she will never forget. As if she didn't recognize her. As if Natalie had turned into a *monster.*

Mom threatened to have Natalie put away. But Natalie wasn't *crazy*. Mom just wanted her out of the way so she could run off with her *boyfriend*. No fucking way.

Natalie boasted about the poison she'd been slipping into her mother's food. That had been in the glass of lemonade Natalie had just poured for her.

Mallory stared at her empty glass in horror.

Afterward, it was easy. Natalie had crewed on *The Happy Daze* her whole life. She knew just how far off shore to dump her mother's weighted body.

And really, it was Mom's fault anyway, the whole thing. *She never should have said she wanted to leave. She never should have looked at me like that.*

As for Crane, he deserved to die. *All* of this was *his fault*.

The night she showed up at his house, she was *prepared* but not *decided*.

He could have altered the course of things *at any point*, even though he was so thoroughly to blame.

He was pleased to see her, which irritated the crap out of her. Acted like they had some kind of *bond*. Because they both loved her mother? It was all she could do not to vomit.

She shyly offered to make them tea, showed him that she had brought a tin of Mallory's favorite blend. She busied herself with setting the kettle on the stove, spooning tea leaves into the mugs he handed her.

The teapot began to sing, a rising whistle. Natalie flicked off the burner and the pot sighed itself to silence. Natalie poured the boiling water into the matched pair of blue earthenware mugs.

Natalie studied the dying man impassively as he gasped and writhed.

Oleander. From his very own nursery. Fitting.

He took my mother away from me. He deserves to die.

He confessed to killing my mother. Then I saw him slipping something into my tea. I switched our mugs without him noticing, just to see, I wasn't sure about anything. And then he just slumped over! It could have been me. He meant it to be me.

She imagined herself in the police interview room, on the witness stand, in the papers. A tragic and heroic figure, the daughter of a slain mother who'd narrowly escaped death by the same cunning, murderous hand.

A heart carved from lapis lazuli sat on Crane's counter. Natalie had been with her mother when Mallory had purchased it. "A birthday present for a friend," Mallory had said, as the clerk put it in a gift box. It sickened Natalie to see it there, proudly displayed. She snuck it into her pocket.

And then Uncle Frank showed up. Natalie tried her story out and liked how it played until Uncle Frank decided he was going to play the hero, dump the body. He sent her home. Natalie went along with it, even as she rued the loss of the opportunity to tell her martyred tale of escaping death to a wider audience. That's *come full circle at least,* she thinks with satisfaction.

Uncle Frank had been so *cool* up until this summer. Natalie had felt a certain admiration for him, especially his brilliant touch of the confession letter "from Crane." *Because Mom had chosen us.* Dad and Jake had lapped that up. Natalie was the only one who knew the truth. *None of this would have happened if she'd really chosen us.*

Who could have foreseen that Uncle Frank would lose his shit so spectacularly? All Dad did was confide in Uncle Frank about Natalie's sketchbooks and his communications with that bitch Dr. Bloom, and Uncle Frank freaked. Thought he was going to be exposed for disposing of Crane's body. Pathetic. But to try to pin Daddy's murder on Jake? For that alone Uncle Frank deserved to die.

Once she saw his eyes, she *knew*. She got him to confess to kill-ing Brian, and after he made his plea—*"It's the best thing for you too, Natalie. We need to keep our secrets"*—she slashed his throat. Just like he had done to Dad. Fitting. Natalie likes things to have symmetry.

She'd relished turning the knife on herself, first slashing at her forearms to make her self-defense story plausible. Next, driving the knife deep into her own guts. A calculated risk.

She was willing to die then, she reminds herself. There's a *rea-son* she didn't. There's a *divine purpose* for her, she's sure of it.

Anyway, the story she'd told Hannah Potter (or whoever the fuck that woman is) was *close enough* to the truth. Natalie won-ders again who *that bitch* really is and what she wants. But then she pushes the thought from her mind, as it interferes with her feeling *gratitude for every day*.

Honestly, look at how well everything's worked out! Natalie's *famous*. She's going to do great things with this new lease on life. *Just watch*. She's all about looking *forward* now, not back.

Natalie checks the time and hurries her steps; she doesn't want to be late to her glassblowing class.

She loves this new medium, reaching with her pipe into the in-tense, glowing ovens, pulling out a molten blob of glass as pliable as taffy, rolling the radiating form against the steel table called the marver, the control she exercises as she forces shapes with her breath.

It's almost like breathing fire. Like being a dragon.

Like being a god.

Catherine

FLOAT

Save your prayers for the living because the dead are already dead.

Who used to say that? Was it Daddy? Father Karl?

I don't pray anymore. But I can't help mourning the dead, can't stop worrying about the living.

"Let's go, Cathy. Let's go."

Jake

HEIGHTS

Jake tries to determine if he is dead center of the bridge. That's what he's aiming for.

He's crossed the pedestrian walkway of the Manhattan Bridge many times, but tonight he takes in the sparkling view of the skyline with a particular rueful attention.

Glimmering buildings, blurred streaks of yellow and red lights on the roadway, inky water shimmering below him. Jake inhales deeply, welcoming the cool that has descended over the city after a punishing Indian summer.

Autumn in the city was one of the things Jake used to love. He used to love a lot of things. But lately he's been picking obsessively at scabbed-over recollections.

Their family vacation in Kauai, for example. That perfect time, the happiest they ever were. Or so he'd thought. But reflection dredged up bitter shards. That day on the boat, for example. After her tears dried, Natalie had whispered to Jake that she had swum "into the jellyfish bloom *on purpose*. Because that crew guy was flirting with Mom, which was *disgusting*."

Other memories flower. So many of them raise questions about his sister. So many of them he just can't *bear*.

He clambers over the chain-link fence and settles into position on the ledge overlooking the East River.

Just a moment more.

He wonders if he will be reunited with his parents on the other side. If there is an other side.

For Natalie, he offers up a prayer to the universe, "Please, do no more harm."

He spreads his arms wide. Takes a step forward. Falls.

A rough hand tugs at the nape of his sweatshirt, hauling him back to safety. Jake wheels around, rocks tumbling out of his pockets and spiraling down to the water below.

He's astonished to see Hannah Potter. Holding on to him for dear life.

BETTER LEFT BEHIND

Was it sheer luck that got me to the bridge on time? Or divine intervention?

All I know is, I wasn't able to get Jake Burrows out of my mind. I tracked him to his apartment in Brooklyn. Found his suicide note. You can figure out the rest.

Now we sit opposite one another in a booth at an open-all-night coffee shop. Fluorescent lights buzz overhead and a lazy fly buzzes my uneaten turkey on rye. I have no desire for the sandwich now, although I was ravenous when we sat down.

Jake's confessed to finding correspondence from Natalie's doctor to their father. In it, Dr. Bloom diagnoses Natalie with borderline personality disorder, along with a heavy lacing of narcissism. The doctor believed Natalie to be a danger to herself and to others.

Jake haltingly added his suspicions that Natalie may have in fact killed Dr. Bloom, who died in a car crash shortly after their last session together. How that speculation has led him to question everything Natalie has told him.

Can you blame me for my loss of appetite? I'm shocked I allowed Natalie to work me so expertly, especially since I was well aware I saw too much of myself in that girl. I'll have to re-examine everything I thought I knew about her. As well as everything I thought I knew about myself.

Jake had ordered only black coffee. He sips at his cup now, but I suspect it's merely to give him something to do with his hands. He shrugs back against the red leatherette seat of the booth, guilt and relief over his betrayal of his sister simultaneously evident on his face.

"So your fears about Natalie led you to that bridge?"

"More or less." Jake stares down at his coffee.

I don't tell my story often, but I do now, in plain, strong language. I leave out a few chapters; some things shouldn't be shared until true intimacy is built, others should remain private forever.

Jake's eyes lift to meet mine. His face registers confusion, disbelief, compassion, and fear in turn.

"Some things are better left behind, Jake. My life has taught me that. It doesn't mean we can't survive them. That we can't move on and find a present that reconciles our past. You are not your parents. Or your uncle. You are not your sister."

"How can you be so sure?"

"I sought you out because I saw something in you."

"What might that be?" He spits it bitterly.

"Compassion. Initiative. Protective instincts. Smarts."

"And I've fucked that up now too, haven't I? Whoever it was you thought you were going to find turned out to be just a suicidal crazy? From a family of crazies, right?"

"You can be your own man, Jake. Chart your own path. It may not be conventional. It may not be what you had planned. But you can get past this. I promise you."

"I'd like to believe you."

"We all make mistakes. Take our hits. It's what we do after that matters. Do we stick our heads in the sand? Give up? Jump off a bridge?"

Our eyes meet and for a split second we share a smile.

"No," I continue. "We learn. We do better. We try to make amends for our past mistakes. So, what's next for you, Jake?"

"The fuck if I know. My calendar after today was blank."

I hesitate. Given what I now know about Natalie, this could be trickier than I'd anticipated.

But also, just maybe, more useful.

"I have an idea I'd like to run by you."

I offer him a job.

If I could tell the story differently . . .
Well, who knows? Next time I might.
There are always countless versions.
Some are even the truth.

Acknowledgments

I am grateful for all the many and varied circumstances of my life that aligned to allow me to write this book. In creating a heroine dedicated to setting things right while trying to battle her own demons, I found I empowered myself.

I must acknowledge my early readers, Kingsley Smith, Hannah Phenicie, Sean Smith, and Janet Cooke, all of whom provided helpful perspective along with their profound friendship.

I also want to thank the many readers who loved *Just Fall* and reached out to tell me so. Writing requires a lot of time in a solitary bubble. Concrete proof that your words and thoughts have excited others is a delicious gift.

As always I want to acknowledge the friends and family who keep me sane and able to present a cheerful disposition to the world (with my blackest thoughts relegated to the page). So thank you to Ed Sadowsky, Jonathan Sadowsky, Laura Steinberg, Richard Sadowsky, Mary Clancy, Robin Sax, Carolyn Manetti, Michelle Raimo, Deb Aquila, Betsy Stahl, Debbie Liebling, Thom Bishops, Matthew Mizel, Sukee Chew, Brenda Goodman, Suzanne Sadowsky, Heather Richardson, Robin Swicord, Pam Falk, Wendy Leitman, Marcy Morris, Lisa Kislak, Shandiz Zandi, Ruth Vitale, Jeff Stanzler, Kathy Boluch, Linda Bower, Debbie Huffman, Judy Bloom,

Alexandra Seros, Ted Sullivan, Andrew Wood, and all the women of the Woolfpack. A special note of thanks must go to the extraordinary Laina Cohn for being my spirit guide through both personal and professional challenges this past year. I have immense gratitude for the "bonus kids" in my life, Arielle and Daniel, Darius and Analia, Ivan and Julia, and my USC students who teach me as much as I teach them. Love and recognition to my husband, Gary Hakman (who now knows enough to get out of my way when I'm writing). I also want to thank everyone at Atmosphere: Mark Canton, Dorothy Canton, David Hopwood, Michael Dwyer, and Frazier.

A good editor makes all the difference, and mine is wonderful. Deep thanks to Kate Miciak for her guidance throughout this process, and for constantly challenging me to be a better writer. And for always suggesting another glass of wine.

I am grateful for the support I have gotten from everyone at Ballantine, particularly Kara Welsh, Kim Hovey, Sharon Propson, Quinne Rogers, Denise Cronin (and her entire team), Loren Noveck, and Julia Maguire. I'm also deeply appreciative of the work my excellent book agent, Emma Sweeney, has done and continues to do on my behalf, and for my film and TV agents at The Gersh Agency, Roy Ashton and Lynn Fimberg.

And to my mom, Jean Thelma Sadowsky, who died on September 17, 2016, I love you and I know you're somewhere watching me publish my second novel with unbridled pride (while asking, "Where's number three?").

I'm working on it.

ABOUT THE AUTHOR

NINA SADOWSKY is the author of the thrillers *The Burial Society* and *Just Fall*. She has written numerous original screenplays and adaptations for such companies as The Walt Disney Company, Working Title Films, Lifetime Television, and STARZ.

Sadowsky served as president of production for Signpost Films, where she worked on such projects as the Academy Award–nominated *House of Sand and Fog*. Prior to joining Signpost, she served as president of Meg Ryan's Prufrock Pictures. Sadowsky was executive producer for the hit film *The Wedding Planner,* starring Jennifer Lopez and Matthew McConaughey, and produced *Desert Saints,* starring Kiefer Sutherland, *Lost Souls,* starring Winona Ryder, and the telefilm *Northern Lights,* starring Diane Keaton. She also produced *Jumpin' at the Boneyard,* starring Tim Roth, Jeffrey Wright, and Samuel L. Jackson, which premiered at the Sundance Film Festival.

She is currently a part-time lecturer at USC's School of Cinematic Arts, as well as the director of educational outreach for the Humanitas Prize's College Fellowships and a member of Humanitas's Woolfpack, an organization of women writers, directors, and showrunners. Sadowsky belongs to International Thriller Writers, Sisters in Crime, and Mystery Writers of America, and is proudly serving on the leadership committee of creative economy promoter Creative Future.

ninarsadowsky.com
Facebook.com/nina.sadowsky
Twitter: @sadowsky_nina

ABOUT THE TYPE

This book was set in Sabon, a typeface designed by the well-known German typographer Jan Tschichold (1902–74). Sabon's design is based upon the original letterforms of sixteenth-century French type designer Claude Garamond and was created specifically to be used for three sources: foundry type for hand composition, Linotype, and Monotype. Tschichold named his typeface for the famous Frankfurt typefounder Jacques Sabon (c. 1520–80).